3

CUPS AND KILLERS

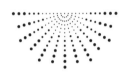

CUPS AND KILLERS

A TAYLOR QUINN QUILT SHOP MYSTERY

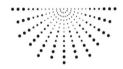

TESS ROTHERY

CHAPTER ONE

*E*verybody dies at that place." Grandpa Ernie frowned in his mirror as he adjusted his bow tie.

"Everybody dies everywhere." Taylor Quinn smiled at the handsome old man. His eighty-seventh birthday was around the corner, and everyone in the town of Comfort, Oregon agreed it was time for him to move to the Bible Creek Care Home, specifically, their memory care wing.

Taylor didn't disagree.

And yet, at two in the afternoon, while using his portable oxygen tank, Grandpa Ernie was his regular old self, and Taylor hated the idea of him not being at home.

Grandpa Ernie gave his well-polished cordovan loafers one last look. "Delma bought me these."

Delma was Taylor's grandmother. She had been gone for eight years now.

"Best shoes I ever had."

"Best wife too." Taylor smiled. Delma had been everything a grandmother ought to be. Soft, warm, dimpled. She baked cookies, sewed quilts, attended dance recitals, kissed boo-boos and founded Flour Sax Quilt Shop, the family business. The business that turned Comfort into an out-of-the-way destination town.

One year and three months ago, Taylor's mom had been murdered. She'd moved back to Comfort to raise her teenage sister and run the family business.

Belle, her sister, was now eighteen and about to start the last year of her undergrad program at the University of Oregon. She was pretty much a genius, though she still groaned and rolled her eyes if she caught Taylor telling anyone that.

Belle was only home for a moment, it seemed. And between running around with her boyfriend and visiting her bio-family in Portland, Taylor wasn't seeing much of her. Next up, Belle was headed to Hungary for the summer to intern at the House of Houdini, a specialist museum on the Castle Buda grounds. Taylor couldn't figure out if Belle's future lay in magic, history, or just getting away by any means possible.

Right now, this exact moment in history, things were the best they had been for the last fifteen months.

Sending Grandpa Ernie away would ruin it.

On the other hand, the increasingly difficult symptoms of what his doctors had recently told her was vascular dementia, caused by several tiny strokes no one had noticed and exacerbated by age, would also ruin what felt like the "golden hour" of their new family life.

"Boggy Hudson considers you his only hope. You have to at least go to the tea." Taylor gave his elbow a gentle nudge.

"Boggy Hudson will probably die."

"Yup. Most likely. I can't think of anything more likely, in fact, than your best buddy who happens to be a good ten years younger than you and in perfect health, dropping dead at the summer evening tea that Bible Creek Methodist Church is hosting at the old folks' home."

Grandpa Ernie turned to Taylor, his bushy eyebrows drawn over dark eyes that held a little mischief. "Watch and see."

"Careful, Grandpa. If he really dies, everyone will think you did it."

He harrumphed into his bushy mustache and led her out.

Boggy's grandson, Hudson, was waiting in the living room.

While tea with their grandfathers wasn't the most romantic date they'd ever been on, it wasn't their least romantic either.

Hudson gave her a kiss on the cheek and then helped Grandpa Ernie into his truck.

She smoothed the fabric of her tea-length party dress before climbing into the jump seat. She felt silly, like mutton-dressed-as-lamb, in the vintage rose-print cotton dress with poufy skirt and sweetheart neckline. She had very recently turned thirty, and this did not feel like the kind of dress a thirty-year-old woman would wear. But Taylor and Hudson had planned ahead, and whatever he really thought about the silly dress, Taylor thought he looked rather delicious in his crisp-pressed blue jeans and seersucker jacket.

"Blue jeans, young man?" Grandpa Ernie shook his head. "I was told this was a formal event." Grandpa Ernie wore his gray wool suit. It was his best, and he had made it himself at the heyday of his career as a tailor. It was beautifully cut and only tugged a smidge around his comfortable waist.

"They're my Sunday go-to-meeting jeans, sir."

"Doesn't his jacket look nice?" Taylor patted Grandpa's shoulder from the back seat. "You made that one for Boggy years and years ago.

"Boggy always was a funny one."

BIBLE CREEK CARE Home sat on the edge of their little town, bordered by the creek. The old folks' home was a sprawling campus of cottages and meeting halls, some connected by open-air breezeways, some by enclosed halls. Bible Creek Care Home arranged several events a year, both to entertain the residents and to let locals see what life was like on the inside.

The tea party was held in the quadrangle, a lush, grassy arena in the center of the campus. A bright early summer sun glinted off the French doors that led to the dining room. Opposite the dining room matching French doors led to the fitness center. Taylor doubted Grandpa Ernie would get much use from the weight room or swimming pool, though he might enjoy the Wii Sports setup.

The tea party tables were hosted by ladies of the local Methodist church and residents, each table laid with a favorite tablecloth and beloved tea set. Spring flowers were just ending as summer flowers began to bloom—a magical moment for gardens in the Pacific Northwest—and the quadrangle looked like a Thomas Kincaid painting.

Hudson led Taylor's party to a table in the center of the quad. Taylor recognized the hand-embroidered cutwork tablecloth as her Grandma Delma's favorite, and a periwinkle china tea set belonging to her dad's mom sat in the middle. Something funny caught in her throat. She was about to have some soft, tender feelings when Grandma Quinny's resonant voice intervened.

"Taylor, you look pale." Grandma Quinny stood from her spot at their table and took Taylor by the shoulders.

"Well, thank you, Grandma." Taylor leaned in for a kiss.

"Don't be defensive. I'm worried. You aren't getting outside enough. I drove past your house earlier this week, and the garden…" Grandma Quinny clucked.

Hudson pulled a chair out for Taylor. "Your grandmother graciously offered to be Grandpa Boggy's plus one."

Boggy Hudson sat next to an elderly lady Taylor had never met before. Her face shone like it had been freshly scrubbed. Her lips and cheeks were pink, and if Taylor was pale, the tiny elderly lady was a ghost, but refreshing, nonetheless. She hadn't been pressed into wearing an adult version of a child's Easter dress, and Taylor was jealous of her teal and gray pants suit.

"Quinny's my date?" Boggy goggled at the elegant, loud woman. "Old Quinn would kill the man who tried that. I'm here with Mrs. Sylvester."

The silver-haired doll of a lady next to him pursed her lips.

"You're just a child. I could get arrested for that. I turned ninety-two on Friday."

"I like a mature woman." Boggy threw his arm around the lady who was almost old enough to be his mother.

"Oh, Boswell." Grandma Quinny took her seat like it was a throne, the flowing chiffon sleeves of her floral caftan billowing as she adjusted herself. "I'm here with my family, to fill up numbers. Angus sends his thousand thanks for sitting with us so that he could supervise what is likely our last harvest of the year." The Quinns lived on a strawberry farm that was mostly a hobby. Harvests were completed by their staff of grandchildren, both young and old.

Taylor finally sat in the chair Hudson was so politely still standing behind.

Then he helped Grandpa Ernie to his seat.

Taylor was curious about this Mrs. Sylvester. The elder lady was a good five years older than Grandpa Ernie, but Taylor still felt like she ought to have known her. "Mrs. Sylvester," she asked, "are you from Comfort?"

"No, no. I'm from Robinette, but it's underwater now. I lived there till they put in that dam."

"I'm not familiar, where is that?"

"Robinette's been gone since the fifties," Grandma Quinny interjected. "Where did you live next?"

"That's when I came here." Mrs. Sylvester's rosebud lips turned up, just a little. "I suppose I'm not new anymore, but only because all the folks that had been here before me are dead." She shimmied her shoulders to help herself sit up straighter. "It's no fun moving to a small town when you're already an old married lady like I was."

"Mrs. Sylvester was the librarian at the grade school." Grandma Quinny's statements felt, somehow, like announcements.

Mrs. Sylvester blushed like she had been complimented.

Taylor wasn't sorry her Grandma Quinny had come to the

tea, she loved her very much, but Grandma Quinny had a way of taking over a conversation.

Taylor caught Hudson's eye.

He took her hand under the tablecloth.

Before Taylor could learn more about Mrs. Sylvester's life, the host of the party, who was also chaplain of Bible Creek Care Home, Pastor Leon Farkas, tapped the microphone. "Good afternoon, friends!" His voice carried across the quad, reverberating through the bright clear air. "Welcome to afternoon tea. Don't worry, there are no dormice in the teapots."

Taylor vaguely recalled a mouse at a tea party in *Alice in Wonderland*.

Grandma Quinny's boisterous laugh triggered a ripple of gladness across the audience.

"Shh!" Mrs. Sylvester held a thin pale finger to her mouth. "That's my boy up there."

"Today's many treats were prepared by Chef Joey here at Bible Creek, and the tea was generously provided by Café Olé, everyone's favorite little Spanish coffeehouse!" A light smattering of applause indicated their thanks.

Taylor's real favorite coffee shop, Cuppa Joe's, had sold out and become Café Olé over the spring. It was nice to have a place to find fresh baked *conchas*, *flan*, and her favorite *tres leches* cake in their little town, but she missed the actual coffee. She would swear on a stack of Bibles that she wasn't fussy, but Cuppa Joe's had been good. Real good.

A little woman in a tall white chef's hat, buttoned-up chef's jacket, and black-and-white checkered pants stepped out of the open dining room followed by two waiters carrying a five-tiered cake. The bright candy-colored decorations were eye-catching, and after a moment, Taylor recognized an *Alice in Wonderland* theme, illustrated with red heart playing cards, pink flamingos, white rabbits, and top hats in many colors.

The crowd erupted in laughs and applause.

Mrs. Sylvester's eyes grew wide and her mouth made a sweet little "o" of surprise.

Grandma Quinny leaned forward, peering as though maybe her glasses prescription needed updating.

Chef Joey helped the waiters set the cake on a table in front of their host. It was a good thing Leon was a tall man, or they wouldn't have been able to see his grinning mug above the dessert.

Chef Joey gently nudged Leon aside with her hip and spoke into the microphone. "Leon didn't know we were doing this, but we wanted to celebrate his fifth anniversary with us. More than just a chaplain, Pastor Leon has been a friend, a handyman, an extra hand for bridge, a van driver for day trips, and someone who always makes us laugh."

Hudson snorted when Joey said handyman.

The little chef gave Leon a side hug.

Leon seemed at a loss for words. He shook his head, mouth open to speak, but said nothing. Then he leaned into the hug, knocking the chef's hat off. Joey rocked under his weight, but Leon seemed to list to the side, pushing the chef into the microphone with a screech of feedback.

"Hold up, it's okay." The chef giggled a little as she attempted to help straighten the big man.

With a groan, and a frantic reach for the mic stand, Leon wavered slowly, then fell face first, smashing the beautiful cake.

The crowd gasped, and white-shirted wait staff flocked to the mess, trying to help Leon stand.

A scream broke through the hubbub, bringing a chill of dead silence.

"Someone call the police!" a young male voice cried out.

Phones everywhere popped up.

Taylor squeezed Hudson's hand tightly and then dropped it. She wanted to get closer to the catastrophe. The buzz in the room was high volume now. Residents were rising from their seats and exiting in a flurry of wheels and walkers and grandchildren's arms.

Taylor tripped over a cane, landing on her knees in the well-watered grass. "Be careful!" The sharp voice was matched by a sharp whack on the shoulder from the cane.

She exhaled, rose, and sidled through the crowd.

The servers surrounded Leon, but Taylor managed to peek between two heads.

Leon lay in the cake, limbs dangling off the table. The black handle of a kitchen knife stuck out from his left side, just high enough to have hit something important. Blood seeped into his yellow shirt.

Taylor wobbled and grabbed the shoulder of a server to get her balance again.

The server turned, face pinched. "Hey!"

It was Dayton, one of her sister's best friends.

"Dayton!" Taylor breathed a sigh of relief.

"Taylor!" Dayton grabbed her hand and pushed their way through the crowd to the privacy of a back hall. "I think I just witnessed a murder!"

CHAPTER TWO

*S*mall but mighty was a description Chef Joey had learned to hate. The way it highlighted her height was condescending.

But she appreciated her ability to take command as the police ushered her and her staff into the dining room to wait for their turns to answer questions.

She settled her staff of cooks and servers into the chairs closest to the salad bar.

"But, Joey, what happened? You were right there." Her assistant, Skye, seemed younger than her twenty-two years as she appealed to her boss.

"My mind was on that stupid cake. I was concerned the table wasn't sturdy in the grass. I don't know what went on behind me while I was talking."

"But you were literally right next to him." Skye's tone was accusatory, this time, but still like a child.

"Yes, I know. Trust me." Joey looked over Skye, to the whole crew. "I was right there, but I wasn't looking at Leon or behind Leon. The police are going to come in and ask us questions. Probably just our names and phone numbers, since there were so many people in the quad. Don't be scared of them. Just answer what they ask."

The small crowd erupted in questions. Joey held up a hand. "Guys, I don't know what they're going to ask. We just have to wait and see. Until then, just sit and breathe and pray this ends well."

"Ends well? Are you crazy? Pastor Leon was murdered." Robin, one of the new servers, piped up. "Murder can't end well."

The server next to Robin had gone green, then drained of all color.

"Dayton, lean forward, put your head between your knees. Robin, help."

Dayton leaned forward.

Robin froze.

"Everyone take a deep breath in through your mouth and hold it. Then let it out slowly through your nose. I don't need any of you passing out right now. Skye, hand these out." Joey grabbed the serving dish full of saltine crackers packets and handed it to her friend. "We'll get through this. I promise."

Skye started the basket of crackers around the group.

Two sheriff's deputies came into the dining room.

"Why don't you come over here with us?" The deputies both had severe, tired faces, though one looked as young as Dayton and the other could have been his mother.

Joey followed them to a table in the far corner of the dining room and hoped no one sitting in the room with her was actually a blood-thirsty killer.

THE SHERIFF MIGHT HAVE THOUGHT he was in control of processing the crowd who had witnessed Leon's death, but Grandma Quinny had other thoughts on the matter. At least concerning the members of her own table. She insisted that Mrs. Sylvester get to talk to the deputies first because of her age and close relationship with the deceased, then Grandma Quinny escorted Mrs. Sylvester to her own apartment, whether the deputies wanted her to or not. When she returned, she cut in again with Grandpa Ernie. The rest of the residents grumbled, but she persisted.

When Grandpa Ernie had given his name, address, and general impression of the night, Grandma Quinny swept him into her new Lexus to take him home—to her home. "You kids go out and have some dinner. Ernie and I will be just fine."

Many hours later, after Taylor and Hudson had spoken with the deputies, they sat in the quiet, dark dining room of Comfort's fanciest restaurant—Berry Noir—a little establishment located at a vineyard just outside of town. They didn't want to talk about the murder they had just seen, but they were only human.

"What do you think Mrs. Sylvester meant when she said Leon was her boy?" Taylor asked, twirling angel hair noodles on her fork.

"That he was her boy?" Hudson sipped the glass of Pinot Noir that the vineyard was known for and frowned.

"But what did she mean? He was way too young to be her son. He had to be our age, right? And she's ninety-two."

"First of all, he was at least thirty-five. But maybe he was her grandson?"

Taylor wrinkled her nose at her slightly younger boyfriend. To her, thirty and thirty-five seemed about the same age. "Probably." Taylor stabbed a broccoli floret and considered it. The way she shushed them while he was talking had seemed so possessive. Maybe he was a grandson she had raised. "Do you know the family at all?"

"I've met her before. And Leon. I do some handyman work there as needed."

"What was he like?"

"Pretty funny. One of those guys that makes you laugh without even trying."

"Was being chaplain his only job? Seems like a volunteer gig."

"Wouldn't know. I'm not Methodist."

The Methodist church ran the old folk's home, and since Taylor wasn't Methodist either, the inner workings of their staff stuff was a mystery to her as well.

As was Hudson.

They'd been dating now for over a year, but not exclusively. That was on her. She'd been given very good advice to give it a year before making major life changes after a significant loss.

Considering her mother had died, she'd moved home to Comfort, and her four-year relationship had ended all in the same week. She qualified for the slow path.

Nonetheless, Hudson had been there for her, pretty much on-call, whether she needed help with a flat tire or someone to go to tea with at the old folk's home. Not to say there hadn't been sparks and romance and fun. There had been. Good fun.

But she'd seen other men, here and there. Her friend, John Hancock, who was in banking, was always up for a night on the town or often had tickets to events he needed a plus one for. She liked their nights out. They were just friends and they both knew it, even if everything they did felt like a date.

And then there was Reg, her friend, the sheriff's deputy. They'd gone out a few times, but she'd kept it casual. Still, she liked him and not just because he'd helped her catch a killer last winter.

She'd never been the kind of girl to say, "I'm not a girl's girl. I like the company of boys better." But she was beginning to sympathize with those kinds of girls. The company of attractive, attentive, interesting men was addictive.

She found herself staring at Hudson's strong face with the scruffy five o' clock shadow and the crinkles around his eyes.

Hudson was four years younger than her but had the kind of face that had looked twenty-five since he was in high school. That and his broad shoulders, muscled arms from all that construction work he did....

Taylor quickly found herself forgetting about the thing with Leon at the place...

"Hello, did I lose you?" Hudson asked with a laugh.

"Yes, but only because you are literally the most attractive man I've ever laid eyes on."

He waved his hand, "Waiter? Check, please."

She laughed and closed her eyes. "What a night, right?"

"Want to go back to my place?"

"Yes." In fact, at just this moment, nothing sounded better. She'd had enough of murder in the last year-and-a-half. Spending a night with this guy sounded much better than going home, barring her bedroom door with a dresser, and letting the PTSD that had come from a few bad encounters with killers have its way with her for the evening.

Her phone buzzed, and though she could have ignored it, she lived in a constant state of alert concerning her sister and her grandfather.

"Have to talk. Please." The number wasn't in her contacts but scrolling back a few messages, she realized it was Belle's friend, Dayton.

"Tomorrow" Taylor's reply was quick.

"tonight please"

She looked up at Hudson with a frown. "I want to go home with you more than I've wanted to go anywhere ever, including Disneyland."

"But?"

"But there's a scared teen who might have witnessed the murder who needs to talk."

"Taylor..." He lowered his voice and his eyelids, a winning combination in her book, "that teen *did* witness a murder."

She chewed her bottom lip and sent another text. *"We can talk tomorrow, right?"* The phone buzzed again.

"Please, Taylor? I'm scared."

She held the phone up for Hudson.

"You've got to go. I understand." He took his last bite of steak.

She replied to the text. *"Where can we talk?"*

"flour sax?"

"I guess I'm headed back to the shop." Taylor scrunched her mouth, not excited about it.

"Can I come?"

Her heart lifted a little. "Yes, please!" If he was willing to stick around through a few minutes of comforting a scared kid, there was still hope for tonight.

DAYTON MET them at the back door of the shop. They slunk in, hushed and shivering, though the June night was still dusky and far from cold.

Taylor flipped the lights on at the back of her shop and filled a paper cup with water from the water cooler. "Drink this, Dayton, and sit." She put her hand on the back of Grandpa Ernie's threadbare corduroy recliner. It was always empty these days as he stayed home with her cousin, Ellery, who was basically his day nurse.

Ellery had been accepted into nursing school for the fall, which was another reason Grandpa Ernie needed to relocate sooner rather than later.

Dayton sat.

A rumbling noise upstairs, like a rolling chair over wood floors, rattled the ceiling. Taylor grimaced.

Hudson gave her a "chins up" kind of smile, though Taylor had a feeling he was as pleased as she was by the noise.

The door to the upstairs apartment creaked open, and Clay Seldon pattered down the steps. "Having a party without me?"

Clay had moved in over the winter. Just for a couple of weeks to get himself together. It wasn't supposed to be permanent. Taylor hadn't wanted her ex-boyfriend, the man who had been her partner of four years, living permanently above her business.

Not long after he moved in, he had convinced her to let him be her bookkeeper too. To pay her back for the free rent.

He ended up taking so much work off her plate she put him on the payroll in addition to the free housing.

All of this rolled around in her brain as she stared at the man she used to love, and the affable half-grin settled comfortably into his friendly face. His flannel jammie pants and sock feet looking every bit at home here as they had in her condo when he had moved in there, "just for a few weeks," so many years ago.

"Hudson." He smiled up at the much taller man.

"Clay." Hudson smiled, the confident look of a man who isn't threatened.

"Sorry, Clay, do you mind? Dayton and I need some privacy." Taylor looked to the stairs he had just come down.

"Sure, I don't mind. Come on up, Hudson. I've got beer."

"I was planning on staying here."

"I think we need to talk alone." Dayton fidgeted, fingers wrapped in the long sleeves of a thin, plaid, flannel shirt.

"Got it. No biggie. I'll take a beer with Clay. I'm just upstairs." Hudson leaned in for a kiss.

The men retreated, leaving her with one of her sister's oldest friends.

She pulled one of the shop's slipper chairs beside the recliner. "What's worrying you?"

Dayton leaned forward and spoke in a quiet, dramatically low voice. "I was in the kitchen when Chef Joey carried the cake out. Me and a couple of other servers."

Taylor waited.

"Two girls left as soon as they finished the stuff they were doing, wiping counters, I think, but I stayed behind for a minute because I had a text from Cooper."

Cooper was the third amigo in the Belle-Dayton-Cooper triangle.

"I was heading out just when Leon got stabbed."

Taylor's breath caught in her throat. "Wait, did you see who did it?"

Dayton's mouth scrunched and eyebrows went up. "Maybe?"

"What did you see?"

There was a long pause as Dayton sorted out what needed to be said. "Right after Chef Joey and some of the guys set the cake on the table, I saw a person with dark hair and a dark suit jacket standing behind Leon, maybe even taking a step toward him. Whoever it was moved to the side, away from Leon, while Joey was talking. Because Joey was talking, I was distracted, but when Leon started to like, fall over, the person in the jacket was gone."

"What do you mean, 'person?' Man or woman?"

"I don't know."

Taylor narrowed her eyes. Was this more of the Generation Z's disinterest in traditional gender?

"I swear! If the person in the jacket was a man, he was a shorter man with sloping shoulders. If it was a woman, it was an average height woman with a very short haircut and a suit also cut for a man. You see what I mean? The person wasn't thin, maybe a little overweight? It was hard to say."

"Could have been a disguise." Taylor drummed her fingers on her knee. She thought if she had been the one to see the mysterious stranger, she would have known if it was a man or a woman, but then, she was still stumped by Dayton.

With a tall, slim, boney figure, small chin but prominent nose, Dayton could easily have been a young man with a baby face or a young lady with the kind of face that other women called "handsome."

"If I was planning on stabbing someone in broad daylight, I'd have worn a disguise." Dayton's words came out stiff and defensive.

"Me too." Taylor wanted to give the kid words of comfort, but she didn't have any. She still woke up at night clutching a sweat-soaked pillow because the woman who had killed her mother had attacked her too.

The one time she had discussed it with Hudson, he had been quick to suggest counseling. She didn't disdain counseling. It had been great for Belle after their mom had died. But she didn't have time. That was the main thing. She just didn't have time.

But it still kept her up at night so she felt like the last person who should be telling Dayton how to get over the fear of murderers. "I assume you told the cops everything."

"Yeah, I did." There was a quiver to Dayton's voice that tugged Taylor's heart.

She had to do something, didn't she?

"But, hon, why do you feel so scared?"

"I think the person saw me."

Taylor ran the scenario through her head as it had been relayed, both to keep herself focused on Dayton's needs and to try and see if the fear was legitimate. "When? Wasn't that person's back to you the whole time?"

"There was a moment right when I first noticed her or him, when the face was turned." Dayton turned in profile. "Like this, and then the person paused and turned away, like they knew they had been seen. Does that make sense?"

"Yeah, it does. If the killer thought they were being watched before they'd stabbed Leon, then they wouldn't have done it. This had to be just seconds after the act." Taylor shouldn't have said it out loud. Dayton wavered and looked ready to faint.

"So, he killed Leon seconds before I saw him…or her?"

"Maybe," Taylor nodded. "But you told the cops this, right?"

Dayton nodded.

"It's going to be okay." Taylor reached out to give a hand

squeeze or something of comfort, but Dayton was curled up, arms tucked in, legs crossed.

"Can I stay with you?"

"Your parents won't like that."

"Please? I'm afraid to stay alone." The words seemed to cost something. The quiver almost broke to a sob.

"Dayton, Dayton..." Taylor reached out again, this time resting her hand on Dayton's shoulder. "You can stay with me any time at all, ever. Whenever for whatever reason. I just thought it might make things hard for you at home with your folks."

"My folks are gone. They're spending the month in Montreal with Dad's cousins. They're supposed to come home in time for me to leave for boot camp, but I'm not going." The frown on Dayton's face looked particularly feminine. "I've never wanted to go into the military. That's all Dad."

"I really don't want you to stay alone. Absolutely come home with me, but...I mean...it's just me and Grandpa Ernie and Belle. Maybe you'd be safer at Cooper's. His dad's a big guy."

Dayton picked at some fuzz on the arm of the recliner. "Yeah. I guess."

"But not tonight. At least tonight you're staying with me. And I can call my cop friend too. We can talk this over with him and see how to keep you safe." Even with Hudson upstairs, the idea of a long chat with Reg made her heart flutter just a little.

She thought briefly that something was really wrong with her as a person but dismissed it. Now was not the time to unpack her troubled heart. Now was the time to be surrogate mom to a scared teen.

She sent Hudson a quick text, and he and Clay hustled downstairs together.

"Tay, if you need anything, I can come over tonight." Clay stood with his feet wide apart and arms crossed over his puffed-out chest. He had never been the biggest man, but he had recently taken up weightlifting and seemed to resemble a tiny rooster next to a stallion, standing like that next to Hudson.

"Thanks, Clay. That's a nice thought, but Hudson already had plans to come home with me."

Clay's face reddened.

Hudson smiled.

Dayton seemed unmoved by the miniature soap opera playing out in Flour Sax Quilt Shop.

CHAPTER THREE

*D*ayton went to Belle's room and Hudson took the couch. Taylor didn't offer her bed, and he didn't ask. The mood just wasn't right for that. Besides, they all felt safer with him down by the front door.

Taylor couldn't fall asleep and found herself digging around Etsy looking for embroidered handkerchiefs.

She could quilt them together for a wall hanging.

It would make a great few episodes of the YouTube show she had inherited with the business.

Taylor had been hard-pressed to find interesting projects her mom hadn't already done, but this was one.

Taylor found thirty-two handkerchiefs. They weren't necessarily cheap, but she needed them, right? She fell asleep with the laptop open next to her on the bed. It might have been good for her if she had kicked it off the bed in the night and it had broken into a million pieces, but she could shop on her phone, too, and anyway, Taylor would probably just use that as a reason to shop for a new computer and get a baker's dozen delivered to the house.

IT WAS EARLY when Taylor woke, bird song sifting through her bedroom window.

She hadn't opened her bedroom window.

She clenched her eyes shut and pulled her quilt to her chin and tried to do a round of circular breathing.

She wanted to think she had opened her window the day before, but she never did anymore. She only and always wanted everything in her room locked up tight before she closed her eyes.

The little breeze that carried the hectic song of the starling into the room was evidence enough someone else had been there. Or still was.

She peeled her eyes open again, one at a time. If a murderer had slunk in here, laying still with her eyes closed wasn't going to keep her alive.

She took three more deep breaths and let them out.

"Hey."

Her heart lunged to her throat. Taylor yanked the quilt fully over her head and screamed.

Feet thudded up the stairs, fast and loud

Her door burst opened smashing the wall.

"What's wrong?" Hudson leapt across the room and landed on her bed.

Shortly before Hudson landed with a thud on her bed, Taylor had opened her eyes and saw Belle, slouched against her closet door with the windmill throw quilt draped over her knees.

"When I got home last night, there was a stranger in my bed." Belle's voice was that of a disappointed schoolteacher.

Taylor wasn't breathing well, so she didn't answer.

Hudson pulled Taylor to a sitting position and put his arm around her. "It's just Dayton."

"Why is Dayton in my bed?"

Taylor's voice found its way out of her mouth and asked, "What time did you get home last night?"

"About an hour ago."

Levi.

Taylor didn't say his name out loud.

She hated that guy.

Weird, overly smart, early college acceptance kid who kept her weird, overly smart, early college acceptance sister out all hours of the night.

Legal adult or not, Taylor didn't approve of this particular teenager spending whole nights with boys. Because of sex. Taylor was a hypocrite, maybe, but Belle was a baby. Her baby sister, anyway.

Thoughts whirled, like they do when your blood is pumping to the rhythm of panic, but Taylor managed to hold her tongue.

"Why is Dayton in my bed?" Belle repeated the question as she folded the quilt and set it beside her.

"Because of the murder." Taylor answered in a firmer, more secure voice, though she couldn't say much more than just that.

"Ah. Got it." Belle rose from her seated position and left.

Got it?

She was so blasé about murder.

Hudson rubbed her back. "You okay?"

Taylor shook her head, but then nodded yes. "From five-thirty in the morning till dark, I'm great. It's just…the other hours that are hard." Taylor glanced at her clock. Five-fifteen. Belle's timing was cursed. "I guess she opened the window when she got here."

"I'll get you some coffee." Hudson was an early riser, like Taylor. A decade of retail life had done this to her, and he was just wired that way. Taylor pulled the pillow over her head and waited for his return. She had a long day of work ahead of her. Hopefully Belle would take Dayton to Cooper's and the three kids could just sort of hang out there. They'd be safe, surely.

Or maybe Taylor could sequester all of them in the apartment and make Clay stay with them. He'd been working out, after all.

He was like a short little bodyguard now. She pushed her pillow to the floor and got up.

Downstairs Hudson was frying some eggs to go with the coffee. Taylor sat at the table and dropped her head to her hands. "Don't say it." She wasn't in the mood for a lecture about her need to find someone to talk about her "troubles" with.

"Got it." He didn't sound pleased.

Belle and Dayton came downstairs together. Belle looked like she had been out all night, as in fact, she had.

Dayton looked like a child. A young girl, to be precise. Wrapped up in a billowy, flowered bathrobe of Belle's with short, pink hair lightly tussled from sleep, and thin bare feet, Taylor had a good idea what Dayton's birth gender was. Dayton's big, cornflower-blue eyes set in a face with sculpted cheekbones and that long, elegant nose, Taylor wondered why Dayton didn't embrace femininity? Few people woke up in the morning looking ready for a photoshoot.

Taylor stood up to get coffee. It was none of her business what Dayton wanted out of life, and Taylor had to chalk her thoughts about a future in modeling up to a lack of coffee.

Dayton got a cup of coffee as well, then followed Belle into the living room.

Their voices carried, though Taylor could tell they were trying to be quiet.

"I stayed because I saw a murder, Belle." Dayton's shivery voice might have been put on. Taylor wasn't sure.

"Who hasn't?" Belle's rolling eyes could be heard all the way in the kitchen.

"Anyways, I like your sister." Dayton's voice didn't carry as well as Belle's, but Taylor caught that.

Taylor smiled.

"I guess you like my pajamas and bathrobe and bed too." Belle laughed, but not happily.

"I'm just trying to not get killed, okay?"

"You have always been such a frigging drama queen."

"Whatever. You need to get some sleep."

"Ugh."

"Would you rather I went back to my empty house and waited for the guy who stabbed the chaplain to find me?"

"Have you lost your mind?"

Taylor couldn't take it anymore, so she joined the fighting teens.

"Dayton's not crazy. We did see a murder, and it sounds like the murderer might have seen…" Taylor hesitated.

"Me," Dayton interjected. "He might have seen me."

Belle's eyes were glued to her phone.

Taylor looked back and forth, wondering if these two were even friends.

"What are you guys fighting about?" Taylor nestled herself into the corner of the couch. "Last I remembered you guys were besties."

"That was then." Dayton's voice did have a drama-for-drama's sake sound to it. Taylor sympathized a little with Belle.

"Did one of you steal the other's guy or something?" Taylor teased.

Belle tilted her chin up.

Dayton's eyes narrowed.

"Cooper?" Taylor said the name with disbelief. "Surely Levi wouldn't like that."

"Who says Belle stole Cooper?" Dayton turned the steely eyes to Belle.

"Do I want to know?" Taylor asked.

"No, you don't. You just want to go make a buck and then spend it."

"Yeah…I'm not a trust fund kid, after all." Taylor referred to the half-a-million-dollar life insurance policy sitting in trust for Belle. Both of them would have vastly preferred their mother over the money, but it didn't change the fact that Belle had a whole lot of money.

Dayton snorted. "At least we know Cooper doesn't love me for my money."

"Whatever. I've got to go."

"At five forty-five in the morning?" Taylor challenged her sister. She was being dumb and deserved it.

"Yeah. I've got to go to bed." Belle stormed upstairs.

"Are you going to tell her what's going on?" Taylor asked Dayton.

"I tried." Dayton stared at the floor.

"Do you want breakfast or not?" Hudson asked. He seemed impatient, which wasn't unusual in the morning, but wasn't pleasant either.

"No, thanks."

"Dayton?"

"Sure."

Taylor followed Dayton to the kitchen. "Can I change my mind?"

"Yes." He set a plate on the table. One egg over easy and a piece of toast. Taylor helped herself to the jam, since it was hers, since this was her house being overrun by people who didn't live here. "Dayton?" she asked as she slathered the toasty wheat bread with some blackberry jam. "I have an idea for keeping you safe today, if you don't have something up your sleeve already?"

Dayton sipped a cup of coffee. "Maybe I'd better see what Cooper is doing."

"Clay works from the apartment upstairs at the shop. He'll be there pretty much all day. I'll be downstairs, you know, running the shop all day too. You could stay with us."

Hudson made a disdainful "humph" sound from his spot at the stove.

"Was that you offering to babysit?" Taylor asked.

"I overreacted last night." Dayton stood. The plate of egg and toast Hudson had just set down was untouched. "I'll hook up with Cooper and then, I don't know. Maybe we'll go talk to the police one more time. But I don't need a babysitter."

"That was the wrong word, I'm sorry."

"I highly doubt Clay would see hanging out with a beautiful girl like Dayton all day as babysitting." Hudson's deep sexy voice was annoyingly sarcastic.

This was why Taylor rarely stayed the night with him.

He really was the worst in the morning.

Dayton cringed.

"He's not too old to notice you," Hudson said. "And some men think newly-legal eighteen-year-olds are fair game."

"You're disgusting." Taylor didn't give Dayton a chance to respond. She did find it interesting that Hudson hadn't been corrected for using the girl label.

"I could be wrong." Hudson shrugged. "I'm not thirty yet. Maybe things change when you get old."

Taylor had turned thirty with literally no fanfare, not so many months ago. She hadn't advertised the day to Hudson, but he had to know.

Dayton looked at her with dismay in those light blue eyes. "Hudson's kind of a jerk."

"You're telling me." Taylor put her plate in the sink and went upstairs. Later he'd probably apologize and say that she had scared him with her scream and that he didn't mean to be such a snot, but you know what? He wasn't the friendliest in the morning. She didn't like it, and she didn't have to like it. Clay was many things, including the loser who hadn't been willing to move to Comfort with her when she needed him, but at least he had the wisdom to keep his jerkiness to himself in the morning.

Three minutes after Taylor got out of the shower, Hudson knocked on her bedroom door. "Hey, Taylor?"

"Come in." Taylor was wrapped in her own girly bathrobe and drying her hair.

"Sorry."

"I know."

"I don't like the idea of you sending that kid to spend all day with Clay."

"He's not a bad guy."

"He's a human though, and she's grown into a stunning girl. I don't want to sound like a creep, but some guys are especially drawn to girls in crisis."

"First off, you seem very confident in your 'girl' assessment."

Hudson laughed a deep hearty gut laugh. Then he paused to catch his breath. But he shook his head and started laughing again. Finally, he took one more deep breath, stopped laughing, and stared incredulously at Taylor. "Dayton? Dayton's dad is my sister-in-law's brother. Were you...were you confused about her being a girl?"

Taylor scrunched her mouth. "No."

He stared, not open-mouthed but just about. "You were confused. The trouble is, you spent too much time in Portland."

"The trouble is, Belle wanted me to be confused. Plus, Dayton's almost six feet tall, right? And anyway..."

He put a friendly arm around her shoulder. Taylor shrugged it off. "So, you've known her since she was born, and you want to protect her from Clay who you feel is definitely a creep. She's a newly legal eighteen-year-old and I'm just old..."

He wrapped her in his arms, this time less "friend" and more loving.

She rested her head on his broad shoulder. A jerk in the morning, yes, but such a strong, kind one.

"You're not old. You're...."

"If you say anything that relates to cheese or wine, so help me..."

"Shoot, we went to high school together." He kissed her cheek and let her go.

"That's better. Even if I was a senior when you were a freshman, we were literally in high school together."

"Don't lock Dayton in an apartment with a guy I don't trust, please?"

"Do you have a better idea?"

He sat on the edge of her bed while she looked through her closet for something to wear.

"Maybe let her take care of her own business?"

"Everything looks safer after the sun rises, doesn't it?"

"Exactly. It's not like someone else is going to die today."

CHAPTER FOUR

*H*udson drove Dayton to Cooper's, and Taylor went to the shop to film with Roxy.

Roxy had her box of hats with her. "Are you sure you don't want to try the pincushion?"

The hat she spoke of was cute. And if Taylor was a sewing-themed clown, it would have been perfect. She forced a smile, much like the one she'd be using in the video. "I'm sure."

"You could use a different one. How about this one? It's cute." She held out a bucket hat made of tattersall patchwork in blues and reds and yellows with a band of faux rope.

"Very nautical. Maybe when we do a compass rose block, we can use that."

"You're not much of a hat person, are you?" Roxy had settled the pin cushion on her head. It was adorable. Taylor could see why she wanted it on video. It looked just like a pin cushion, right down to the hat pins sticking out of its top.

"I just don't think I could pull it off, to be honest."

Roxy tilted her head and considered Taylor. "You looked great in that beret, a long time ago, but it doesn't really go with what you're wearing."

Nothing did. Not that Taylor had a busy print on, because

she had learned not to do that. But today she was sporting their brand-new Flour Sax polo shirt in dusty rose with the logo in a faded lime green with a khaki collar. It was far from stylish, but the colors were correct for the kinds of printed fabric sacks flour and feed used to come in. For that reason, the shirts looked nice with the stock they carried.

The shirts didn't look nice with any of the bright, bold, or whimsical hats Roxy had in her tote.

"We'll find a great hat one of these days." Roxy shut her box of hats. Her grin was infectious, and Taylor was almost recovered from her cranky morning.

Since Clay took over bookkeeping and Taylor focused on advertising, their sales had gone up considerably. Roxy had been given a raise, and they had even hired back Willa, the sweet grandmotherly lady who had been their part-time help when her mom was still alive. Willa would be in later today to run a class.

For the last several years, Grandpa Ernie had spent his days in the back of the Flour Sax, in a little living room like area, or wandered the shop visiting with customers. As an accomplished tailor, he could answer questions and sell fabric as well or better than any of them. But now that he spent his time at home with Ellery, Taylor had expanded their classroom space. His recliner had a place of honor in the corner, next to an expanded coffee bar.

Customers asked after him. Some ladies really missed the old guy, but mostly their regulars were excited that they were offering classes again and that they could fit more than six at a time.

Taylor exhaled and tried to get her mind back to the task at hand. Today's video was risky. Instead of a handy how-to, Taylor was giving a tour of their classroom space and talking about how classes go. She didn't know how their YouTube followers would respond, but she was ready to mix things up a bit.

Comfort, Oregon was a quilt town, and four shops lined Main Street: Bible Creek Quilt and Gift, which offered Churchy style fabrics and gifts; Dutch Hex, which was almost a direct copy of her store except Amish themed, and Comfort Cozies. Some of the ladies, well, technically just Carrie from Comfort Cozies, had been asking if Taylor would tour all of the stores for her show.

On the one hand: no.

Roxy and Taylor weren't doing all this work to benefit the other stores.

But, on the other hand…maybe?

If viewers liked the tour of the classroom, Taylor could tour the other classrooms. They were trying their best to be a destination town with nothing but the four quilt shops on one side of Main Street and the Antique Mall on the other side. Anything that got quilters to town was worth it. But if viewers didn't respond well to a tour of her own classroom space, there was no way she was touring someone else's shop.

As they filmed, Taylor stumbled over words as well as furniture. She took over an hour to get enough footage for their final fifteen-minute video.

"I guess it's better you weren't trying to keep a hat on your head." Roxy gave her a sympathetic pat on the back.

"There were a lot of sewing machine cords…." Taylor pointed to the floor, though she knew she had tripped over her own two feet as much as anything else.

"Jonah is sending some video for you to approve later today." Roxy's son Jonah, who was going into his senior year of high school, did all their editing. Belle managed the behind-the-scenes things at YouTube, the uploading and money, and so on.

"That's great. Tell him I appreciate him."

"Trust me, he knows."

YouTube revenue had returned almost to the levels it had been for her mom, now that they had regular video going out. But it would probably never be what it had been. Laura Quinn had just been better at it. Better at everything, really.

Taylor looked out the window at the sunny day in Comfort.

By the time her mother had been thirty, she'd had a husband and a ten-year-old. A year later, she'd be a widow.

Taylor thought about her dad every day, even if it was just a little. She didn't know exactly how much losing him when she was eleven had done to gild his image, but it had to be quite a lot. A firefighter, he'd been killed on the job, tragically, and not just Taylor, but the whole town remembered him as a hero.

She once overheard her Grandma Delma say she felt sorry for any boy who'd try and marry Taylor. No one could live up to her father.

She could see him in her mind's eye: tall, broad shouldered, holding his firefighter helmet under his arm, his baggy fireman britches held up by suspenders, walking toward her.

No, he probably hadn't had any flaws.

None worth remembering anyway.

If Dad had been snotty in the morning, no one remembered.

The bells above the door jangled as someone rattled it. They didn't open for several more hours, so Taylor planned to ignore the noise, but she glanced that way and spotted Sissy Dorney on the other side of the door.

Sissy was Cooper's mom.

Cooper was Belle's closest friend.

And after helping Sissy find out who had killed her aunt Reynette, Taylor realized Sissy was likely one of her closest friends.

She let her in.

Sissy had a way of coming in like a whirlwind. She was tall, but not that tall, blousy, but not really fat. A hairdresser, but more often than not her own hair was a shaggy mess of dark roots and frizzy curls. "Tell me what's wrong with Dayton. I can't get a word out of the kid." Sissy was dressed for work in a black tunic over matching pedal pushers and black clogs for a long day on her feet.

Taylor was on her feet most of the day as well, but at least

Taylor got to walk around. Sissy owned her own shop just around the corner from Flour Sax.

Taylor patted her head self-consciously. She needed her bangs trimmed, and if she was going to stick with highlights, she needed to get in and get them touched up.

It was only nine. They didn't open till eleven. Taylor had planned on consulting with Clay about the books beforehand, but couldn't get the idea of him wanting to be a bit...overly protective...of Dayton out of her head.

Poor Clay.

He had no idea what nefarious things Hudson had suggested.

She had no desire to spend time with Clay this morning.

"Let's head over to Café Olé so we can talk."

"I can't stand that place. Let's go to Reuben's and get a real breakfast instead." Sissy wasn't wrong to suggest it. Reuben's Diner was a solid morning choice.

"Whatever you say." Taylor led Sissy back out, and Roxy locked up after them.

Reuben's was busy and noisy. The perfect environment for sharing secrets. They took a booth in the back. Sissy ordered a pancake platter and Taylor had a coffee and cinnamon roll.

"She told you about the murder?" It felt funny calling Dayton "she" after all this time. Almost sacrilegious.

Sissy lifted an eyebrow, then just smiled. "Yes, *she* did." As far as the teens were concerned, Sissy was the expert. She had three kids of her own: Pyper, Cooper, and Breadyn ranging in age from twenty to thirteen. "She told me some dramatic story about a man in disguise who had a knife and how she thought he saw her, but don't you think if all that was true, I'd have heard it on the radio this morning?"

"I was there. It's true. Didn't Hudson corroborate her story?"

"She was with Hudson? Hudson East?" This time her eyes narrowed. "I suppose he's only about six years older than her, but at eighteen, that seems pretty old."

"He's more than six years older than her..." Taylor did the math fast, though it wasn't hard. Hudson was...eight years older than Dayton.

"Don't tell me you're still seeing him. Aren't you living with Clay again?"

"Sissy, where are you getting your gossip? First off, Clay rents an apartment from me. Second off.... no. There's no second. Clay rents the apartment above the shop. I live in my house with Grandpa Ernie and Belle."

"Sounds like a good cover story to me."

"Does the whole town think I'm living with Clay?" Taylor set her coffee down and stared at her friend.

"Dayna, Dayton's mom, saw you out with some guy in a suit, with messy hair. Messy hair for men is not in style. So, she says you're not living with Clay. I've heard you're living with him, but you aren't faithful."

"Humph. I'm not unfaithful, and I'm not living with Clay." Taylor chewed on her cheek in annoyance. Clay was a good bookkeeper, and once or twice they'd gone out to dinner to talk business. That was all. Except sometimes he came over for movie night with the family. But *that* was all. Except for that one time, when she was really, really tired and they had been up all night doing inventory and he had kissed her. Well, she had kissed him. But she had been really tired, and that was all it had been. And it wasn't cheating. Because she didn't have an actual boyfriend, Clay or Hudson.

"But you *are* seeing the boy with the messy hair?"

"You can only mean John Hancock. First off, his hair isn't 'messy,' just sort of tousled. And yes, we go out on occasion."

Sissy's smile looked sly, like she had set Taylor up for that confession. "So, it's off completely with Hudson then, is it? Because I heard you were seen at the tea party with him yesterday."

"You heard I was at the tea party with Hudson, but you *didn't* hear that Leon, the chaplain, got a knife in the back?"

"I did hear you and he were there together, but I thought you were living with Clay and refuse to believe you are a cheater."

"Thanks for that, I guess. But seriously, when I said he dropped Dayton off at your place, you assumed they were together? She's a child."

"She's a beautiful young woman."

This so closely reflected what Hudson had said that it caught Taylor off guard. Maybe Sissy was going the long way around to tell her something she was refusing to notice on her own. After all, eighteen was legal, and it wouldn't be the first time a man in his mid-twenties went after an eighteen-year-old rather than a thirty-year-old. "I am dating Hudson." There was a firmness to her words, as though she were staking a claim in him. "Just, not exclusively."

"Casually?"

"What's wrong with that?"

Sissy looked Taylor up and down like she had an expiration date. "And what about Reg?"

"What about him?"

"Are you also casually dating him?"

"Is that not what 'casually dating' means? I had been under the impression that if you were not a couple with any particular person you could date anyone you wanted."

"It's your life."

"Yes, it is." Taylor sat up, stiff. It was her life, and it was none of the business of the good people of Comfort. "You didn't hear anything on the radio about the murder, and no one is talking about it around town?"

"I'm hardly a gossip, Taylor." Sissy gave her a lemony look.

"As you aren't a gossip," Taylor's voice dripped with sarcasm, "let me tell you what I know." Their waitress, one of the many Reuben cousins who started their work lives in the family diner, interrupted with their breakfasts. Taylor was thankful for the moment to compose herself. "Chef Joey was honoring Leon's service to the care home with a fancy cake. She was making a speech, and while she was talking, he slumped over, first onto her and then he crashed into the cake. Everything got chaotic with people getting up and trying to leave. When I got close enough to see what was going on, I spotted a knife in his back." Taylor sipped her coffee.

Sissy was hardly spellbound, but nodded for her to continue.

"Dayton was behind the action. She saw a shifty person who might have seen her. She thinks the person was in the right place at the right time to stab the chaplain. The person was dressed like a man, but was petite, so might have been a woman in disguise. The person disappeared in the mess that followed the stabbing."

"Well, that does match what Dayton claimed. Do you have anything new to add?"

"Just that Dayton is scared. What are you going to do about it?"

"I'm not her mother." Sissy took a long gulp of her coffee.

"She could use a stand-in."

"You do it. You don't have your own kids." Another up-and-down look from Sissy.

Taylor did a little quick math and realized that Sissy had at least two of her kids by the time she was thirty.

"Dale will be thrilled." Taylor rolled her eyes. Dale had once made empty threats about Taylor's family destroying Dayton's future.

"He's not here, is he? Maybe this will soften him to you and Belle."

"Why is he making her join the military?"

"To pay for college. Not everyone comes into money like you two did."

This time Taylor stiffened, and it was permanent. They hadn't "come into money." Their inheritance came at the cost of both of their parents' lives.

"Just because it was a tragedy doesn't make me wrong."

Sissy shrugged. "I miss your mom something awful. She was a good friend."

Sissy had hardly been on her mom's besties list, but Taylor granted that when someone died, they grew in importance in your life. "Dayton seems to hate the idea of the military."

"Kids are so unreasonable. She'll be fine once she gets through boot camp."

Taylor shrugged. "Is Dayton at your place with Cooper?"

"I don't know. I headed straight out. I think Cooper needed to go to town today. Maybe he'll take her with him."

"Let's hope so."

DAYTON WAS on her mind all day as Taylor worked. She tried not to pester the girl, but texted her twice just to check in.

Dayton replied the first time with a thumbs up and the second time with a simple *"K."*

At closing time, Taylor texted Belle. *"Is dayton staying with us or cooper tonight?"*

"Dunno." Belle's response left much to be desired.

"Can you ask her?"

"I'm not going to be there."

Taylor curled her lip in disgust at the phone. Not that the phone was impressed. She had locked up the shop for the night and was alone, except for the sound of Clay's footsteps upstairs. Ellery would be with Grandpa Ernie for another half hour, so Taylor headed up just to say hi.

She knocked on his door, but didn't wait to be let in. He looked up from his phone in surprise when he saw her. "You heard?" He held out the phone.

"No. What's to hear?"

"There's been another death at that old folk's home."

CHAPTER FIVE

*T*aylor sat down with a thunk, the hard, wooden dining chair an unforgiving surface. Another murder? Her throat felt like it was closing. Instead of letting panic get the better of her, she closed her eyes, took a deep breath, held it for seven seconds, then let it slowly out her nose. Circular breathing. Her mom had taught it to her after her dad had died. Looking back, Taylor could tell she'd needed professional help. Her mom hadn't been equipped to deal with the panic attacks she'd had after the fire.

She pulled herself to the present. Thinking of past trauma was just another way of escaping current challenges. She refused to let her brain betray her that way.

The thing was, it was an old folks' home. There were bound to be deaths there. She didn't need to immediately panic.

Clay was staring at her, not worried per se, but definitely curious.

"Are you back yet?"

"Yeah."

"Good. I hate it when you disappear like that. I was telling you something important."

"An old person is dead?"

"Not an old person. One of the CNAs was found in the closet. It's all over the news."

"Sissy hadn't heard anything when we spoke this morning."

"They found her an hour ago."

"By 'news,' do you mean it's all over Facebook?"

He passed his phone to her without comment. His Facebook feed had exploded with the news. "I follow all of the quilt stores and a lot of quilters. It's good for business."

"No one is saying anything useful." Taylor gave him his phone back. The ladies of the Comfort, Oregon quilt world were all posting the same link to a spot from the radio station.

Cricket Jones, had recently moved to Comfort for the job, had been found in the closet dead. No means were mentioned. There were no real details about Cricket except that she was sweet, good with the elderly, and in her mid-forties. Taylor wanted to know the good stuff. Was this woman a drug user? Did she have a violent ex? Where had she lived before Comfort? Who did she spend her time with? Was she even a quilter? "Wait, let me see that again."

He gave it back.

Cricket had been tagged in several of the memorial posts, so Taylor clicked her name. Her friends list was private, her photos were private, and the "about" page wasn't filled out. Useless. She gave it back again. "I should call Reg and find out what's going on." Taylor got up to leave.

"Did you come here for a reason?"

"What? No." Taylor looked at Clay for the first time. He was sock-footed and in a t-shirt and boxers. His thin short hair was a little messy, but not in a stylish way that John Hancock managed. "Sorry."

"Weirdo."

She caught his last word as she left but didn't give it much thought. Reg would know more about this Cricket woman, and he'd also know if she should be worried about Dayton or not. She called him, but there was no answer.

TAYLOR GAVE Reg another call the next morning. There was still plenty of time before the shop opened, so she made herself a cup of coffee in their Keurig and settled into Grandpa's golden-brown, threadbare, corduroy recliner.

Reg answered his cell on the first ring. "Hey you, it's early." He had a sexy voice in the morning. A little gravelly, a little slow. She'd not heard him in the morning before.

"It is, I'm sorry."

He cleared his throat and his froggy voice returned to normal. "It's nice you called. I was thinking about you."

"I was thinking about you too." Taylor tucked her knees up and rested her chin on them. She had been thinking about him, but not necessarily in the way he meant. He didn't have to know that.

"Are you free this evening? I want to drive off with you somewhere far away and show you something marvelous."

"Reg!" Taylor laughed, embarrassed by what he might want to show her.

Like Hudson, Reg was a broad-shouldered, strong manly-man, and it occurred to her he might really be something marvelous to behold.

He laughed, too, a bit chagrinned at what her horrified tone implied. "I just mean some waterfall or mountaintop. Something to impress you."

"You're something else." She sighed, his romantic idea hitting a sweet spot. She'd never understand how she'd come across such a richness of single men in such a small town when all she'd managed to find in Portland was Clay.

"So, are you free?"

"I can be. Belle will be home tonight, so she can stay with Grandpa."

"I'll pick you up at seven-thirty."

"Should I dress for an adventure?"

"Better dress for dinner out, instead. I'm not sure I can drum up a good adventure in one day."

"Basically, the same then?"

He laughed. The Pacific Northwest was notoriously casual.

That was part of what made going out on dates with John Hancock fun. He always dressed for an occasion, so Taylor did too. Very unlike the rest of the world they lived in. Her mind did a quick, whirlwind comparison of the two men.

At least John Hancock knew where he stood, firmly in the friend zone.

Usually.

"See you at seven-thirty," Reg said.

"Wait! Before you go?"

"Yeah?"

"Do you know anything about the murder over at Bible Creek Care Home?" Taylor sat up to knock the romantic notions out of her brain.

"Oh." The disappointment in his voice was acute.

She hadn't called him about a crime or a murder in months and months, so she didn't know why he was upset about this one.

"I've actually been off all week. Vacation time."

"Oh." Now her disappointment was obvious.

"Is dinner off if I can't give you inside scoop on a murder?"

"No, of course not. Let's go away together and be amazed by some super delicious food."

"Thanks, Taylor. See you at seven-thirty." He hung up.

She scowled at her phone. Dinner with Reg would be nice, it always was, but to be brutally honest with herself, she'd rather eat with Hudson or John Hancock, or…even Clay.

Poor Reg.

THE DAY WAS long and quiet. Few customers, and Roxy had the first half of the day off. Taylor missed having Grandpa Ernie around to chit chat with, so she called him at noon, an hour after they'd opened.

Ellery answered.

"Hey, Elle, can I talk to Grandpa?"

"Sure..." She paused. "He's a bit tired, though, just so you know."

"Has he been on his oxygen yet this morning?"

"He won't. He says he's just fine."

Taylor closed her eyes for moment and sighed. "He can be a pretty stubborn patient, can't he?"

"Very much so."

"Did he eat?"

"Yeah, a little breakfast, then a midmorning snack. We're about to do lunch."

"I'll give it a try, anyway."

"Who's this?" Grandpa Ernie answered like Taylor was a solicitor with a thick accent.

"Just Taylor, Grandpa. Just wanted to say hi."

"I'm the only tailor in this family."

"Taylor, your granddaughter."

"I know what they named you, but it's a dumb name for a baby girl. Your dad was an idiot. Thought I'd like it. I said they should have named you after Delma. That's a real pretty name for a lady."

"It is. Delma's a beautiful name."

"Then your mother named that baby Belle. Like a bell? What's wrong with her?" He was certainly in a mood, but he seemed to remember who everyone was.

"I picked that one, Grandpa. Belle was my favorite princess."

"You don't know any princesses."

"She's in a movie. She was my favorite Disney Princess."

"Dumb thing to name a baby. What are you going to name the next one? Fabric because you work in a fabric store?"

"No one's having a baby, Grandpa."

"That's right they aren't, because none of you are married. That's why."

"So, having a good morning?"

"No."

"I hear another person died at the old folks' home." Taylor could have kicked herself for saying this. It was what popped into her head because she figured Cricket was having a worse day than Grandpa was, but this was not the thing to say to make him want to move there.

"I told you that's where folks go to die."

"Well, I mean…"

"It just goes to show, young lady. You want me to move there so I'll die. I don't need to move because I have my own house. You're the one who needs a house."

Though Taylor had inherited her mother's house, where she lived with her grandfather and where Belle stopped by on college breaks, she did not correct him.

"And I don't need a babysitter. You say she's a housecleaner, but she certainly doesn't clean the house all day long, and she's always yelling at me about oxygen."

"I doubt she yells at you, Grandpa." This conversation was less satisfying than the call to Reg had been. When another call beeped through, she was filled with relief. "Gotta go, Grandpa, sorry.

"I bet you're not."

She switched to the other call. "This is Taylor."

"Taylor!" The sonorous tones of her Grandmother Quinny greeted her. "So glad to hear you. It's a terrible thing about young Cricket at the care home. You really can't send your grandfather there."

Taylor sighed. This call was not the escape from her grandparent problems that she had hoped it would be. "I promise I won't move him till the murder is solved."

"And who's going to solve it? That Leon was killed right in

front of all of us, and they didn't catch the guy, and now Cricket? She was a lovely thing. She was your cousin Danielle's husband's niece."

"Adam's niece? He's not much older than I am, and Cricket was in her forties, wasn't she?".

"Wait, you're right. I think she was his aunt."

"Maybe his sister or his cousin?"

"No, not that…. well, anyway, she was practically family, and she died in such a terrible way. I don't want any of you going around there anymore."

"Ellery won't love this change of plans." Taylor began to pace the store, stopping at each shelf to wipe imaginary dust from the little bit of wood that showed in front of the bolts of fabric.

"Bible Creek Care Home isn't the only place you can send him." Grandma Quinny was always so confident.

"Grandma, I'm sorry, I'm at work. Can we have this conversation later?" For the last year and a half, Bible Creek Care Home had been *the only place* and if Taylor didn't send Grandpa Ernie there, then she was a fool. Not just according to Grandma Quinny, but to everyone else in town. Even Clay, who really had no idea what was what, was on team "send Ernie to Bible Creek Care Home."

"It doesn't look busy in there."

"Excuse me?" Taylor scanned the sidewalk outside her front door. A waving hand across the street caught her eye.

"Phyllis at Artifact Antiques called and said she had an old plow your grandfather would like, so I'm just headed in to buy it.

"Does Grandpa Quinny need a new plow?" His collection of pioneer farm equipment was beginning to outgrow what had seemed like an ample acreage.

"Does anyone need a new antique plow?" She laughed, that rich, full sound. "Of course not, but he'd love it, so I'm going in after it. Then I'm coming into Flour Sax to discuss this situation with you like an adult. Things need to be arranged for Ernie before Ellery starts school. We all know this."

They did all know this, but Taylor had the distinct feeling that no one in this town believed she knew it too. Taylor wondered at her mom's fortitude. How had she lived as a widow all those years with this kind of mother-in-law?

Grandma Quinny dragged the tiny old wood-and-rust plow across the street with her and leaned it up against the building before she came in. "Mary Badel over on Shriver and 9th has a bed open in her adult foster home. Ernie can move in there."

"That seems silly." Taylor stood up, tall. "If he's just going to live in a house and have care, I might as well hire a proper nurse and let him stay in his own home." She didn't want to slight Ellery, who had done a great job caring for Grandpa Ernie, but she did want to put Grandma Quinny in her place.

"Don't be absurd. That's far too expensive. Mary is very good, and the others that live there will be company for him."

"Maybe he doesn't want company."

Grandma Quinny laughed again. "Now you're just being stubborn. Of course, he does. He's always had a home full of people and a business to run. He's bored to tears and becoming impossible. I try to take him out at least once a month, but he's been just plain rude the last two times."

Considering the call Taylor had just endured, she knew her grandma was right.

"Bible Creek Care Home is better. As soon as they find out who killed those two people, it will be perfectly safe."

A couple of thin middle-aged men in matching Hawaiian print shirts had stopped to look at the plow.

Grandma spotted them, tossed her silky floral scarf over her shoulder, and thrust herself outside, hollering, "Young men, that is not for sale!"

Taylor wished the young men, or anyone really, would come in and keep her busy so she didn't have to fight with her grandmother.

She didn't see herself as some kind of detective just because she had helped solve her mother's murder, a cold case related to it, and the murder of Sissy's aunt. But catching whoever was responsible for the deaths at Bible Creek was in her best interest, and as Taylor watched her Grandma Quinny haul the antique rust to her car, she realized she was going to get herself involved. Not just for Dayton's sake. For her own.

CHAPTER SIX

*R*eg showed up at seven-thirty.

With Belle and Grandpa Ernie settled comfortably with a pizza, some soda, and a cowboy movie, Taylor slipped away.

Reg had dressed for a night out. Taylor was impressed. It wasn't Hudson in a seersucker jacket cute, or John Hancock in a black suit for the opera, but it was nice. Khakis. Plaid button-down. He looked like a tech guy applying for a job.

They drove up the valley to a little place just outside of Dundee and stopped at a vineyard with a restaurant. These were plentiful in their region and usually guaranteed to please.

"I know there's nothing remarkable about a vineyard." Reg held the door open for her, bristling with excited energy.

"No, it's great." Taylor had changed from her Flour Sax get up into a cotton skirt with a little swing to it and a fitted tank that matched without being matchy-matchy. She had found both in her mom's closet.

"You haven't seen anything yet."

The restaurant was at the top of a steep hill, perched on a long, shallow ridge. The hillsides were covered in grapevines. The narrow stone building had wide glass doors that opened to a large shop full of bottles with a tasting bar on one side. Reg led her through to the restaurant on the other side.

Taylor froze in the entry, her breath stopped. "Wow."

He took her hand. "I'm glad you like it."

The restaurant seating was an open-air series of patios and decks nestled into the side of the hill, each holding only two or three tables, and every table with a mesmerizing view of not only the vine-covered hillside, but the whole rolling valley with the glistening snake of the Willamette River below.

A hostess all in black seated them on a patio three sets of stairs down the hill. Taylor took a long deep breath of the clean valley air. "How did I not know this exists?"

"It hasn't very long, and then only from Memorial Day to Labor Day."

"You've done it." Taylor picked up the menu, and hoped the food tasted as good as it sounded. "You've managed to do exactly what you wanted to do. I'm amazed and impressed."

"It's not really much different from home." He shrugged, a little embarrassed.

"When was the last time you got to sit on top of the world and view it all like this? I don't ever."

He sat up a little straighter and smiled. "Taylor, I'd really like to see more of you."

She bit her tongue to keep herself from saying anything she'd regret.

"We get along great. We've been seeing each other now for a while..."

"It's just since Mom..."

He reddened.

"It's not you, Reg. I really like you."

"Never mind. We haven't even eaten yet. Order something from the expensive side, it's vacation after all." His face stayed red and his manner was guarded, hurt even.

Reg and Taylor had met ten years before, when he helped her with a little case regarding her friend Isaiah's dog. They hadn't kept in touch, her being a freshman at Comfort College of Art and Craft at that time and him being a newly-minted sheriff's deputy. It hadn't even occurred to her to try, as an eighteen-year-old girl. They didn't have a long and deep back story, but they had run into each other last winter. And she did like him.

"I talked to some of the guys at the station about the situation over at Bible Creek Care Home." He changed the subject.

Taylor shivered and sat up. Then a wave of guilt washed over her. This was a nice guy. A very nice guy. But she really did only want him for the one thing.

He seemed to spot her increased interest, and whatever hope had been left in his eye died out. "Jones, the victim they found this morning, had also been stabbed. She had been shoved in the closet. That's all they know."

"You don't have to…."

"You wanted to know."

The waitress came, and they ordered. Taylor couldn't bring herself to order from the expensive side of the menu.

When the food eventually came, it was unremarkable. Good, but all winery restaurants were good. The conversation was stilted. He didn't bring up the murder, and she couldn't make herself ask. They didn't stay for a dessert.

On the way home, he stopped at the sheriff's office. "Give me one sec and I'll see if they know anything else."

"Seriously, Reg, you don't have to."

"I brought you all the way out here. It's the least I could do."

She put a hand on his shoulder. "I ate dinner with you because I like your company, not to get juicy police gossip from you."

He didn't unbuckle. "But you aren't interested in anything more than dinner." He stated flatly.

"I didn't say that." Taylor smiled, trying to look romantic, but not feeling it.

"You didn't have to. Is there someone else?"

She bristled. It wasn't really any of his business. That feeling alone should have told her all she needed to know about her own feelings.

After so many years with one man, dating had seemed new and fun, but it was also new and confusing. Stupid Clay for having kept her out of the game for so long.

"I'm thirty-four years old. I had my wild years a decade ago. I like you because you're serious. You're not a child."

She worked to maintain her composure. There was something so unflattering about the sound of that.

"I'd like to settle down, have a family."

"Then you should." Taylor clenched her hands around the strap to her purse. "But I'm not there yet. There's just been too much change in my life already."

"Don't take this the wrong way, Taylor, but you're not a kid."

"Now you've said that twice." She pulled on the strap of her purse, but it wasn't satisfying. She wanted to wring his neck for pointing this out. Twice.

"I thought, at your age, you'd also be interested in settling down. My sisters both had a couple of kids by the time they were thirty."

"Good for your sisters." Taylor crossed her arms. "We're not in the same place, Reg, so I guess this was a lovely last dinner."

"I guess so."

He drove her home.

She wanted to stomp her way into her bedroom and slam the door shut.

But she was much too old for that.

Clay was a ditherer who abandoned her when she needed him most. Hudson was a jerk in the mornings, Reg…Reg thought Taylor was too old to be single and needed to settle down and have babies.

The whole mess of them could just go rot. Only John Hancock and his uncomplicated invitations to do interesting stuff in the city was worth anything.

Too bad she wasn't in love with him.

Dating would be much easier if she was just in love with someone.

Belle was snuggled on the couch under the princess-themed nine-patch quilt Taylor had made her when she was little. It was the first twin-sized quilt Taylor had ever made. So, so, so many corners to match. It had put her off patchwork for a very long time.

Belle's eyes were glued to her phone, and despite the blast of chilly night air that must have hit her when Taylor opened the front door, she didn't look up.

Taylor kicked off her sandals and took the other side of the couch, tucking her feet under the edge of her quilt.

"Men are awful."

"Cricket Jones had been dating the Chaplain." Belle still didn't look up from her phone.

"That's not quite the non sequitur that it seems, is it?"

"What if her ex, or maybe his, killed them both in a fit of jealousy?"

"Then it would be safe to let Grampa Ernie move there…"

"Exactly."

"Long night?" Taylor asked.

"Very. He refused oxygen, refused pizza. Got mad at the movie, took himself to his room, but refused to go to bed."

"Thanks for staying with him."

"You should just marry Clay and get it over with. Then he could move in here, I could have the apartment, and the two of you wouldn't have to go out on dates because you'd live together again."

"Is that what you think marriage is?" Taylor closed her eyes, but she could see that future so clearly, so comfortably. She opened her eyes again.

"Obviously not, but it's what marriage can be, if necessary."

"And you've decided it's necessary."

"You love him."

"I used to." Taylor yawned. She was exhausted. Nothing

about the day had been satisfying. She was ready to lock herself in her bedroom and sleep it away.

"You still do. Love doesn't really die, it just sort of fades to the background if not tended. And he loves you, or he wouldn't be here still."

"Enough, Belle. I'm going to bed."

"I'm not wrong."

Taylor gave her a nudge with her toe, a snuggly person's version of a kick, got up and went to her room. She flipped on the light, and noticed a big lump in her bed

Dayton.

Fine. If this was the game Belle was playing, Taylor could play it too.

She headed down the hall to Belle's room, but that bed was also occupied. From what Taylor could see of the head that was poking out just a bit from under the covers, Levi, the boyfriend she didn't approve of, was here.

Taylor headed back downstairs.

"Who said you could have a boyfriend stay over?" Taylor crossed her arms and glared at her.

"I'm eighteen."

"This is literally my house."

"Oh, calm your tits. He's got the flu and his parents are on vacation. I'm not going to have sex with him tonight. And if it's anything like the flu that went around all winter, it will be at least five days of celibacy."

"Belle, you shouldn't be so casual about this stuff."

"We've been together two years, Taylor. You want to complain about casual, what about you and that string of men you have coming around?" She yawned and stretched out on the couch.

"You've got to be kidding me, Belle. Where am I supposed to sleep?"

"I'm sure Clay has room."

Taylor went back to her room and changed into jammies in

the dark so she wouldn't wake Dayton. Then she grabbed a couple of quilts from the chest at the end of the hall and went back downstairs to stretch out on Grandpa's recliner. It was like a sleepover, but where Taylor was an unwanted guest in her own house.

She definitely needed to get to the bottom of this murder situation. Too bad she had alienated her connection with the sheriff's office.

THE NEXT DAY was Taylor's day off. She woke with a crick in her neck and a kitchen under siege.

Levi, in a white terry bathrobe that had grubby cuffs, sat at her place at the kitchen table, head resting in his two hands, breathing his germs all over the jelly jar.

"Excuse me?"

"Hi." His voice was mostly gone.

"What are you doing up?"

"I don't really know. Where's Belle?"

"Asleep on the couch. Get out of the kitchen. The last thing I need is my elderly grandpa to get the flu."

"Shots." The word came in a midst of coughs.

"Yes, he's had the flu shot, but there's more than one kind going around."

He coughed again, his thin elbow bent in front of his face, an insufficient guard from his germs.

She stalked out of the kitchen and shook Belle awake. "Get your sick boyfriend back to bed, then decontaminate the kitchen before Grandpa gets up."

Belle rubbed her eyes and then got up silently.

Taylor thundered up the stairs, not caring if her heavy footfall woke Dayton, though when Taylor saw her crumpled up in her bed, she changed her mind. She grabbed some clothes and went to the bathroom to shower and dress.

She avoided contact with the sicky and her sister and escaped the house. But she was keenly aware of the need to eat and maybe consume a lake full of coffee. On the way to Café Olé, Taylor Googled the Bible Creek Care Home to see who she could talk to at the office. Cricket dating Leon was a good place to start on her investigation, and she was ready to make some ground. Someone named Karina Wyandotte was listed as resident concierge, so Taylor decided to ask for her. She needed to ask Belle how she'd found out about Cricket and Leon, but not right now. Right now, she was too irritated.

She had finished her filling and only lightly sweetened pink *concha* by the time she got to the front office of the care home. The lady at the front desk was petite, maybe only five feet tall. Tiny little hands flew over her keyboard, but she had big, big hair to compensate.

"How can I help you?" she asked, without stopping in her typing.

Taylor set her paper coffee cup on the counter next to a name plaque that said, 'Karina Resident Concierge.' "I have some questions about resident life."

Her hands kept at it. Taylor wondered what kind of typing a resident concierge needed to do that was so urgent.

"Sure, go ahead." Her eyes were on a paper held upright in a clip attached to her monitor.

"I have a grandfather who really ought to be in a memory care home. That's something you have here, right?"

"Yes." Still the fingers went. The light click-clacking had a bug-like quality to it that made Taylor feel itchy.

"And do those residents get the same access to, say, entertainment that the regular ones do?"

"Yes, though there are some differences."

Taylor leaned on the counter casually. "What kind of differences?"

Karina picked her paper out of the holder and slid it out of sight. "Memory care patients can attend any Bible Creek Care

Home planned event on the campus, but there are outings that we don't take them on as we don't have the funds to bring the appropriate staff. Also, each building hosts its own smaller events. They are planned and run by the residents, not by the business. That means the memory care wing has events that the other residents don't go to—it's not as though the memory care is being left out, you understand."

"Sure, that all makes sense." But it wasn't getting her anything useful. "What about, say, church?"

"Memory care residents need to be signed out by someone on their approved list, but if they are, they're welcome to do whatever they want on their own time."

"But there's no chapel here?"

She pursed her lips. "Listen, Taylor...."

Taylor stepped back.

"You were here when Leon died yesterday. You know we're a family in crisis right now. I'm sorry if you still can't decide what to do with Ernie."

"Hold on, I didn't mean to offend."

"I'm sure you couldn't help it. I've spent hours talking to Mrs. Quinn, and even your mom, a couple of years ago. And now you need to be convinced. You're all a bit exhausting."

"But regarding chapel, will Leon be replaced?"

"Does Ernie even go to church?" Karina's professional polish was gone now.

Taylor gave her a long look. Karina was a little younger than Taylor, but she felt like she ought to recognize her, but not even her name rang a bell. "Karina, I'm sorry, we got off on the wrong foot. I did come here to talk about Leon, but I chickened out."

"You're wasting my time."

"He seemed like such a great guy."

She cringed in disbelief. "He's a big quilt-shopper, I guess. You've certainly never visited chapel."

"Was he friends with Cricket?"

Karina stood, her tiny hands pressed against the desk. "We

were all friends with Cricket, and if you don't mind, I'm going to lock up. The boss said I could. I was stupid not to."

"Can I buy you dinner to make up for this?" It was a desperate offer.

"Dating Hudson isn't enough? Now you want to take me out, too? Ha. Isn't that ironic?"

"What? Not a date. Just to talk or whatever."

"Yeah, sure. Dinner out with Taylor Quinn, because I want everyone to talk about me."

"Is everyone talking about me?" Taylor was developing a headache.

Karina laughed out loud, a surprisingly attractive, musical laugh. "Like you didn't know. Poor, tragic, heroic Taylor. Everything in life is out to get her, but she doesn't let it hold her back. She's a hero. Look at everything she's given up for her sister. Yeah? Well, what about everything she's taken?"

Taylor stared hard at the livid face of the young woman in front of her. She hadn't paid much attention to underclassmen when she was in high school. Or maybe Karina was from another town....

"Are you saying Hudson dumped you for me? Because that's absurd."

"Is it? Is it absurd he'd date a Wyandotte girl? I know we're not epic town heroes, but we're not trash."

"That's not what I meant."

"Hudson and I were a couple till you got here, yes. We had dated for two years. Then you got back. Poor, poor Taylor. The girl who can't catch a break. Doesn't she work so hard? Isn't she industrious? Isn't it amazing what she accomplished even with her dad dead?"

Taylor inhaled sharply. "Calm down."

"Excuse me?" Karina's hand was on her hip, and she leaned forward, though the front counter was a sizable barrier to her petite frame. "Even my parents thought your dad was the town hero. Saved a baby, didn't he? From that fire? And then went back in for the parents but didn't make it? I'm surprised that wasn't the baby your mom adopted."

"You can go to hell, you know that?" Taylor snapped. All of the rage from the morning was going to go to this tightly-wound person talking trash about her dead parents. "If I ever hear you talking about my parents again, I'll...." Words failed, but it didn't matter. The threat was there, in her face.

Karina lunged across the counter, but the desk was too wide and the counter was too high and she was too short. She knocked over her monitor and slipped back down to the floor, tangled in the cords.

Taylor left.

But she wasn't going to give up.

CHAPTER SEVEN

$\mathcal{T}$aylor stormed across the facility to the quadrangle where they'd had the tea party. She didn't know one building from the other and hadn't gotten herself a map while she was having her friendly chat with the devil.

She hovered near where their table had been. Somewhere in this facility was Hudson's Grandpa Boggy, and somewhere else was that little Mrs. Sylvester. The one who had called Leon "her boy." She'd be the one to talk to, but if she wasn't around, Taylor would settle for Boggy.

It was past the breakfast hour, but too early for lunch. There was a chance someone in the kitchen would know where she could find them.

Taylor rapped on the French doors to the dining room, mouthing "Knock, knock." She tried to sound friendly even though she was pretty rattled.

"We're not open today." A woman approached the door and, though it was locked, Taylor could make out what she said. After looking past Taylor, and seeming to scan the quad, the woman in the white chef's jacket opened the door.

"No resident meals?" Taylor asked.

"We're delivering bag lunches and dinner plates indefinitely. You saw the deputies at the front door, I assume."

"I did. But maybe you could help me...I want to find a certain resident."

The lady wore a name tag that said "Frida." Taylor recognized her but wasn't sure from where. She might have once worked at the school cafeteria. Or maybe the College. The whole chef's jacket thing seemed familiar.

"Taylor, right?"

"Yeah. How are you holding up, Frida?" Taylor said her name because it was on the tag and seemed like the friendly thing to do.

"Not well. I just can't believe someone would do that to her."

"To Cricket?"

"Yeah. She never harmed a fly."

"Was she a good friend?"

"She was everybody's friend. She'd give you the coat off her back and then give you all the cash in her wallet just in case you wanted to buy a different coat."

"I'm so sorry. There's just been so much death. I was hoping to go visit Mrs. Sylvester. She had said something about Leon being 'her boy,' so I thought she must be hurting."

"Probably so. He was very popular with the older ladies. He was fun, but kind of a man child. The kind you wouldn't want to be married to, but everyone wants to mother."

"Interesting that he went into the ministry."

Frida's whole demeanor was one of grief. Taylor wanted to ask her to sit down, but Frida blocked the door. "He was good natured and cared about people, I guess. But I figure he had to be a chaplain because no church would put up with his shenanigans for very long."

"Shenanigans?"

"He was the kind of guy that thought he was a comedian. Jokes, pranks, sarcasm. I don't know. I don't think anyone would ever hire a guy like that to pastor a church."

"Did he have several places he, um, chaplained?"

"Got me. I just know he was here all the time glad-handing the old men and getting mothered by the old ladies."

"You don't seem surprised he got knifed in the back."

Her face froze. "Oh, I was surprised. I was. I hadn't seen that coming in a million years. And yet, when compared with Cricket's death, it doesn't really seem all that surprising. I could see any number of people wanting to stab Leon in the back."

"Anyone in particular?"

The frozen look left her face. "You're kind of into murders, yeah?"

"I wouldn't put it that way."

Frida sucked on her bottom lip. "I don't know. You get people arrested. I wouldn't want to name anyone to you without feeling really sure about things."

"I mean, I'm not a cop. I can't really arrest people."

"But aren't you dating a cop?"

"Excuse me?"

Frida rolled her eyes. "And Hudson East and a banker and have some boy toy stashed above your store? And last I heard some college kid stays nights at your house..."

"At least one of those boys is dating my sister!"

The two women stared at each other and then, like a cork bursting, Taylor started to laugh.

And Frida laughed.

"It's absurd. A single lady can't even go on a few innocent dates in this town."

Frida was still laughing but managed to choke out a few words. "I bet a day's wages you have no idea who I am."

Taylor held up her hands in surrender. "I've been very preoccupied the last year."

"I worked in the kitchen at the high school when you and Chef Joey were there."

"I did remember!"

65

"Sure...." Frida rolled her eyes. "I don't care who you date, but some folks do. This isn't Portland."

"I ran into Karina already." Taylor leaned on the door. "I really don't think Hudson dumped her for me."

"The timing is suspicious."

"Clay, the guy I have stashed in the apartment above my store, is single. Maybe I can introduce them and make things even."

"Oh, dear God." Frida laughed again. "I'm single, you might as well introduce him to me."

"Anytime, Frida. I'd love to shut the gossips up."

"And I'd love to lose twenty pounds. I work in a kitchen. It's not going to happen. You live in Comfort, Oregon. Your dreams aren't going to come true, either."

"But no gossip for me about who might have wanted to see either Leon or Cricket dead?"

"I'll tell you this much. There are people you say you'd love to see dead that you wouldn't actually kill. Leon falls into that category. Then there's folks like Cricket who you'd take a bullet for, but then, that's only because she'd do it for you. So, you ask yourself, did she take that knife for someone else? Or could someone really be so dark and evil they'd kill the world's nicest person?"

"That is a very, very good question."

"I'm not allowed to give directions to resident's rooms. Especially if they're in memory care." Frida nodded slowly, like Taylor was getting the information she needed. "Especially now. The place is on lockdown."

"Got it. Thanks for your time." Mrs. Sylvester was in memory care, apparently, but it didn't matter, the place was all buttoned up.

"I hope to see you around after Ernie moves in."

"Anytime." Taylor, on the other hand, did not hope to see Grandpa Ernie move in.

She went back to the front door, smiled nicely at the deputy who she recognized from stops in to see Reg, and went to the front desk.

Karina was gone. An older man sat at the desk, handsome in a gray-in-the-temples kind of way.

"How can I help you?"

Taylor wondered briefly if this man was in on the gossip, and if so, did he fall into the camp that saw her as a tragic orphan or the one that saw her as a tramp?

"I'm here to visit Mrs. Sylvester."

He nodded. "Good. Good. I'm glad to hear it. May I see your ID, Taylor? Just a formality."

She chalked the caring stranger up as one in the "tragic orphan" camp.

He looked at the driver's license briefly, then gave it back and pushed the guest registry book to her.

"I just need to know what room."

He told her the room number and gave her a map of the building.

Mrs. Sylvester's apartment in the memory care wing had a little table in front of it filled with ceramic Sylvester the Cat figurines, and right in the center of the figurine display was a decorative mailbox that said "Mrs. Sylvester" on it.

Taylor knocked.

A reedy little voice invited Taylor in.

"Good morning, Mrs. Sylvester, I'm Taylor Quinn, Ernie's granddaughter."

"I know who you are."

Her apartment was a sort of studio and very comfortable. An adjustable hospital bed was in one corner, made somewhat private with a little half wall. Across from that was an electric heater that looked like a fireplace. And the wall by the door held a pseudo kitchen. The cupboards were clean, white painted wood, with a granite counter on top. The kitchenette had a tiny little dorm fridge, as well as a microwave, coffee pot, and an electric kettle. Taylor wondered if all of those were safe, but supposed the professionals knew what they were doing.

"Can I make you some tea and cookies?"

"That would be lovely." Taylor took a seat in a small, plaid, wingback chair that was positioned across from a matching love seat.

Mrs. Sylvester took a tube of chocolate chip cookie dough from her fridge, scooped four spoonfuls onto a dish, and put it in the microwave. Then she filled the kettle and turned it on. "It's a convection microwave," she said proudly, "so it bakes like a real oven. My boy got it for me."

"Leon?" Taylor asked, thankful the transition had been so easy.

"No, Carl. My son. Leon, oh, poor Leon, can you believe what they did to him?"

"It's heartbreaking. I remember you saying he was your boy yesterday, so I wanted to come see how you were doing."

The microwave chimed, and Mrs. Sylvester took the plate out.

They smelled like proper chocolate chip cookies. Taylor was impressed. Maybe she ought to put a convection microwave in the apartment above her shop. Seemed safer than having the full kitchen up there above all her flammable fabrics. She hadn't worried about it till Clay had moved in. The two kitchen fires he'd started in the condo in Portland left an impression on her.

Mrs. Sylvester brought her a cup of tea in a small pink china glass and two cookies on a matching saucer. She moved gingerly and sat on the edge of the love seat. "I say Leon was my boy," she said after adjusting the pleats of her dove-colored wool skirt, "but he was actually my sister's boy. Her grandson. It was such a delight to find he was our chaplain."

"Were you and your sister close?"

"Yes, very close, when we lived in Robinette. A close-knit community is good for families."

"And after?"

She clucked sadly. "We moved here, Merlin and I, because of the mill in Willamina. But my sister and her husband moved to Oklahoma to work for a mill there. I was just crushed."

"How did Leon end up all the way back here?"

"I wondered the same thing. He went to seminary in Oklahoma, but he said when he looked at the various ministry jobs available, the one in Comfort called his name because he knew he had family. Isn't he sweet?"

"Very sweet." Taylor thought of her Grandma Delma. She'd been one of six sisters. The girls had also spread around the country for work and husbands. Taylor remembered her grandma going to visit a sister here or there, now and then, but none of them had ever come to Comfort, and Taylor wouldn't know where to start if she needed to find any of them now. "Did Leon play favorites since you were here?"

Her pale white cheeks glowed. "Oh, he did! He was terrible. He'd come have tea with me every Tuesday at three. Cookies and tea."

Taylor nibbled the microwaved cookie. Mrs. Sylvester seemed very aware and capable for someone in the memory care wing. Perhaps that was why she was allowed so many cooking devices. "You'll miss him terribly, I suspect."

"Yes, very much." Her pale blue eyes sparkled with tears.

"And now with the terrible news about Cricket Jones, everyone must be very upset."

"What terrible news about Cricket?" Mrs. Sylvester set her cup down with a shaking hand.

"Oh! I'm sorry…" Taylor set her cup down too. It was not her place to tell the residents what had happened.

"Cricket Jones? The young lady who was so fond of Leon?"

"She must be just devastated…" Taylor offered, hoping Mrs. Sylvester was at least confused enough to think that was what she had meant all along.

"Yes, I suspect so. I called and left a message for her to come over on Tuesday for tea and cookies. I thought it would be a comfort to both of us."

"Mrs. Sylvester…I think I need to be going, but before I do, could you remind me what room Boggy Hudson is in?"

Mrs. Sylvester frowned and tilted her head. "Boggy…"

Taylor tried to remember Boggy's real name, the one Mrs. Sylvester had used. "Um…. Boswell?"

She brightened. "Yes, young Boswell. He's such a scamp. He lives just off Creek Street with his father and stepmother."

Mrs. Sylvester had slipped away, lost in the past somewhere, her lucid moment over. Or maybe she hadn't been lucid at all. Maybe she only thought Leon was her nephew…it was hard to know.

Taylor didn't try to find Boggy this time. She wanted to do a little Googling, and that would be best done at home over a proper lunch. While she was heating water to make macaroni, Hudson called. "Ellery, could you take over?" Taylor waved her phone at her cousin.

"Sure thing."

Taylor took her call upstairs.

"Taylor…"

Taylor was about to reem him out for the scene Karina had made, when she paused. He had left Karina for her. He hadn't cheated on anyone. And it wasn't Taylor's business who he had dated previously. And since Taylor had been the one to insist they were just casually dating, she really didn't have any room to holler at him.

But she still wanted to. "I was ambushed today by a broken-hearted house elf."

"House elf?"

"Yes, a tiny, angry, little elf of a person who works at Bible Creek Care Home and believes I destroyed her world."

"Ah. Sorry about that."

"Obviously I want to be angry with you, but I realize that's absurd."

"Thanks, I guess." He sounded down.

"What's up?"

"Can I see you tonight?"

"Of course."

"You won't be out with anyone else?"

"Nope, that dance is free for your name."

He sighed.

"Don't be like this."

"Sorry." His Eeyore tones were hard to listen to.

"Don't be moody. You know how it is." Taylor paced her room. How was it, exactly? She wanted to have her cake and eat it, too, that's how it was. And it didn't sound very nice when she put it that way.

"Let's just talk tonight, okay?"

"I really want to see your grandpa," Taylor said before he could hang up. "You want to come with me?"

"I'm on a lunch break, not a day off."

"When's your next day off?"

"Let's just talk over dinner. Can I pick you up?"

"Sure, why not?" She paused, a little sick with the feeling she was in trouble. But she hadn't really done anything wrong, had she?

"See you tonight. Is seven too early?"

"Not at all."

Taylor hung up and paced her small bedroom. She didn't have time in her life for moody young men with expectations. And part of the fun of dating Hudson was that he was too young for expectations. What twenty-six-year-old man was mooning over not getting married?

In fact, just considering that idea made her realize she was worried about nothing. Karina Wyandotte had gotten under her skin. She felt guilty, but that didn't mean she was guilty.

Something else was bugging Hudson, and Taylor couldn't guess what it was.

As for Reg, somewhere out there was a girl desperate to jump into marriage for the sake of having a ring. He wouldn't even have to wait for true love.

She was tempted to call John Hancock and see if he wanted to eat at that fancy cliff side vineyard restaurant with her. She rarely called him and when she did, her ideas were rarely impressive to the pseudo-sophisticate and his trust fund.

But she didn't. She'd see how the conversation with Hudson went first.

She had plenty of day off still, and though she had learned the two murder victims had been seeing each other, she was far from any kind of solution. Plus, she hadn't heard from Dayton, the stealer of her bedroom, all day. Taylor had forgotten her, but on seeing the messy sheets and quilts, she remembered and worried.

She sent the teen a quick text. Simply, *"where are you?"*

Dayton replied just as fast. *"w/cooper."*

Taylor exhaled. While not a recent convert to weightlifting like Clay, Cooper was at least young and energetic. And he cared about Dayton. He wouldn't let a killer stab her in the back and shove her in the closet.

Taylor sat on her messy bed and opened her laptop. She needed to learn a little bit more about Leon and Karina.

FOR AS LONG AS Taylor had been at the computer, she had little to show for it. Leon Farkas was on the Bible Creek Care Home website with a mini bio. Graduate of St. Paul School of Theology, hailing from Oklahoma. Happy to join the family at Bible Creek. No mention of his actual family, Mrs. Sylvester. A handful of other sites promised more information, but they were all behind a paywall, and she didn't know which one would give her a virus and which would give her the info she was after.

Cricket Jones was a local. She showed up on a community bulletin board from the late 90s. She commented on the Comfort

Facebook Page. She posted pictures of the creek glistening in the sun to her Instagram. But there were no pictures of her and Leon together. Her Facebook page was private. She was listed on the alumni page for the high school, but she was older than Taylor by about fifteen years and younger than Taylor's mom by about five. Taylor didn't know her.

She should have.

If she hadn't moved to Portland so long ago, she would have.

When she went downstairs, Ellery, Grandpa Ernie, and the macaroni were all gone. Ellery had left a note that they were going for a mid-afternoon coffee at Reuben's.

Taylor sat on her front step and texted Dayton.

She responded, "*Still good.*"

Taylor texted Belle.

She didn't respond.

There was so much day left, Taylor itched to fill it with accomplishments. Achievements. The satisfying feeling of having gotten something done.

She drove to Eugene, an hour away, and went to the mall.

Hudson was coming by tonight and in a terrible mood. Maybe if she had something new to wear, it would cheer him up.

Shopping would certainly cheer her up.

WHEN HUDSON CAME by to pick her up, not only did Taylor have a new pair of jeans that fit like they were made for her and a pair of wedge sandals that improved the look of the jeans, but her highlights had been attended to and she had a fresh manicure. French tips, because she had heard it might come back in style and wanted to be ahead of the curve.

She wore a layered, flowy, silky, spaghetti strap tank that hung loose and showed just enough of her lacy bra, if she leaned forward.

Still, as they drove off to dinner, he was quiet.

"Can you tell me what's up now? Please?"

"I'm trying not to make a big deal of this, but small towns gossip."

"True, they do." Thoughts of what Belle and Karina had accused her of ran through her mind. "But you don't live in Comfort, so it can't really bother you too much.

"My family does."

"I'm sorry. I shouldn't have gone out with Reg last night. I don't like him as much as I thought I did."

Hudson stopped slowly at the red light as though her words had no effect on him.

"But this does seem like an overreaction, don't you think? We're both seeing other people."

"Reg? You ate with him?" Hudson shrugged. "I guess people talk about that. I was thinking of Cricket."

"Don't hold back. You know I'd like to talk about this. I got to talk to Frida, remember her from the school cafeteria? She works at the care home and had plenty to say."

"What did she say?" Hudson pulled into the parking lot of a diner on the far side of Willamina.

Taylor was glad she had gone for jeans, but still felt over-dressed. "Wonderful things about what a caring, generous, good woman she was."

"She was."

"Did you know her well? She's quite a lot older than…us."

"I didn't date her, if that's what you're worried about. She was twenty years older than me." He turned, his eyes mournful. But he lifted one eyebrow, just a little. "I'm only interested in one older woman."

Taylor laid her hand on his knee and spoke softly. He was clearly hurting, but he'd never get it off his chest if he waited till they were inside. "Hey, Hudson. What's bothering you? I've never seen you down like this."

"Cricket Jones was everything Frida said she was. She was also almost my stepmom."

"Ah." She squeezed his leg slightly. She knew what this kind of grief felt like.

"It was years ago, when I was in elementary school. She lived with us. Honestly, it's a bit blurry. I think she was my babysitter for a while, and then my dad fell in love with her. He proposed with all us kids there, and she stuck around another five or six years. Then moved on. We missed her, but I get it now. Relationships don't last forever."

"Help me understand what gossip has to do with this."

"I was working at the high school today. Repair work to the ramps on the portable buildings. I grabbed breakfast at Reuben's on my way in. The family behind me said Cricket killed Leon and then offed herself."

"She couldn't have. She was stabbed in the back and shoved in a closet." Taylor spoke softly, trying to offer him some comfort even with the horrible words.

"She was found in a closet and stabbed in the heart," he corrected.

"That would be a particularly vicious kind of suicide. I can't imagine she did that to herself. It must have been murder."

"Someone at the table argued that side. They said Cricket and Leon were both murdered because they had broken up a marriage."

A picture of Karina's fury came to her mind. She seemed like she would have killed. "Had either of them been married before they met each other?"

"I don't know. I didn't even know Cricket was living in Comfort." Hudson stared into the distance through the windshield of his truck.

"Let's get some food in you."

"Thanks for listening. I have a mom, of course. A good one. But Cricket was good too. She didn't deserve this." He didn't make a move to leave the car, so Taylor picked up his hand and kissed it.

"Thanks for always being there for me, Taylor. I know I'm

awful in the morning, and I know you're not looking for a boyfriend. But you really are the best."

She kissed his hand again, then she kissed his lips. She might have kissed him all evening, but a family in a minivan pulled up and a passel of kids poured out.

"Shall we eat?"

He looked at Taylor, and at her suggestive shirt, then started his car. "We can do better than this."

TAYLOR TEXTED Belle that she wasn't coming home tonight.

Belle responded *K*.

CHAPTER EIGHT

*T*he next morning Hudson wasn't being a pain. Taylor was swaddled in his down comforter, sipping coffee from a hand-thrown mug.

Hudson lived in a large airy home with a view of Moon Creek just outside of Blain, a community so small it made Comfort feel big. His home was quiet and modern, but in a hand-hewn kind of way. He had built it himself, for the most part.

She couldn't see herself living in this house, way out here, or raising a family in it, but she couldn't see him anywhere else.

"Are you going to try and find out who murdered Leon and Cricket?" Hudson asked.

"Yes."

"I'd like to help." He sat on a bench made from a slab of pine resting on cast concrete pillars. "For Cricket's sake."

"We've got to learn more about Leon. He's the mysterious one. I'd like to talk to more of the staff at the old folks' home, but that door is barred to me by the angry gatekeeper." Taylor sipped the coffee and watched him closely to see how he'd react.

"You think I'd do any better?" He was nonchalant, almost too much so.

"Go see your Grandpa. He can take you to visit his friends. Ask lots of questions about Leon. Sign into the visitor's sheet and go about your business. Smile pretty at Karina and compliment her about something."

"Come with me."

"That would be ideal, but I think Karina would make a stink if she saw us together."

"Why? It's not like you're my girlfriend." He turned his gaze away from her with a frown, then left the room.

Nope. Taylor wasn't. He was right. Karina really had no business being so nasty.

Taylor didn't owe Karina an apology for Hudson deciding to move on, and she didn't owe him anything, either. Though, after last night, Taylor wondered if maybe she owed herself.

If this wasn't true love, she didn't know what was.

She dropped back onto her pillow and closed her eyes.

After dinner, they had driven back here, lit a fire in the stone fire pit at the back of his property, and watched the stars fill the sky while they talked about their families, what it means to be family, and what their hopes were.

It was late when they went inside, and though they kissed and snuggled, Taylor somehow fell asleep in his arms, and he didn't wake her.

When she woke the next morning, she was still wearing her date clothes, and the aroma of fresh-brewed coffee meant he was in the other room.

Nothing had happened. Nothing, if you didn't count the heart bonding and the trust that they had built.

Her heart pattered at the thought of it. Perhaps, just perhaps, she really was falling in love with Hudson East.

She joined him in the kitchen. "I really do want to go with you to talk to your Grandpa and his friends."

"Good. Also, Karina had a different view of that relationship than I did. For example, I thought we had been a couple for a year."

"Funny, she said two."

"That's what she said when I ended it too. But a few dates don't make a couple, right? You know that at least. We were only a couple after we decided we were. It didn't take long for me to realize that she was way too high strung for me. I tried to let her down gently, but it turns out, I was too gentle. She started counting us as a couple a long time before I did, and she didn't realize we weren't together. Just thought I'd been busy working, I guess."

"Not till you and we started seeing each other, I suspect."

"Exactly."

"Can I ask what you said to her when you let her down gently? So, I'll know how to recognize it myself?"

His eyes twinkled. "But we're not a couple."

"Still, it's good to be prepared."

"Don't judge too harsh. I was trying to be kind."

"Out with it." Taylor refilled her cup, ready for anything, and very curious what a man like Hudson considered gentle.

"I said that it was really sad when you liked someone but realized it just wasn't working."

"Followed by?"

"No, that was it."

"Are you sure there wasn't a goodbye kiss and a parting look?"

"This is probably where I screwed up. I said it at the beginning of the date, then took her out for dinner."

"Tell me you didn't stay the night with her that night."

"No, I didn't. As far as I knew, we were done."

"Did she act like her heart was broken over dinner?"

"I assumed she felt the way I did, and our friendly dinner meant we could still be friends."

"This is very good information for me. I will keep an eye out for a comment about relationships in general manner followed by a nice dinner."

He laughed. "If you ever agree to be mine exclusively, I plan on making it stick."

Taylor rolled her eyes, but her face heated up nicely. Maybe this was love...maybe it would stick. "I have to get to the shop today. Call me later and let me know when we can go see your grandpa and friends." Taylor looked down at her silky date-night top. "I've got to go get dressed for work."

He leaned over and kissed her cheek. "Will do."

TAYLOR TEXTED Dayton when she got home.

Dayton replied, "*Still at Coopers,*" so Taylor let it be.

She wished dinner with Reg had gone differently. She'd feel so much better about everything if she had the solid advice from the deputy to help her take care of this scared kid. Especially now that Cricket was dead. For all Taylor knew, Cricket had also caught a glimpse of the killer.

But so long as Dayton didn't run around alone and stuck by a family that cared about her, surely it would be okay.

Probably.

Maybe.

Taylor pondered this all day as she rang up customers and restocked shelves. Around three, Clay came downstairs dressed like he had a business meeting. He stopped at the register and leaned on the counter like it was a bar.

"Going somewhere?" Taylor asked, eyeing his khaki trousers, button-down shirt, and navy blazer.

"The bank."

"Oh?"

"You need a business loan."

"Excuse me?" Taylor narrowed her eyes at him.

"Your mom hadn't taken out a loan in ages. You've been using all cash. Do you know what your credit rating is right now?"

"When you have plenty of cash, you don't need a credit rating."

"But it's a good time to get one, for if you need it later." He loosened his tie a bit.

"You're not authorized to take out a business loan for us, you know that, right?"

"Thought I'd pick up Ernie on the way."

"You're insane, get back upstairs." Taylor flung a small roll of cotton floss at him. She knew he was lying, because they both knew Ernie would never leave the house with him.

"I have a date?" Clay said it with eyebrows raised, like a question.

"Try again, this time make it believable."

"I thought I'd see what kind of mortgage I could qualify for."

"And you need to do that in person? The internet isn't good enough for you anymore?"

He shrugged, looking a little embarrassed. This one must have been the truth. "I think it would be better for me to talk in person. My credit rating doesn't really exist. Never had a credit card. Dad gave me that old car. I lived with you."

"And you had all those scholarships for college. Dang, you don't have a credit score, do you?"

"Nope. Thought I'd drive into McMinnville and see what interest I could get. Unless maybe your buddy John Hancock could help me out." He offered her his affable grin.

"Try your luck in McMinnville first. John isn't in the mortgage business."

"Got it. See you." He gave her a jaunty salute and left behind a jangle of bells.

Clay was exhausting. It would be nice to get him out of her apartment. It might make folks stop talking too.

Later, when Taylor closed up, John Hancock called. "U of O symphony orchestra is doing the Alan Thicke retrospective again —it's a mini-symphony of theme songs. I thought it was right up your alley. Are you free next Saturday? It's a fundraiser."

She bit her bottom lip. That did sound right up her alley. Symphonies are the stuffy kind of fancy, and though she liked a fancy night out, the music could get a little dry for her taste. Television theme song symphonies, on the other hand, were fancy and fun.

Then again, if she was really and truly falling in love with Hudson, would she go to any kind of symphony with John Hancock?

John was just a friend. A person needed friends. "Yes, definitely. That sounds like a blast."

"Fantastic. If you don't want to meet me there, I'll have to come by pretty early to pick you up. That okay?"

"Of course."

"Like, four pm early. We'll eat after."

"That's perfect. See you Saturday."

She felt guilty as she swept, dusted, and generally cleaned the shop.

Going to a concert with a friend wasn't cheating.

Especially if you didn't have a boyfriend.

She'd have gone with Belle or with maybe Sissy Dorney. And since Belle and Sissy were the only two people Taylor could think up to go to a concert with, it showed she really did need her friend John.

Stupid puritanical world making her think it was wrong to just enjoy life.

Like Taylor had to want to be settled down and married just because she was thirty.

She *didn't* have to, and she resented how much room it was taking up in her brain.

But last night, and this morning...love, like, real love, had seemed very close at hand.

If only John Hancock had been gay. Then she could go to whatever fancy event he could come up with and no one would mind. Or if he was her cousin or something.

These were small towns. She should start telling people he was her cousin.

She stifled a laugh.

They held hands an awful lot for cousins. And they had been seen kissing in public once or twice.

Stupid John, being so much fun.

Instead of going home, she texted Belle to make sure she was there to relieve Ellery. Then she went to Sissy Dorney's house.

Sissy was putting some kind of macaroni dish on the table for her family. "Want to join us for some goulash?"

Taylor's lip curled in spite of her best intentions.

Sissy laughed. "Trust me, it's good."

"Sure, if you don't mind answering some questions."

"Then grab yourself a seat."

Her youngest, Breadyn, was dressed for karate, Dayton and Cooper were absent, and so was her husband. "Where is everyone?"

"Is that the first question? It's not very interesting. Hubs is working late, Cooper is also working late with his dad, and Lord knows where Dayton is. I've never been able to keep track of that kid."

"But she was supposed to be here. She said she was."

"I'm sure she was at the moment you asked."

Sissy finally sat down with a heavy sigh. "It's been a long day on my feet. I always thought opening my own salon would mean I could do more sitting in an office and less actual work, but it turns out, no."

"Mom, can I have some white bread?" Breadyn looked at the goulash with deep disappointment.

Up close, it still didn't look great, but it smelled good. Like Hamburger Helper but with more vegetables. "Mmm. Looks delicious." Taylor gave herself a heaping spoonful."

Breadyn scrunched up her face but also took a scoop.

"What did you really want to know?" Sissy asked.

At the moment, what Taylor really wanted was to know

where Dayton was, but she skipped to the other stuff anyway. "Anyone you know live at Bible Creek Care Home?"

"Sure, lots of people. I set up a mobile salon there once a month."

"What did everyone think of Leon?"

"Everyone loved that guy. The ladies especially. They talk about him nonstop. He has a way with them."

"And what did you think of him?" The goulash was decent. It tasted like childhood.

"I thought he was a shmuck. If one of my daughters ever came home with a person like that, I'd throw him out of the house. But he was good for morale, I guess."

"He'd been there a long time." Taylor had cleared her plate and was taking seconds.

"That he had."

"No complaints?"

"None I ever heard." Sissy also took seconds.

Breadyn just moved her noodles around her plate with the tips of her fork.

"Did the old guys like him as much as the ladies?"

"No, of course not. Jealous old coots. But some of them liked him all right. He was a good listener, if it suited him. And lots of men like to tell their war stories or their hunting tales or just reminisce about the good old days." Sissy rolled her head from side to side until it cracked. "Don't try that at home. You can hurt yourself."

The motherly caution made Taylor laugh softly. "Had you ever heard anything about his life before he got here? Back in Oklahoma?"

"Not that I can think of. I tried not to get cornered by him. While folks told me he was a good listener, it seemed to me he only loved talking."

"Did he have a particular obsession he'd go on and on about?"

"Besides Jesus?"

"He was a Methodist chaplain. I'd suspect that much at least." Taylor set her fork on her plate. She would not eat thirds.

"He was a very big sports fan. The Ducks and all that."

"But you're a Ducks fan, too, aren't you?" Sissy's daughter Pyper attended University of Oregon.

"Sure, but I know when to shut up about it."

"While he sounds unpleasant, I can't see anyone wanting to kill him over it."

"And yet, he's dead. Taylor…" Sissy sighed again and closed her eyes. When she opened them, she leaned forward, "you were a big help with my aunt Reynette, and I appreciate it, but I am beat off my feet with work right now and can't join you in some new detective thing."

"No, sorry. Of course." Taylor sat up, awkward all of a sudden. Sissy wasn't a close friend, she guessed. All the more reason not to turn away invites to hang out with John Hancock.

"Now, don't get offended. I like you fine. Glad to share dinner. But I'm putting in long days right now and just don't have it in me."

Taylor stood and picked up her plate. "Seriously, not offended. I appreciate this conversation, though. It was a big help."

"You know I don't like to butt into things that are not my business—"

A snort from her daughter interrupted her.

"That's enough out of you." Sissy swatted at her daughter with a laugh. "I don't like to butt in where I'm not invited, but sometimes you have to. And I think you aren't going to solve any issues with your inner person by doing this. I always thought your mother ought to have had you in counseling after your dad died. And now you've lost her too. And Ernie can't be far behind. Let the police take care of Leon's business and you go take care of yours."

Taylor swallowed hard and kept her mouth shut till her brain

TESS ROTHERY

thought of something not rude to say in response. "So, you hadn't heard about Cricket?"

Her voice dropped, "What about Cricket?"

"She's dead. Knife through the heart. And till they find out who, what, when, where, and why, I suspect Dayton is still in danger."

CHAPTER NINE

*B*readyn, go to your room."

"But, Mom, I'm hungry." The tween started to scarf the food she'd been ignoring.

"Then take it with you. The adults need to talk."

Breadyn left the food at the table but didn't argue about staying.

"Who would kill Cricket Jones? All she ever did was work hard and take care of people."

"If she was as great as everyone says she was, then the person who killed her wouldn't hesitate to kill someone who might have seen the murder."

"Dayton is convinced she was a witness, but I'm not. Anyone could have been walking behind Leon when he was killed. In fact, lots of people probably were, which would be part of why the killer thought they could get away with it. You were there, wasn't there a crowd?"

"Yeah, there was. It got crowded around the scene really fast. So, there must have been more folks behind him than Dayton recalls. But I wasn't back there. I was at my table."

"I'd say the killer was dressed like staff so he could blend in."

"Sure...that's plausible." Taylor was ready to accept any

ideas right now. Maybe it was the person Dayton saw who looked like he or she was in a disguise, or maybe it was someone else, disguised so well no one noticed. Taylor pulled out her phone and sent Dayton a text.

"The trouble is, Taylor, I really am about to fall asleep right here at the table. Why haven't you gotten that cop you're stringing along to help you?"

"He cut the string." Taylor didn't correct her. Why bother?

"Call him again. This is more important than your hurt feelings."

"My feelings aren't hurt." Taylor thumped her phone with her thumb. She was irritated by the way her harmless intentions had led to discomfort, but that was the same thing as having hurt feelings.

"Tell that to the red that just poured into your cheeks. I'm not saying you wanted to marry the guy, but no one likes to get cut off."

"Fine. I'll text him." And Taylor did. Just a quick one asking for help.

"What else have you done to get to the bottom of this?"

"It's only been a couple of days."

"In a couple of days, the murderer could be out of the country." Sissy yawned, shook her curly-haired head and then yawned again.

"If my only goal is to protect Dayton, then I guess that's a good outcome."

"You need to talk to Leon's wife."

Taylor blinked in slow motion. "Hold on, I heard he was involved with Cricket."

"Oooh." Sissy ran her fingers through her hair, making the short, thick waves stand on end. "Then I guess we have one suspect."

"Surely he's not married. You must be thinking of someone else."

"I've been introduced to his wife twice by him. But it was

years ago. Maybe they've split up. Definitely check there. If he was seeing Cricket, his wife might have a lot of thoughts on that."

"Got a name?"

"Annie Farkas. Don't know what it was before they got married."

"Does she live in Comfort?"

"They used to live in this little cabin out in Happy Hollow, but I don't know. If they split up, she could be anywhere."

"Fantastic." Happy Hollow was a tiny little place in the Coast Range Mountains, about forty-five minutes from Comfort. Taylor could probably hit up every "little cabin" there in an hour or two, but she didn't relish the idea of bothering a bunch of folks who like to live out of the way where people can't bother them.

Her phone pinged, and her heart lurched. Dayton, finally.

But it wasn't. Just Reg. *"We can talk."* It wasn't the warmest message ever, but at least he responded.

She followed up immediately. *"do you have time tomorrow?"*

"Meet me for coffee by the Sheriff's office at 6."

"Will do. Thanks." She sighed. "Okay, Reg is going to talk to me tomorrow. Let's hope it's not too late."

"Go home and see if you can scrounge up info about Annie Farkas. I'll call Dayton. She knows better than to ignore my calls." Sissy rubbed her eyes with the ball of her hand.

She did look beat, if Taylor was being totally honest. "Thanks. I owe you one."

Sissy shrugged. "Come have dinner again anytime. You're always welcome."

Funny thing about Sissy. Sometimes Taylor felt like Sissy liked her as a person; sometimes Taylor wasn't feeling it. But she knew that the invitation to eat with her anytime was sincere. This was the safest house Dayton could be in, and Taylor needed to get her back there.

Even though Sissy promised to get in touch with the kid, Taylor texted once more before she headed home.

🦢

"I CANNOT BELIEVE the nerve of that woman." Karina Wyandotte sat in the Bible Creek Care Home Kitchen with the skeleton crew who had been preparing the sack lunch meals since the two murders. First thing Tuesday morning, just as the sun was starting to rise, and the place had the surreal feeling a school campus has during the weekend.

"I think she means well." Frida passed a coffee to Karina. "She's pretty good at solving murders."

Chef Joey rolled her eyes. "So are the cops."

"I just can't believe you entertained her at all, much less answered her questions and sent her talking to residents." Karina was in a scolding kind of mood.

"What makes you think I sent her talking to residents?"

"Joey?" Karina passed the question off.

"I've been visiting Mrs. Sylvester every afternoon, and *she* said Taylor Quinn came to see her and had a lot of questions about both Leon and Cricket." Chef Joey poured herself another cup of coffee. She needed several to keep up with kitchen hours. Food was her one true love, but she had never been a morning person.

"I've never trusted the cops." Skye had been sitting back, observing. "Not after the trouble Marco got into." Marco was her husband. None of the crew knew exactly what his trouble had been, but it involved immigration detention. He was home now, but things had been hairy for several months the previous year.

"So, like me, you think it's good of Taylor to be looking out for Leon and Cricket," Frida said.

"I guess I don't know her well enough to say for sure, but I'm glad someone's doing it, and, frankly, I don't have the time or energy or anything." Skye patted her belly, which was ever so slightly round.

"What?" Frida's eyes popped.

"Yup. I'm just telling people now, but that's why I've been so exhausted and pukey."

Frida ran across the room to hug her friend.

Karina exchanged a look with Joey, but Joey wasn't in the mood for spinster-sisterhood.

"If I were Cricket's family, I wouldn't want some amateur messing around with the investigation. That's all," Joey said.

"*Some* amateur, or this one?" Skye asked. "I can understand why Karina is salty about Taylor, but what beef could you have?"

"None." Joey caught Skye's eye and gave a big, fake smile. "Beef has too much cholesterol for this kitchen."

Frida laughed. Skye giggled. Karina gave Joey a long once-over, but Joey ignored it. She had as much love for Karina as she had for Taylor. And for the same reason.

Why was it girls like that—pushy ones, no talent ones, women who just sort of existed but never contributed—made men like Hudson fall in love with them? She'd never understand the male mind.

"So how is Mrs. Sylvester now that her boy is gone?" Frida asked.

"Mrs. Sylvester is sad, but you know how it is with the dementia patients." Joey left it at that. The others nodded. Everyone who worked at Bible Creek Care Home knew what it was like with the memory care patients.

Joey went to the pantry to count non-perishable protein snack types. Not that she needed to, but she needed to be away from the ladies for a moment to think.

Taylor was out of line, snooping around Bible Creek Care Home. This was Joey's territory. Taylor didn't even have family living here.

A light knocking on the pantry door made Joey turn. Karina stood there looking like she knew everything in Joey's mind.

"I don't know or care why you hate Taylor Quinn. But I think our mutual dislike would be better served if we teamed up."

Joey frowned at the small, intense woman. "I don't know what you're talking about."

"Suit yourself. But if she gets that Ernie Baker moved in here, you'll never see the end of her."

Karina left, her heels clicking down the linoleum hall.

If Joey could have her way, she'd keep Ernie Baker out of the care home and get rid of Karina Wyandotte too. She sighed. It all sounded so dramatic, but she wasn't plotting more murder. Just daydreaming. For example, Karina Wyandotte was the kind of girl who'd embezzle or commit petty theft. It would be delightful to catch her with her hand in the cookie jar. But it wasn't like she'd set a trap for her or anything…

Joey stared at the Rubbermaid full of cookies that had been left over from the tea party. The residents each got one in their lunch sacks. Sometimes she and her skeleton crew had a couple with their coffee.

No, she wouldn't hope to catch Karina with her hand in the cookie jar. But she sure wished something would happen to get that woman out of her hair.

"Joey, Earth to Joey." Skye waved a dish rag in the direction of her boss.

Joey started, then offered a wan smile.

"How many residents died here last year?"

"Edith Baycock, Deirdre Johnstone, Evelyn Rupert, and Josiah McCobb."

"So, four, yes?" Skye asked.

"I guess."

"No, it's four. I counted. But you didn't count. You remembered. You remembered their names. They were your friends. This place is a sad place to work, even when there isn't a murder, and you need to get out. Can't you take a little vacation? I think we're all capable of making sack lunches."

"Oh…" Joey hadn't taken the toll of losing her friends into account when considering this job. After all, when she started, none of them were friends. That only came with time. "I don't know. I ought to stick around. The police might think it's weird if I just disappear."

"Then just take today off. I promise we can handle it. Go, get your chef's hat off literally and figuratively."

Joey looked around her spotless pantry. Everything was lined up for a day's worth of sack lunches. Her team could handle it. "Okay." A heavy sigh escaped. "You're right, you know. This is a really sad kitchen to work in. Right now, I'm terribly worried for Maureen Voytich. She broke her hip a month ago and her recovery has really been hard. I don't know if she'll make it." Tears formed as she spoke the fear she had been keeping locked up. Maureen was a lovely woman in her late eighties. She'd already had two heart attacks, and the broken hip had almost taken her. But her laugh always rippled through the dining room making everyone else smile. And she told the silliest jokes imaginable. It would be so quiet around Bible Creek Care Home when Maureen was gone.

"Go, get out. Get some fresh air. Come back tomorrow. Or don't."

"Thank you." Joey thrust her arms around Skye for an impulsive hug. She needed to get away. Maybe an afternoon off would feel good. But if it didn't help, she'd call the boss and ask about taking a longer break.

JOEY WENT STRAIGHT to Café Olé for a cup of *café con leche,* a beautiful half milk/half coffee drink that warmed the cockles of your heart. Once there, she couldn't turn down a dish of flan, either. But the coffee shop was crowded. She stood, awkwardly assessing the small space full of people she didn't know. How had she lived in town all this time, but still only knew the residents of the care home?

"I've got a spare seat." A nice-looking man with a crooked

smile stood from his table. "If you don't mind sitting with a stranger."

"Oh. Um…"

"I'm very chatty," he said, "so we won't be strangers long. Anyway, I'm kind of new to town and need to meet folks. You can be one of the first."

"Sure. Thanks." She sat on the edge of the chair opposite this fellow.

"I'm Clay Seldon." He held out his hand.

She set her things on the table. "I'm Joey Burke. Nice to meet you."

CHAPTER TEN

*R*eg was waiting by the front door of the sheriff's office in McMinnville when Taylor arrived at six in the morning that Tuesday.

"Let's go across the street." He nodded in the direction of a Starbucks.

They walked through the misty morning. It would burn off, and the day would be warm. The weather report promised it. But for now, Taylor shivered in her Flour Sax Quilt Shop polo shirt.

She ordered herself a coffee—just a regular one. Reg didn't have anything. The place was crowded, but they found two stools at the bar that flanked the window.

"I assume you want to know more about the Leon Farkas murder."

"And now Cricket Jones too."

He looked grim, his mouth a flat line in his otherwise ruggedly handsome face. "Well?"

She held the warm paper cup in two hands. She'd had several thoughtful and important-seeming questions in mind, but they felt shallow and worthless now that she was free to ask them. She swallowed hard and went ahead with it anyway.

"First, I've heard mixed reports about his marital status. Do you know?"

"Legally separated."

"Ah. Um...has anyone talked to his wife?"

He didn't respond, his eyes were guarded and trained on the sheriff's office across the street.

"I've also heard he was dating Cricket. They were both stabbed. Were the knives similar?"

He still didn't respond.

"Okay. Then how about this one: Who has contacted the sheriff to talk about the final disposition?" Terms like that were all too familiar to Taylor, having gone through the loss of her mother not so long ago.

Reg nodded, remained quiet for a minute, then responded. "His wife, Annie Farkas. The divorce wasn't finalized so she's still the next of kin."

"I see. But, also, possibly a suspect?"

"I can't tell you police secrets about an open investigation. Especially a double murder. I wouldn't even be able to tell a wife the kinds of things you're asking. But Annie being the next of kin is an issue of public record. I'm sure if you hunt for her you can find a way to contact her."

"And what about Cricket Jones? Who's her next of kin, according to public record?"

"Her parents, Clark and Bethany Jones."

"Wait! I know them!" She almost dropped her coffee. "They are the cutest couple ever. They quilt together. I've met them at the shop a ton of times."

"I've got to go to work." Reg glanced at his watch.

"It's so early." She frowned. This wasn't a friendly chat. This was barely a worthwhile chat, and she'd left her house at five-thirty in the morning to have it. "Can't I ask just a couple more questions?"

"I don't know why I said I'd meet you. Maybe I thought...." He looked at her with softened eyes for a minute, but then they grew cold. "I've got to go to work."

"Thanks for your help."

He left. She didn't walk out with him.

Dating around sucked. That was one thing she'd learned in the last year and a half. Relationships weren't necessarily easy, but this dating around business was for the birds.

Nonetheless, she wouldn't have learned about Cricket's parents if she hadn't kept in touch with Reg some way or another, and somewhere in the database of the Flour Sax Quilt Shop she had their contact information. She could call them immediately and offer her condolences. In fact, had she realized this couple had lost a daughter, she would have done it anyway.

TAYLOR HAD MODERNIZED Flour Sax Quilt Shop's mailing list earlier in the year, so it was a cinch to find Clark and Bethany Jones' contact info. She waited till it was a polite hour to call, but didn't rehearse what she was going to say. She didn't need to—she honestly loved those guys and felt awful for them.

Bethany answered on the first ring.

"Bethany? This is Taylor Quinn from Flour Sax Quilt Shop."

"Taylor, nice to hear from you." Bethany's voice was soft and sad.

"I can't tell you how much I am feeling for you," Taylor said, after a quick greeting.

"Of all the people in the world who could, it would be you."

"Do you remember when your daughter was involved with Doug East?" Taylor was glad Hudson's dad's name came to her quickly.

"Oh! Doug. Yes. He was a nice man, a bit older than her. It took him a while to win over her father."

"His son, Hudson is…a friend of mine. And he is really broken up over this."

"I haven't thought of little Hudson in years. He was such a

pill, but we had so much fun playing grandma and grandpa to him. He was with his mom all the real holidays, but we did our best with April fools." Her voice cracked. "Cricket never got to be anyone else's mommy."

"I don't have words. I'm just so sorry."

"After what you went through, darling, your few words mean the world to us. I can't believe you even thought to call."

"Is there anything I can do to help? I know there's so much to do for a funeral, especially when the death was…a tragedy."

"Our son and daughter-in-law flew in yesterday and will be helping us with everything, but it means so much that you called."

"After talking to Hudson, I just…had to." She knew she wasn't telling the whole truth about the call, but she found herself saying it anyway.

"Thank you, darling. Thank you."

They ended the call. She had a yen to call Hudson, talk to him about the intimate things of his childhood life. Get to know his inner man in a deeper way. But it was the middle of the morning and he was off somewhere swinging a hammer and bringing home the bacon. And for a young man in his mid-twenties, he was remarkably good at both. His spacious, modern home in the hills flitted through her mind. How had he managed all of that in such a short time? Most of it he built himself, and he knew who to hire to do the things he couldn't. But he'd had to work hard and plan wisely and save up to create a home like that. Hard work and dedication….

She had paused the YouTube filming schedule after the murder of Leon. She knew it was a bad decision, but she didn't like filming and took any excuse she could to take a break. Still wasn't fully comfortable. Was always aware she was but a poor imitation of her mom. She wasn't remotely as hard working and dedicated as Hudson was.

YouTube income had increased since they began regularly filming and posting, and it was an important supplement to their business income. Just a month ago they'd had a packed house for a class based on one of her mother's projects—quilters had come from around the country for it. The next class was scheduled for August, and they had booked space at the Comfort College of Art and Craft to accommodate the expected crowd. Quitting because of "stress" was foolish.

She texted Roxy.

Roxy replied with a thumbs up.

A short twenty-five minutes later, she was at the shop. They didn't have much time before they needed to open at eleven, but it was something.

"Sorry." Taylor held her hands up in surrender. "You know how hard this is for me."

Roxy gave her a friendly side hug. "I know. Life is full of hard stuff, isn't it? I respect you so much for continuing this, and not just because it helps my son pay his bills." Her high school son did all the editing, and the wages he earned paid his car insurance and whatever extras teenage boys needed.

"I don't have a plan. I just know we need to do it."

"Then let's not film just this minute. Let's look at the plan you've been working on and talk our way through it."

Taylor's filming notes were in a binder at the desk at the back of the shop.

"You wouldn't have texted if you didn't want to do this." Roxy didn't seem phased by Taylor's reticence.

"I know. I've gotten lazy, I think."

"Hardly."

"I just mean…I spend all day thinking about who killed Leon Farkas, or who I'm going to dinner with, or what's going to happen to Grandpa Ernie. Now that Clay does all the accounting and we've got Willa back to work with you…I don't know. I just feel very distant from the shop."

"It's not your shop." Roxy's words were devastating even though she said them without judgment. "Your grandma founded it. Your mother left her indelible stamp on it. You've been saving it, true, but it's not like it was your creation or your passion."

"And yet, it sort of is, isn't it? All I did in Portland was manage a Joann's, and I called that my passion."

"But it wasn't rally about the fabric, was it?"

"I do have a degree in fiber arts from the craft college." Taylor was beginning to feel defensive.

"I'm not doubting your qualifications. I promise. There's no one else in the world I want running this place. But from the style of fabric to the YouTube program, none of this exists because it's what you would do, is it?"

Taylor looked across the many, many walls of vintage reprint thirties fabric. "No."

"You've brought in a few new fabric lines, but even though they aren't exactly what your mom had before, they are almost the same."

"It's what the shoppers want."

"But what do you want?"

Almost like her mind refused to take life seriously, John Hancock, Hudson East, and even Clay all came to mind. "It doesn't really matter, does it?"

"You've got a bad case of the megrims, I'm sorry to say. And filming today, or even going over the film schedule, won't help."

"Let me guess, it's time I start seeing a counselor to deal with my grief."

"It's not a bad idea, but they might not have an opening this second. How about we make some popcorn and watch your mom's videos and cry together a little?"

A laugh escaped.

Roxy smiled softly. "I love you, Taylor, but I miss your mom so much it hurts. Every day."

"I'll make coffee to go with the popcorn." This time she gave Roxy a hug. It was easy to think that all the grief in the world always belonged to her, but it wasn't true. Laura Quinn's death had left a lot of people lonely and hurting.

They were a wreck when it was time to open the store, but it was a good kind of wreck. Red-eyed from crying and tummy ache from laughing and talking and remembering. They didn't get through a single video without stopping it to talk about something it reminded them of.

For the rest of the morning, she could hear her mother's voice in her head reminding her that you get what you pay for. The integrity of the materials is what makes the integrity of the quilt. And the person. This was implied with the lift of Laura Quinn's eyebrow, and the knowing look she gave the camera. If a person didn't have integrity, if they weren't a good, quality person on the inside, no one should be surprised to see their life fall apart.

HUDSON STOPPED by right after Flour Sax opened at eleven. "I've got a bunch of salvage stuff to drop off across the street." He jerked his thumb at the antique mall across the way. "We've been fixing up an old Queen Ann in Junction City. Deirdre at Comfort Memories has first dibs on all the good salvage."

"Lucky her." Taylor had managed to pull herself together after the emotional release of her morning with Roxy.

"This time, for sure. Lots of good stuff. I was just wondering if you were up for lunch, since I was in town."

Taylor loved the old-fashioned way Hudson would come in and see her, or call, instead of texting little invites like this.

Roxy was within listening distance and nodded with a sappy smile on her face.

"Sure, what time?"

"Give me about an hour to unload. I thought we might take Grandpa out and talk to him a little about Leon."

"Ooh. I like." And she did. The idea of distracting herself with the investigation was even better than a lunch date. No need to come up with small talk.

Exactly an hour later, Hudson and Taylor took a comfortable

stroll to Bible Creek Care Home to collect Hudson's grandpa, Boggy. He was waiting with his windbreaker and a khaki bucket hat. "Well, well, well! I didn't know I'd have good company today." He gave Taylor's elbow a little squeeze.

"Grandpa, what's your poison? We can go to Reuben's or the dining hall or the bar."

"The bar?" His face lit up. "You know, I haven't been to the bar in at least a year. But you'd take a lady there?"

"It's not so bad at lunch time, Boggy." Taylor blushed. It was so sweet, this idea that she might be too delicate to go to a bar.

"Then let's go. I could use a beer. You know what they've been doing here?" He walked them out, locking his apartment as he went. "They've got us on short rations. Sack lunches. Sack lunch for breakfast—it's got yogurt in it. Sack lunch for lunch, which is fine, except they never give us bologna. Sack lunch for dinner. That's just an insult. Who wants a cold dinner? I don't."

Boggy was stronger, fitter, and a bit younger than Grandpa Ernie. The gentle walk across their small town to the nicer of the two bars didn't strain him at all. "They promised us good times at this old folks' home, and what's good about sitting alone in your apartment eating a cold sack lunch three times a day?"

"Literally nothing is good about that," Taylor agreed

The atmosphere of Loggers, the nicer of the two bars in town, wasn't all that nice. The dimly lit, dark interior smelled like stale beer and dirty frying oil. The knotty pine walls had been shellacked long ago and were golden and greasy. The tabletops felt sticky, though they looked clean. The dusky atmosphere couldn't hide that the oxblood vinyl booths had been repaired with duct tape or that the chipped linoleum floor was also held down with the silver plastic repair magic. But Boggy sat down with a happy sigh and took a deep breath. "Smells like despair in here, kids, but it's better than eating alone. And they don't serve beer at Reuben's."

The waitress—a regular at Flour Sax—brought them their menus. "Good to see you, Boggy, and you, too, Taylor." Suzanne smiled a wide, gap-toothed grin. She had the quirky looks of a super model or a small-town girl. There was something special about her that life in the city would have ruined. "And Hudson, right?"

"Yup. Good to see you."

The men each ordered a Budweiser and burgers, but Taylor got a Coke with hers. "I'm headed back to work after this."

"Can you imagine cutting yardage drunk?" Suzanne laughed.

Taylor smiled, but didn't laugh. She hated the feeling of being drunk and avoided it.

"This is what I'm talking about, Son." Boggy leaned forward and stared down his grandson. "Good food and the company of beautiful women. How am I supposed to get that if they keep feeding us sack lunches in our rooms?"

"Any word on when dinner service will resume?" Taylor wished she had discussed this with Reg. She assumed the residents were in their locked apartments to keep them safe, but she didn't know if Bible Creek Care Home decided that was how they needed to do things or if the police had.

"Not a word. And we were supposed to go to Spirit Mountain tomorrow. Leon took us once a month."

Comfort, Oregon bordered the Grand Ronde Reservation, and their Spirit Mountain was one of the most popular casinos in Oregon.

"That sounds exciting." Taylor nibbled a French fry. While a day at the casino did nothing for her personally, the loss of that outing would be a big deal to the residents. "But, are you telling me the chaplain used to take you all gambling?"

"He took us for the buffet. Whatever else we did was up to us. Chaplains in general are very nonjudgmental." Boggy grinned. "I liked the craps table. Simple fun. Mrs. Sylvester always gave me a five to play in the slots for her. Magically, she always won ten." He winked.

"Anything for the ladies, right, Grandpa?" Hudson chuckled.

"What else did Leon do?" Taylor asked.

"He was a smart cookie." Boggy narrowed his eyes in thought. "Always had some fun idea. It's hard to come up with stuff for us old folks to do, you know. No mountain biking or jet skiing. He set up one of those computer sports games in the rec room, though, and we have bowling competitions in the winter. In the summer we putt-putt in the quad."

None of that sounded like it would get Chaplain Leon Farkas killed though. "Any other outings? Overnight trips?"

"No, but a few of the classier folks go see the school plays at that little college in McMinnville."

"Obviously you go."

He grinned. "I can be classy when it's warranted."

"I bet all the employees loved the guy." Taylor decided to turn the conversation from the residents to the staff. She just couldn't picture any of the folks like Boggy going in for stabbing. Especially stabbing and shoving the body of Cricket Jones in a closet.

CHAPTER ELEVEN

*J*oey floated back to her apartment. She hadn't met a friendly stranger under the age of seventy-five since taking the job at Bible Creek Care Home.

The warm glow of the early summer sun on her face, the fresh air as she walked down the long driveway to the apartment she lived in above the garage of her bosses' house, the happy feeling of a sweet mid-morning treat all combined to make her wonder if she believed in love at first sight.

It was nonsense.

Silly.

She didn't believe in it, but hadn't the world looked absurdly dark and impossible before Clay welcomed her to his table at Café Olé? And hadn't it turned into an amazing place of wonder and hope just seconds later?

Once safely behind her own door, she allowed herself to laugh out loud. Surely she hadn't fallen for Clay on first sight. But she had the loveliest feeling that, given enough time, she might very well fall deeply in love with him and find that this morning, this very morning, was the morning she had met the love of her life.

She flopped backward onto her futon, a silly, happy smile on her face, ready to dream about wedding dresses that suited the petite bride. She had just decided on a very long train when her phone rang.

"Yes?" She hoped it was Clay. They had exchanged numbers, after all.

"Joey. This is Karina. I hear you have the day off." Karina Wyandotte sounded desperate, dramatic, and excited.

Despite knowing Karina could sound like that for the most foolish reasons, Joey felt her pulse increase. "What's wrong?"

"Nothing is wrong, necessarily, but you and I need to talk. Are you at home? I can come over."

"Yes, fine…" Joey sat up and glanced around her. The place was clean enough for Karina.

"Fine. I'll be there in ten minutes."

Ten minutes was enough time to decide between white, ivory, or blush for her imaginary wedding dress, so she dropped back down, closed her eyes, and let herself dream.

Karina let herself in and strode to the armchair like she was running from something.

Joey sat up, shocked. Karina hadn't been over before, much less let herself in.

"What's going on?"

"Do you have any coffee?"

"Um, yes, of course." The apartment was a studio, one wall of which was a kitchen. Joey took the few steps necessary and filled the kettle with water and the French press with beans she had ground that morning.

"Sit down, you're making me nervous," Karina ordered.

"I can sit down or make coffee. You're going to have to pick one or the other."

"Ugh. Fine." Karina turned the chair to face Joey. "Let's take care of the Taylor Quinn situation now, while we can."

Questions tumbled in Joey's mind, fighting with the happy dreams of Clay Seldon for primacy. She was pretty sure Clay was the ex everyone had said was living with Taylor, but she wasn't going to hold it against him.

"We both have the day off. How often does that happen?"

"Rarely." The kettle was taking forever to boil, Joey tapped the side of it with her pointer finger and wondered if Clay liked girls with painted nails. Kitchen work meant hers were rarely painted. "What exactly do you want us to do today? I thought you just wanted to try and keep Ernie Baker from getting an apartment?"

"That's definitely on the list, but we could do anything, anything at all. Remember, she's a man-stealing homewrecker who doesn't deserve Hudson East."

Finally, the kettle whistled. Joey filled the French press and set her watch for four minutes. "But I don't want to do anything crazy, Karina. I mean, nothing we could get in trouble for, right?"

Karina sighed, exasperated. "What kind of trouble are you avoiding? Arrest? Sure, we can avoid that. I'm not here to get a record."

"Okay, so what are you talking about then?"

"Hudson is done with me, obviously," she sneered. "And I wouldn't take him back if he begged. But, darling, you are a hot piece, did you know that? I say we get him to take you out. He'd do it. He's never been able to say no to a pretty girl or a sad girl. You're more than pretty—prettier than Taylor, if you ask me. And though you're not sadder than her, God bless the person who ever is, you did just lose a couple of friends to murder. Let me give you a makeover, then we'll hunt him down and start to turn his head."

Joey pinched her mouth. This she would have loved yesterday. And every single day before yesterday. But today?

Her mind did a compare contrast, vector graph of Clay and Hudson. Clay was new. Clay represented hope. Hudson was the one she'd had a crush on for most of her life. "I don't hate the idea. But how do we find him? How do we make this work?"

Karina poured out a plan to track Hudson down while Joey

poured the coffee. Eventually it was Joey's turn to talk again. "But, why limit ourselves to Hudson? I met Clay this morning," her face warmed nicely as she said his name.

"Oh, did you!" Karina's eyes sparkled. "And you want to go in for both at once?"

Joey shrugged, embarrassed. "If Taylor can date around, why can't I?"

Instead of answering, Karina picked up her phone. She poked around, and when someone answered she said, "Hey Sissy, we need an appointment for Joey Burke. Yes, right?" Karina laughed. "I agree. The sooner the better." There was a pause. Joey shifted uncomfortably. "Perfect. See you in an hour."

"Who knows," Karina turned her conniving smile back to Joey, "maybe we can hook that policeman too."

THE MAKEOVER WAS PAINLESS. Her hair couldn't go too short because she liked to be able to put it all up in the kitchen. But when Sissy was done, it looked cleaner, neater, healthier. It didn't hurt that she gave it a non-permanent color wash, just a deeper brown to make her fair skin look ever so slightly more ivory. Then Sissy did her eyebrows, and threading hurt far less than tweezers had ever done. Another stylist at the salon did her face. The fake eyelashes that made her eyelids feel heavy seemed a bit much, but she couldn't deny they looked amazing paired with a "natural" face and red lip.

"I feel like I'm going out somewhere fancy," Joey laughed as she left with Karina.

"You are. My closet." Karina lived in a large house half a mile outside of town. It had once been a derelict, but Karina had bought it for back taxes and during her two years of dating Hudson, he had helped her fix it up, like an HGTV show.

Kind of like she was doing with Joey.

That said, the clothes in Karina's closet, though they were

about the right size, were not right at all. Karina had a miniature hourglass figure, and though Joey was also shorter than average, that was all they shared. A decade in the kitchen meant Joey was what she liked to call "cuddly sized."

"Well, that's a wash." Karina stared at Joey in one last dress that she couldn't zip up the back but still managed to be loose in the bosom. "You do have something nicer than bleach spotted t-shirts and jeans, right?"

"Sure. I've got something." Just barely, but she did.

"Good. Put something together for later tonight, and we'll conquer Hudson. You're ready?"

"Sure." The plan was simple enough, as far as Joey was concerned. She just had to show up on time and let Karina throw a tantrum with her as the subject. Apparently, the makeover and Joey's big brown eyes would do the rest. The part Joey wasn't sure entirely of was Karina's ability to get Hudson to the right place at the right time.

Karina gave her a big hug and then pushed her out the door. "Okay, get out of here then and don't mess up your face or your hair. I'll see you tonight."

"See you." They had walked from her apartment to the salon and out to Karina's house. She wondered how she was going to keep her face and hair nice on the two-mile walk back. As the wind whipped her expensive new hair on her way home, she didn't care. Karina was a madwoman, and nothing was going to come of her plan. Right before she turned onto Main Street, she peeled the fake eyelashes off.

Clay worked for Taylor at Flour Sax.

Perhaps today she'd take up quilting.

CHAPTER TWELVE

$\mathcal{C}$lay whistled his way back to what he called his work-live space. Joey Burke was a doll. An absolute doll. Dark and mysterious.

Taylor was a dishwater blonde.

Joey was petite and soft where Taylor tended to be tall and hard.

Maybe this Joey was exactly what he needed to get over his broken heart.

Not that he was looking for the next love of his life, but he wouldn't turn it down if Joey was as great as she seemed at first glance.

Joey had been quick to give him her number, so he suspected the interest was mutual.

He'd wait a day then text. Dinner at Berry Noir should be a good way to start things. Followed by who knows what. He'd find out.

Taylor was hard at work in the shop looking dishwatery, tall, and wearing the unflattering polo shirt everyone had to wear at Flour Sax now. She looked tired. Pretty, but tired. A little sympathy tugged at his heart. He wanted to feed her and send her to bed. But since he couldn't, he pushed her out of his mind.

Yup. He needed someone new to think about, and the pretty, dimpled face of chef Joey fit the bill. He tried to keep her in mind as he made his way through Taylor's store and up to Taylor's apartment.

He was just settling into his armchair with his laptop to get some work done when he got a text from Taylor. "Team building tonight. Loggers. Everyone needed. Flour Sax is buying."

He responded with a thumbs up.

He didn't hate going to the bar with the team. Willa was a dear old girl who treated him like a favorite son. Roxy was a firecracker and only ten years older than him. He'd considered taking her out on more than one occasion and still thought, if he got stuck in Comfort forever, a man could do worse than Roxy Lang.

And then there was Taylor. Sure, she looked a bit worn out today, but who wouldn't with all she had going on? She could use the night out more than all of them put together. A burger to fill in the hollows of her cheeks, a drink to get her to relax. If there was music, he'd get her out on the dance floor and show her team building.

It was always fun to be the only man in a group of women at a bar.

He went back to work not thinking about escaping from Comfort or about romancing Joey. Just happy that he had something fun to do for the night. One day at a time. It was usually the best way to take things and rarely failed for Clay Seldon.

Well, it had failed once.

Just that time he'd decided to wait it out and see if Taylor really meant she was selling their place and moving.

But it usually worked out just fine.

THE EVENING ATMOSPHERE at Logger's wasn't much worse than for lunch. The crowd was bigger, which was always nice. And everyone seemed to be in a good mood. Taylor smiled at her little crew. She had been inspired by her outing with Hudson and Boggy. Willa, the dear who had come out of retirement, had a parent living at Bible Creek Care Home. Maybe, just maybe, Willa knew something about Leon and Cricket that could crack the case.

Seated next to Clay, who looked unusually happy and young tonight, Willa looked tired but happy. She wore a quilted vest, all Flour Sax fabrics, over her Flour Sax polo. Her reading glasses perched on the end of her nose as she read the menu boasted a beaded chain. The shadows under her small dark eyes made Taylor think she'd better get on with her plan.

"Where are we at with guild business right now?" Roxy didn't look at the menu, instead focusing her attention on Taylor. "I know they had some big quilt hop scheme, but I hadn't heard anything much about that recently."

"The only thing on schedule right now is the Cascadia Quilt Expo." They had a big—very big—event coming up. Taylor had a to-do list as long as her arm, since bringing the expo to town had been her idea.

"Are we going to talk about it on the show?" Roxy was always good for reminding Taylor she could weave their various business ventures together.

"Bad idea." Clay jumped in. "We need to focus on evergreen content. Nothing time sensitive. Play the long game on YouTube. The highest earning videos are still Laura's work."

It pinched a little to hear him say that, but it was true. Taylor's mom's videos were still more popular than hers. "You're probably right. But maybe we can do a Facebook live or one of those other things that disappears after a while."

Willa yawned.

"We need to get this lady a Coke before we lose her." Clay dropped an arm around Willa's shoulder.

"Back again?" Suzanne was still on shift and welcomed Taylor and party with some surprise.

Taylor shrugged, "When something's working..."

"A Coke for my dear friend." Clay patted Willa's shoulder where his arm was resting. "And a PBR for me. Ladies?" He indicated it was Roxy and Taylor's turn. Taylor also had a Coke. Roxy also had a PBR.

"Ready for food order?" Suzanne asked.

"Not yet. Give us a few." Taylor eyed Loggers' entertainment options. She really wanted to get Clay and Roxy off doing something so she could have Willa to herself. The pool table was busy, but there were several dartboards.

"I really want us to have a little fun together tonight." Taylor shut her menu. She'd have a burger and fries. It didn't need a lot of thought. "A meal together, conversation, maybe some darts. Something to remind us we have each other. It's been a hard couple of weeks in Comfort."

"Fellowship." Willa nodded at her. "You ought to come to Bible Creek Methodist on Sunday night. Prayer and singing and potluck. Very good fellowship."

"Do you bring your marmalade cookies?" Clay asked like a child.

"Sometimes." Willa rolled her eyes at Clay. "Move your arm. You're crowding me."

He gave her shoulder a squeeze and then released her. "I'll come if you bring the cookies. And I bet Roxy would, too, am I right?"

Roxy smiled indulgently. "I do like the marmalade cookies."

Willa's face brightened. "If that would get you two in church, of course I'd make them."

Taylor looked around to see if Suzanne was coming back with their drinks, but she was nowhere to be seen. She happened to be looking when the door swung open and Joey Berk and Karina Wyandotte walked in.

They didn't seem to be together as they took seats at either end of the bar.

Suzanne made it back with their drinks and took their food order.

"Service here is slow," Clay said. "How about some darts?"

Taylor could have kissed him for reading her mind. The thought warmed her a little. She missed kissing him.

"I'm in. Willa?" Roxy stood.

"No, no. I'm worn out."

Clay took Roxy's arm and walked with her to the other side of the bar. She didn't need help walking, despite her limp, but she didn't seem to mind.

The door swung open again, but this time Hudson entered, looked around, then joined Karina at the bar. He hadn't noticed Taylor.

She didn't want to think about what he was doing there with the insane firecracker he used to date.

"Uh-oh." Willa clucked. "Those two used to be very much in love." She also hadn't missed the sight of Taylor's almost-boyfriend meeting another woman at the bar.

"I've heard."

Willa leaned forward. "Take some motherly advice, dear. You don't have forever to make up your mind."

"Sure..." Taylor tried to train her eyes on Willa and not keep glancing at the bar, but it was hard.

"Boys like Clay are a dime a dozen. Men like Hudson are rare. Don't let him get away just because Clay is familiar."

"Of course not..."

"I feel you dragged me out here for some purpose." Willa rested her arms on the table.

"You see right through me." Taylor sighed, and smiled apologetically. "Your mother still lives at the Bible Creek Care Home, right?"

"Yes."

"Don't even!" The yelling voice interrupted every conversation in the bar. Both Taylor and Willa turned.

Karina was standing at the other end of the bar now,

teetering on a pair of stiletto heels, her face red as she screamed at Joey. "Don't you dare pretend you have any feelings for Leon or Cricket."

Joey's face went pale. She seemed to wobble on her chair.

A blur of khaki passed as Clay ran to her side. He held out his hand as though he could keep Karina away. "Hold on, hold on, hold on. Calm down." What he lacked in eloquence he made up with in sincerity. "Joey is minding her own business, and I suggest you do as well."

Taylor was confused—did Clay even know Joey? She scanned the room. Roxy stood next to Hudson, nodding at something he was saying.

Hudson stood, and he and Roxy joined Taylor at the Flour Sax booth.

He lifted an eyebrow. Taylor shook her head, not knowing what was going on.

Voices were quieted and things had seemed to calm down when Karina shouted again. "She can't have everyone in this town!" She flung herself at Joey and pulled her hair. Clay hadn't gotten between them, but from the side, wrapped his arms around Karina, pulling her away.

"Should I intervene?" Hudson asked Willa.

"She's your date," the older woman spoke with disdain.

"Not a date." He held up his hands in surrender. "She wanted some pictures for a memorial wall to Cricket. From when I was a kid. Said she'd buy me a beer to pay me for it. I told her she didn't have to."

"Sounds like a date to me." Willa frowned.

"It's okay," Taylor soothed. "Hudson can accept a thank you beer whenever he wants."

Hudson didn't look as pleased with Taylor's good attitude as she thought he ought to look.

"What set her off?" Taylor asked.

"You got me. As far as I know, Joey was just sitting there,

drinking alone. She didn't even say hi, and I've known her since grade school."

"I wonder what men Karina thinks Joey is trying to steal..."

"Clay?" Hudson asked with a pointed look at Taylor.

"Who would she be stealing him from? I set him on the curb with a 'free' sign more than a year ago."

Hudson gave her joke a half-smile, half eye-roll and checked his watch. "I have a busy day tomorrow and an early start or I'd ask if I could steal you from your party."

"It's a nice thought."

"But she hasn't drummed me for information yet," Willa supplied. "And, sadly, she's not going to get to tonight. I'm too old for bars. But if she comes to fellowship at church with me, I'm sure I can think of answers to whatever question she has about Leon. That is what you wanted, isn't it?"

Taylor nodded.

"Hmmm." Willa's eyes narrowed. "Then come to fellowship. There are a few of us there who might know exactly what you want to know."

Willa slid out of the bench seat and stood with a groan. "Taylor child, I know you need help, but I am giving you my two-week's notice. Surely there's someone young in this town who won't mind standing all day and going to bars at night."

"Let me walk you out." Hudson offered Willa his arm, and they left together.

The little fight seemed to have died out. Clay had taken Joey to another booth, and Karina sat back at the bar nursing a beer.

Taylor considered the scene before her. Joey was a bit on the young side. Twenty-five to Clay's thirty-four, but that wasn't the worst age difference in the world, and if it got him out of her hair, all the better.

Suzanne brought four burgers to the table that now only Roxy and Taylor were sitting at. "Take one home to Jonah," Taylor offered, digging into her dinner. "And if Clay's hungry, he'll come get his himself.

Clay and Joey left the bar together, though he did grab his burger from Taylor's table and offered her an apologetic half grin.

As she watched him walk out, she had a twinge of loss. There he went, the man she…. She stopped herself mid-thought. How long was she going to allow herself to wallow? Sure, a year and a half ago she'd had all sorts of visions about their future together, but at least he was still alive, and if she wanted to pass the time of day with him, she could. Unlike Leon Farkas or Cricket Jones.

THE LIGHT in the apartment above Flour Sax glowed through the gap in the curtain as Taylor drove past. She wondered if Joey had gone up with Clay. She wondered if they'd have an embarrassing good morning as Joey tried to slip out the back the next day. Then again, as a chef who ran breakfast, she'd be long gone by the time Taylor and Roxy were filming the next morning.

Taylor longed to call Hudson, but he had an early morning, too, and calling Hudson because she missed Clay was a level of not-coping-well that she didn't want to fall to.

Instead, she texted Dayton, the scared young adult she hadn't heard from in a while.

As if by miracle, Dayton replied. "Safe. Don't worry. Hiding."

This was exactly the kind of message that would make Taylor worry.

BELLE JOINED Taylor at the breakfast table the next morning. "You know," she said as she poured a cup of coffee for her sister, "I'm getting kind of worried about Dayton."

"Funny you should mention that." Taylor passed the phone over, opened to the cryptic message from the night before. "When are her parents coming home?"

"They aren't. Last I heard they are putting the house on the market and moving permanently to Montreal."

Taylor's heart seemed to stop. Poor Dayton. "They can't just abandon her here, can they?"

"This is all from Cooper, who heard it from his mom. Well, she didn't tell him, but he overheard her talking to Dayna— Dayton's mom. I guess Sissy was pissed. She said they had to send the kid a plane ticket. Cooper couldn't hear the other side, but his mom said a bunch of stuff about how they can't force her to join the military, and they can't abandon her here with no job or money. You get the picture."

"They have to come home to pack up their stuff though, right?"

"You'd think. Cooper didn't get those details."

"I'd better add seeing Sissy to my to-do list. How about dinner tonight? She said we're always welcome."

"Sure, better than your cooking." Belle grinned. Maybe getting out of Comfort for some world travel soon had put the mercurial teen in a good mood. If so, Taylor hoped Belle would have a lifetime of great adventures and only come home when she was happy.

Belle excused herself, carrying a plate of dry toast and a glass of water.

Taylor stared after her. It took her longer than seemed right to remember Levi was upstairs with the flu. This couldn't continue. She had to get rid of that kid somehow.

Taylor sent Ellery a text asking if she could stay a little later with Grandpa Ernie and got a thumbs up. She had to head to the shop for filming, so she did the washing up quick and then put on her YouTube face. More make-up and hair product than her norm, but she'd noticed she wasn't herself recently. She was a sort of shadowy, hollowed-out version of herself, but not in the "I've started running" or "I went vegan" kind of way. She was sure she was eating enough, and she was treating herself, too, so there was no way she was losing weight due to neglect.

What she needed was a nice long day in town with an unlimited credit card. That always put the roses back in her cheeks. Until then, she just hoped Jonah could work some magic when he edited the video. Get some life in her eyes, if that was possible.

At the shop, she just bumbled around. She was early for filming. She had sort of wanted to catch Joey sneaking out of Clay's apartment.

Joey, as she found herself saying several times since the deadly tea party, was a nice girl. She liked Joey. Missing the closeness of her childhood best friend, Maddie Carpenter, because of a misunderstanding regarding Belle's grief counseling, Taylor longed for a girlfriend to fill the void.

Roxy showed up at nine, right on time. If Joey had been upstairs, she'd left before Taylor got there. No friendly teasing this time. But if she was brave, she could face the dragon at the front desk of Bible Creek Care Home and pop over to say hi. After all, considering the tantrum Karina had thrown at the bar, Joey and Taylor had something they could bond over—a mutual enemy.

CHAPTER THIRTEEN

arina Wyandotte sat in her office chair, spinning it side to side in agitation. Her plan hadn't worked last night. Her vicious attack—and it had been a good one—on Joey had somehow thrown Hudson into Taylor's arms. It didn't make sense. Joey had texted that the attention from Clay must have been just as good—surely that would make Taylor jealous, but why would she be jealous that Joey had the attention of a mealy-mouthed little man like Clay when she had Hudson on a string, and that string was wrapped around her finger?

Karina wanted to go to the kitchen and give Joey a real piece of her mind. If Joey had an ounce of brains, she would have gone straight to Hudson for protection when she saw he wasn't coming to her. How hard would that have been? But having it out on Joey wouldn't be a good use of her morning. Besides, there was a mid-morning staff meeting for department heads. After that she could have a few quiet words with her new friend. She could put her right.

Mid-swivel, her boss Van Rexel came in. A tall, handsome man in his mid-fifties, he had become a sort of goal for Karina. Not him personally, but him as a type. Van was very rich, and quiet. He didn't seem like the kind of man who'd make a fuss around the house for his wife. He was well-dressed, today in khakis that flattered his bottom, and a gold shirt that showed off his tan. His hair was silver, but thick. Like the old guy on Mad Men. And his eyes, also a sort of silvery gray, sparkled with amusement whenever he spoke.

She would have liked to make him her target. He was a catch —but someone had already caught him. And the divorce had been acrimonious, to say the least. Marv's new wife was a disappointment, in Karina's opinion. She ought to have been a sexy young blonde, but, instead, she was about his own age with short silver hair that kind of matched his. She golfed too. At least his first wife had been housewifely and made cookies for the staff.

"Earth to Karina." Marv's eyes sparkled, almost like he was laughing at her. She wasn't sure if she'd been staring at him or past him, but it didn't matter. She was young and pretty and didn't golf or cook, so she wasn't his type anyway. "The mid-morning meeting is important. The sheriff is coming in to update everyone on the investigation and give us our new parameters. While the department heads are meeting, I need you to run to town and get a few things." He slid a list across the tall counter that separated Karina from visiting family.

"At your service."

"Good, keep up the good work." He made a finger gun and a clicking sound as he left.

Roxy and Taylor filmed an indifferent video about keeping your scissors sharp. Even Roxy looked defeated at the end of it.

"Your heart isn't in this right now, is it?"

Taylor put away her many pairs of scissors and didn't reply.

"We were doing really well all winter and spring." There was an uplift at the end of Roxy's words that should have been, well, uplifting. "But this murder…"

"And with Dayton off hiding somewhere." Taylor traced the blade of her Ginghers. "My heart's not in it. That's a good way of putting it."

"Is there something you've been wanting to do that you've been too busy for? Someone you'd like to talk to? You might as well. I'm in today, and Willa is as well. The shop doesn't really need all three of us."

"I'd love to finally talk to Leon's wife. I bet the whole mess could be cleared up in that one conversation."

Roxy laughed. "You don't think she'd just admit to murder, do you?"

Taylor scrunched her face. "No, but I bet she's the only one who really knows what Leon would have been killed for. She might not even know she knows it."

"Then go ask. Why not?"

THE FARKAS' house in Happy Hollow was exactly what you would picture for a place called Happy Hollow. It was tucked off Three Rivers Highway, down a long gravel drive that rounded at the house to make it easy to leave again. Sheltered by the Evergreen forest of the Coast Range mountains and encircled by a velvety green lawn, it was an illustration of bucolic rural living.

The house itself was small and Sears-kit styled in the Tudor tradition with peaked roof and arched doorway.

Taylor parked in the rounded drive and took a deep breath. She didn't know if Annie was grieving the loss of her almost-ex-husband or relieved. And she didn't know if she'd let a stranger in to ask probing questions, either. Taylor knocked on the cheery lime-colored door and hoped at least Annie would be home.

An elfish tween girl with hair in small buns all over her head opened the door.

"Hi," Taylor faltered. She hadn't expected there to be kids.

Hadn't even thought of children. "Is, um, is your mom at home?"

The tween narrowed her eyes, then turned and hollered over her shoulder, "Moooom!"

Within seconds a slim, elegant woman with sleek, golden bobbed hair came to the door. "Yes?"

"Hi, um, Annie?"

"Yes?" Her face was neutral. No signs of recent weeping, no signs of shock at seeing a stranger at the door. She stood behind her daughter, patiently waiting for Taylor to state her business.

"Hi. Um. I...." But Taylor was at a loss for words. She didn't know Annie, didn't have anyone to introduce them, and stood staring at a kid who maybe ought to have been devastated by the recent loss of her dad.

Those feelings, those panicked feelings from all those years ago, rolled over Taylor. But she too had been able to present herself as calm during the day back then. Maybe this tween was the same. Able to holler for her mom now, while the sun was shining, but broken into a million pieces at night on her own.

Taylor rallied. She knew about grieving kids. She could do this. "I was wondering if we could talk about Leon."

Annie sighed heavily. "Maeve, head to your room for a few, okay?"

Maeve skirted around her mom and left.

Annie took a step as though to join Taylor outside, then changed her mind and opened the door wider. "Come in. I have coffee, how do you take it?"

Taylor followed Annie to the kitchen.

"First of all, I'm so sorry for your loss. I wasn't aware that Leon had kids."

Annie inhaled slowly, but not in frustration or anything like that. She sounded instead like she was fueling up for a long talk.

The kitchen was small by McMansion standards, but had room for a round pine table and four chairs. Taylor sat and

Annie poured coffee from a percolator into a blue and gray handmade ceramic mug. "Cream or sugar?"

"Cream, please."

Annie took a small paper carton of half-and-half from the fridge and brought it to the table with the mug, then she sat. "I'm sorry for whatever he's done."

"You misunderstand." Taylor sipped the coffee. It was strong but not bitter.

"Ah. Then I had better let you talk." Annie had a mug that matched Taylor's. They were both lovely glowing things with thick rich blue glaze and delicate sides, though the clay itself felt sturdy in her hand.

"I'm sorry for not introducing myself. I'm Taylor Quinn. I live in Comfort and run Flour Sax Quilt Shop."

Annie's eyes went soft. "Oh, yes, you were in the news recently. I'm so sorry about your mother."

"Thank you."

"You helped with that other investigation as well, didn't you? The death of Reynette Woods? I have one of Reynette's quilts. It's beautiful. I'm not a quilter myself," she stroked the side of her mug with her thumb, "but I appreciate beauty in all art forms."

"Yes, she was very gifted."

"I assume you must be here to offer to help me find out who killed Leon." Annie sighed as though the idea made her tired.

"I was really wondering if you could help me. You see, I was there when he was killed as was a dear family friend. That friend thinks she saw the killer and that the killer saw her. I know, it sounds melodramatic, but she's young. And she asked me to help her. To look into it. The sooner the killer is caught, the sooner this girl feels safe."

Annie lifted an eyebrow and nodded. "I see. That does change things."

"So far everyone I've talked to either loved Leon with their whole heart or begrudged him the love everyone else gave him, but not enough to kill him. Especially in such a dramatic matter."

"And as his ex-wife, I'm maybe the only person you could think of who would want to see him dead."

"Not at all. You're the only person I could think of who knew him long enough to know why someone else might want to see him dead."

"The police have spent considerable time here with me. Don't you think their resources are better than yours?" Her words weren't judgmental. Tired, but not impatient. She seemed curious. That's how it felt to Taylor. Annie didn't seem to mind the intrusion, but she hadn't made up her mind to help yet.

"Reynette was killed over money—the potential loss of it, anyway. My mother was killed by a woman who, well, she was deranged, but what spurred her to kill was the idea that Mom had hurt her daughter or damaged her in some way. Is there anyone in Leon's life who might have felt something like that?"

Annie smiled. "Do we know any deranged people he has harmed? Not offhand. None I can think of anyway. Do I know anyone who would benefit financially from his death? No. No life insurance policies. No savings."

"Is that why you separated?" It was a bold question, but something about Annie's tone, her open body language, and the way she made eye contact, but not too much of it, made Taylor think she could ask a personal question like that."

"Yes." Annie set her cup down. "Leon was very charismatic, but not wise. And he was overtly friendly, but not kind. It was a difficult relationship for me, made worse by his gambling."

"Was it an addiction?"

"I don't think so." She paused. "No, I really don't. He claimed it was, like you do when you want sympathy for your bad behavior, but he wasn't racking up debt behind my back to fund the gambling, and he wasn't out every night doing it. No... he just slowly but surely frittered away our life's savings and didn't mention it."

"What was the final straw?"

"He's in the ministry and that doesn't pay well. I'm an artist, a potter," she nodded at a hutch full of pottery that matched the mugs they were drinking from, "and that doesn't pay well, either. Every penny we had saved through the years had come as a sacrifice. No sports for Maeve or Orrin, for example. No summer camps, either. I work in my studio behind the house and so we were a one-car family for several years as well, though I briefly taught pottery at Comfort College of Art and Craft. He said it didn't pay well enough to justify the expense of keeping the second car. I agreed, though I miss it."

"Were you able to start again when you separated?"

"No. The position was filled. The last straw was when I realized the savings, not much, mind you, but safely in mutual funds for retirement someday, was just gone. All of it."

"That seems like it could point to addiction."

"The marriage counselor agreed. But I don't think so. He went to the casino with his residents and just lost the money there. Over and over and over. At our age, we ought to have had more, I know, but you don't have to be an addict to lose thirty-thousand dollars in five years of trips to a casino."

"I see."

"But the loss of thirty-thousand to gambling is devastating when it is literally all you have."

"And there wasn't a life insurance policy? Not through his work?"

"If Bible Creek Care Home insured him for their own gain, I don't know about it. They certainly didn't insure him for us. And neither did I. He had a congenital heart defect, and the premiums for a life insurance policy weren't affordable."

"Annie, I'm so sorry to make you dig through all of this again."

"It's to be expected. The police have been here several times, as I said. The pastor from the church wanted to talk it out with me. I've been fielding calls from the media."

Taylor shook her head. "Still, a nosey citizen seems like one too many to me."

"When you care about someone, as you care about your young friend, sometimes you have to do things that are inconvenient to others."

Annie's grace made Taylor uncomfortable, stiff and awkward with guilt. "When Leon gambled," she turned the conversation, "he lost, so it's not as though there was some hit man out looking for him because of his absurd winnings."

Annie smiled, her eyebrows crinkling in humor. "If he had to be dead anyway, I sure would have liked it to be for that reason. I could use some ill-gotten gain about now."

"What about the residents? Did they win much? Or was someone losing so much they got angry at him?"

Annie shook her head. "I don't know much about the residents. Once the kids got to school age and could take the bus, I had to give up the car, and so I wasn't around to get to know them."

"He never took you with him on his field trips?"

"If he had, how could he have gambled away our life's savings?"

"True."

"Gambling was his weakness. But it wasn't weak enough to bother the owner of the business or the denomination that ordained him. I made some calls before we separated. I thought if I had the support of the church, maybe we could save the marriage."

"I'm shocked that a religious body would condone gambling."

"They said that because he had confessed it was an addiction, they would never hold it against him."

"That's weird. I would never hire someone to work at Flour Sax who had confessed to a gambling addiction."

"Churches are different. They often reward people who

admit their sins like that. It encourages the congregation, I suppose." Her eyes flicked briefly to the hutch of pottery.

Addictions came in many sizes, and Taylor wondered if Annie regretted her decision to be an artist—and she wondered if she'd had any real control over that decision. "What were you hoping his, um, bosses would do about it?"

Annie frowned, her eyebrows drawing together. "I wanted him removed from his position as chaplain. I thought it was too much temptation. He needed to have a more boring job where his ego wasn't being fed by the adoration of grateful residents all day long. He needed work where he wouldn't be the center of attention. I don't know what it ought to have been, but they told me his gift was clear and that he was needed and that the residents would be bereft without him."

"Did he at least cancel his trips to Spirit Mountain?"

"No. He said that God would give him the strength to not gamble and that the residents didn't have to suffer because of his weakness. The bosses ate that up. He was reformed, redeemed, and sanctified all at once."

"And that's when you separated?"

"Yes. If the church wasn't going to look out for his wife and children, I had to do it on my own."

"Did you know his aunt, Mrs. Sylvester?"

"We'd met."

"Is there anything I ought to know about her?"

"She adored her great nephew."

"I feel like I've interrupted you to no good end." Taylor stood. "But thank you for your time. And let me know if there's anything I can do to help."

Annie smiled gently. "It's a lovely thought."

"Oh, one more thing." Taylor remembered suddenly that there might have been a problem just as bad as the gambling in Leon's life. "What did you think of his relationship with Cricket Jones?"

Annie's face reddened. "Cricket was lovely. Honestly. If you had to have a stepmom in your family, she was a good one."

"But?"

"But I do wish the relationship could have waited until the divorce was final."

"Did it wait until you were at least separated?"

"One wonders." Annie's face, still pink, was otherwise calm and clear.

She walked Taylor to her car and said goodbye.

Out back of the charming picture-book house nestled gently in the Happy Hollow was a studio and a kiln where Annie had been able to build her dream life as an artist as her husband slowly but surely took it apart again, bit by bit.

Even if he had been cheating on her as well, Annie Farkas didn't seem like the kind of woman who would kill.

Taylor drove back to her shop wishing there was something she could do for the sake of his kids whose grief and pain she understood much more than his wife's. There was still plenty of day left at the shop. She was thankful for something practical to keep the sympathetic grief at bay.

Karina Wyandotte paced the hall at the Bible Creek Care Home. Her errands had been run and the place was still on a sort of modified lockdown. The phones weren't ringing, and there was nothing to do but stew in her frustration at ruined plans. She had an ally in Joey Burke, an ally to annoy the crap out of Taylor Quinn. But Joey wasn't a very impressive ally. She'd had a simple job and biffed it.

But maybe it wasn't Joey's fault. Maybe the trick to getting between Hudson and Taylor wasn't in romance.

She smiled to herself and transferred the desk phone to her cell.

If Hudson loved anyone in this world, it was his Grandpa

Boggy. And if Boggy loved anything at all, it was lots of attention from girls who flirted. From the elderly Mrs. Sylvester, who could have been his mother, to the high schoolers who bussed tables in the dining room, if Boggy could get a giggle or a blush out of a female, he was a happy man

Karina sauntered down to Boggy's room. Today all she had to do was make a bored old man happy. In the long run, she could slowly but surely poison him against Taylor Quinn.

If Boggy didn't like Taylor, Hudson would give up on his single-minded pursuit.

Sure, it didn't mean she'd get him back. But she was past that. If she couldn't have him, neither could Taylor. That was all that really mattered.

Boggy didn't answer on the first knock. For a second, Karina felt fear. It surprised her. She knocked louder and hollered his name. After what felt like forever but was probably just a couple of minutes, the door opened.

"Well!" Boggy looked pleased. "If I'd known you were coming over, I wouldn't have fallen asleep. What kind of trouble can I get you in?"

"I just thought I'd pop over and say hi. With the dining room closed, I don't get to see anyone."

"Come in, come in. I've got coffee on."

She came in, happy with her success, happy that Boggy wasn't dead. Just happy in general.

He poured her a mug of strong black coffee and settled himself in a recliner. "Did you abandon post this morning or is someone doing all your hard work?"

Karina waved her phone. "I abandoned it. But the calls will come to me if anyone calls."

"You know, kiddo, I always did like you. You're both clever and lazy, like me." He grinned.

She knew he meant it as a compliment, but she stiffened. Clever and lazy were too on point.

"This is just a social visit, but if you have any thoughts you'd like to share about how we've been handling the, um…"

"Imprisonment of free people?" He lifted an eyebrow.

"Ah."

"This is ridiculous. Open the dining room. Open the rec facilities. We pay good money to live here and can't use any of our stuff."

"At the same time," Karina remembered the surprising fear that something had happened to Boggy while she waited for him to answer the door, "we've had two murders. We've got to figure out how to keep everyone safe."

"Real sad about that Cricket," Boggy said. "You know she's a homewrecker?"

He looked wistful as he said it, which also surprised Karina. "She stole my Michelle's husband from her. But you know that because you almost married Hudson. Doug East was never any good. A drinker, mostly. So my Michelle was better off without him. But when I saw that Cricket running around here, I wasn't real happy about it."

"Are you saying that Doug left your daughter for Cricket?"

"Sure am."

"I bet you would have liked to kill her yourself."

He shook his head slowly. "I was really mad, and I bet my daughter would have liked to stick a knife in her, but like I said, Doug never was any good. It didn't take me long to figure Cricket did us a favor. But you know how homewreckers are. She got tired of Doug and moved on. Who knows how many angry wives are out there?"

"Very true." Karina was pleased with the turn of the conversation. How easy it would be to explain that Taylor was a homewrecker too. That she had slipped right in and stolen Hudson from her.

She was about to say just that when her phone rang. She made an apologetic grimace and answered it. "Bible Creek Care Home, this is Karina."

Mrs. Frida Calloway was on the other line. There was a

mouse in her apartment. Karina shivered. "I'll get housekeeping out there right away." She called housekeeping, who said they'd go set a trap.

By the time she was done, Boggy was half-asleep.

"Sorry about that."

"Hmm? What?" He roused a little.

"Sorry about the interruption. We were talking about home-wreckers..."

Boggy clucked. "If I told you all the times women tried to steal me away from my darling, you'd never believe me." He grinned.

"Just like Taylor Quinn." She frowned, hoping she looked young and sad.

"Oh, I don't know. Girls try to distract Hudson, but he's pretty set on that one. Real good girl too. So sad about her being an orphan. Did you know she took me to a bar yesterday? For lunch. God bless her for even thinking of it. But that's the Bakers through and through. You know her grandpa is Ernie Baker. Best man who ever lived in this town. Did I ever tell you about what he did during the war? Korea. He's too young for World War II."

Karina couldn't stifle the distaste. She pulled her phone out. "Oh, no! Oh, Boggy, I'm sorry. I've got to run. I can only hide from work for so long."

He nodded and stood carefully, as though his joints weren't as kind to him as they used to be. "I tell you what, Karina, you get that Ernie Baker to move in here and you'll be my favorite girl in the world. Might even marry you." He winked.

She giggled though it wasn't convincing and hustled back to the office.

Wasted.

But just because she didn't achieve her goal today didn't mean it wasn't possible. Taylor Quinn had a weakness. Everyone did. She just had to find it and exploit it in such a way that it turned Hudson's crush into disgust.

Shoot, even apathy would work at this point.

CHAPTER FOURTEEN

*C*lark and Bethany Jones entered Flour Sax reverently, as though it was a sanctuary.

Taylor spotted them immediately and joined them in the corner where her mom's videos streamed day in and day out. "Taylor, we really couldn't thank you enough for the call. We just wanted to come by and say so ourselves." Bethany picked up a stack of fat quarters that had been folded like triangles, stacked like stars, and bundled. "We wanted to come and support you the way you have supported us."

Taylor took the fabric from her. "You do not have to buy things from me."

She picked up another. "Let us, please."

"It's a baby quilt set. Mother Goose themed."

Bethany set the fabric down again and looked around. The Flour Sax Row by Row hung behind the register. Seven years of rows her mother had designed. The last, music themed. "Do you have a kit with all of the rows? I would love to make it, to remember Laura."

Taylor led them back to the classroom. "We do, but you don't need to do that. Can I get you a cup of coffee?"

"Okay." Clark led his wife to the recliner that used to be Grandpa Ernie's throne, and she sat.

Taylor put a hazelnut pod in the Keurig. "I'm so glad to see you. Can I buy you dinner? We're closing in an hour."

Willa was putting the shop back in order already. Unlike Roxy, who enjoyed a lengthy chat after the door was locked for the day, Willa liked to get it done and get back home.

Taylor wasn't keen to ask Ellery to stay late again, though. "Grandpa Ernie would love to see you. We can take him down to the diner and have a meal together."

"You do too much for everyone, Taylor." Clark's voice deep and gentle, fatherly, though not at all like her own father's had been.

"Make yourself comfortable." Taylor gestured toward a stack of quilt magazines. "As soon as we're closed up, we can collect Grandpa Ernie and have a meal."

The last half hour or so of closing dragged on as she worried over Cricket Jones' parents. It didn't seem right that they had driven to town just to buy an expensive quilt kit in support. Their minds shouldn't have been on her call at all right now. Something was wrong, and as the minutes passed, her idea of what it might be grew to absurd levels. By the time they were collecting Grandpa Ernie at her house, she almost believed they had killed their own daughter to cover up her role in Leon's death. After all, she had learned with her own mother's death that some parents would do literally anything to protect their children.

And maybe they saw death as preferable to a murder conviction.

Taylor tried not to let her fears show as they settled into their booth at the local diner, but she was stiff, uncomfortable, and knew they could tell.

"Real sad about your kid," Grandpa Ernie declared after the waitress, Aviva Reuben, had given them their menus and water glasses.

"If anyone would understand our pain, it's you, sir."

Taylor had introduced Bethany and Clark to Grandpa Ernie, but she wasn't sure if he remembered them as the passionate quilting couple who had supported the business for years and years. At this hour, she was never sure exactly what he remembered.

"This one wants me to move into that old folks' home," Grandpa Ernie continued, "but I told her people die there. Now we all know it's true."

A flicker of confusion crossed Bethany's face and Clark gave her shoulder a rub. He seemed to recognize the dementia that had changed their old friend. "It's a good home, Ernie. I have an old friend who lives there. That's how Cricket heard of it."

Grandpa Ernie harrumphed into his mustache.

"His son is considering him moving to the memory care wing." He gave his wife's arm another gentle stroke, and she seemed to understand the clues he was giving.

"Did Cricket like working there?" Taylor asked.

"She did. She'd had some career troubles through the years, though she was very well meaning. You know she was actually a stay-at-home mom to Hudson, way back when. I think the end of that relationship—with Doug East—really hurt her."

"But that's in the past," Bethany murmured. "Nothing is hurting her now."

"I like Hudson," Grandpa Ernie said. "Wish Taylor would just marry him. He's a real man."

"Oh!" Bethany brightened. "You hadn't said. You didn't say. If you married Hudson, you'd almost be a granddaughter."

Taylor suppressed an impatient facial expression, or at least she hoped she did. "It's a lovely thought. You know, I'm sure he'd love to hear from you. No one ever forgets their grand-parents."

"Oh, ho ho." Clark looked proud, but tried to brush the idea off with a wave of his hand. "We haven't seen him since he was a child, surely he's forgotten us."

"He hasn't. He spoke so warmly of your daughter, truly loved her like a mother. He would love to hear from you."

Bethany's eyes sparked with fresh tears. "We wouldn't even know how to find him."

Taylor wrote his number on a napkin and passed it to Clark. Funny that she knew it by heart, as she never had to dial it. But she did. "Call him. Anytime."

"Now?" Bethany asked, looking at the number with gratitude.

"No, not now. We're having dinner now. No phones at dinner." Grandpa Ernie slapped the table with a shaky hand. "You kids are all the same."

Bethany Jones tucked the napkin into her purse. "Thank you, Taylor. We'll call him."

"Bet you didn't know my kid was a detective." He turned an approving look on Taylor. "Her mother and I never thought she had it in her. Never was book smart, our Laura, but she solved two murders. Now, who was it? Tell them whose murders you solved, Laura." He nodded firmly at Taylor.

Her face scrunched into a chagrined smile of apology. "Not long ago my friend's aunt passed," she said. "Maybe you heard about Reynette Woods?"

"The quilter, yes. We followed that case on the internet."

"On Facebook," Bethany nodded. "I'm in a group that follows murders to pray for the families and for justice."

"What an interesting idea." Taylor sipped her water, watching Bethany closely. Another thing that she had seen warp people around her was an intense desire to do anything for attention online. At least that was a part of what had gotten her mother killed. "They must be a comfort to you right now."

"Oh, yes, so much. I have been getting so many messages of support, and their prayers lift me up. You don't even have to be a Christian to be in the group. Some of our members are Catholics."

"Aren't there some Jewish folk in the group, too?" Clark asked.

"Yes! Some messianic Jews are in the group. It's so wonderful when people can put aside their differences to help one another."

Taylor held her opinion to herself. But inside she was kicking. Since when were Catholics not Christians?

"Her phone's been blowing up with messages. Messages from Facebook all day long. I made her turn it off for the drive here so she'd talk to me for once instead of that online community."

"Gotta be careful on the computer," Grandpa Ernie said. "People are out to get you."

"Very true, sir," Clark said. "Never give your banking information to anyone online."

"Or your social security number!" Bethany piped up. "I couldn't believe our poor Cricket got bit with that one. She seemed so young and smart."

"The crooks are getting smarter every day," Taylor murmured, though she also couldn't believe someone in their mid-forties had given away a social security number on the Internet. She wondered what had actually happened that had made Cricket tell that story to her parents.

"Crooks are everywhere. Laura may be a detective, but she steals from me. Every month she steals my social security check. You can't trust anyone."

Grandpa Ernie's agitation was growing.

"Pardon me." Taylor was sitting on the outside of the booth. "I need to get to the car and grab something." When he got this bad, it was a clear sign he needed his oxygen. He had refused to take it into the restaurant, but his portable canister was in the car. It wouldn't take long to grab it. "If Aviva comes back, tell her I want a patty melt and side salad, please."

Mere minutes later Grandpa was plugged into his oxygen. His eyes cleared and his words made a bit more sense—he called her Taylor as he hollered at her. But he was still angry, this time that Laura used to steal from him, and that Taylor forced him to stick rubber tubes up his nose.

They ate quickly. Taylor paid the check and they left in their separate cars. As she made her goodbye, she paused. "Mom never stole from him. He just can't grasp the concept of automatic deposit."

Clark shook his head. "I only wonder what new thing will befuddle me in ten years' time."

"And…it could happen to anyone," Taylor added. "The social security thing that happened to Cricket. But since her info was, um, stolen, I'd try and be extra sure that no one is using it now. You'd hate to start getting those terrible collections calls now that she's gone."

"I hadn't even thought. Oh, Clark, let's get home and search that on the Internet and find out what we need to do."

"Good idea. Thank you, Taylor, and for dinner as well. You shouldn't have. We'll be back, you know, and you won't be able to stop us from showing you how much we appreciate you next time." They drove away in their comfortable little Beetle. A twenty-year old car now, the kind Taylor had thought was so, so cute when she was a little girl.

BELLE WAS HOME when Taylor returned with Grandpa Ernie. She hovered in the background as they hung their coats and got Grandpa settled in front of the TV in his room to watch the golf channel they had recently discovered.

The second Grandpa Ernie's door swung shut, Belle started in on Taylor. "We've got to do something about Dayton. You promised to help her."

"I'm trying, but it's not like I'm a trained cop or anything."

"Just look at this." Belle passed over her phone, opened to a text conversation that looked like it was between Belle and a bot.

Over and over again, no matter what Belle had said or asked, all Dayton replied was, "I'm safe. I'm hiding."

"That's like what she said to me."

"Exactly. Don't film tomorrow. Take me to the sheriff instead. We need to report this.

"I couldn't agree more." She sent a quick text to Roxy cancelling their morning appointment.

TAYLOR DIDN'T ASK for Reg at the sheriff's office the next morning. She wasn't even remotely inclined. In fact, if she never saw him again that would be great. Her face heated up at the thought of him, in fact. But why was she embarrassed? She hadn't slept with him, led him on, accepted expensive gifts.

She'd have to parse out the complications of her heart some other time.

Dressed in what looked like a Target uniform of khaki pants and red sweater set, Belle was the picture of efficiency. She wasn't chatty or even very friendly. She drove.

Taylor wanted to ask her about the surprisingly dull and old clothes she was wearing but didn't bother. As she was wearing dark jeans and that pastel Flour Sax polo she was beginning to regret ordering, she was hardly one to comment on fashion choices.

Reporting Dayton Reuben as a missing person was disturbingly normal. The deputies didn't drop their jaws in shock as Taylor laid out the story of the scared young adult who had witnessed a murder and whose texts seemed to be written by someone other than her. In fact, they seemed tired.

But at least they hadn't been dismissive.

Taylor and Belle left the sheriff's station feeling defeated.

"I guess we're on our own." Belle leaned on the car rather than getting in.

"They are going to look for her."

"How hard, though? They made it clear she's an adult with the right to move on with her life and not communicate if she wants to."

"It's a murder." Taylor popped open the car door and got in.

Belle followed her.

"They will take it seriously." It was always funny to Taylor how she could say things she didn't mean to Belle, just to make her feel better. "But that doesn't mean we have to stop. Let's keep looking, keep asking questions."

Belle nodded, her face looking young and scared.

They stared at each other. This wasn't a game. They weren't playing. Two people were dead, and though they both had mixed feelings about Belle's old school friend Dayton, they very much did not want her to be the third.

"If our main goal is to protect Dayton and we were thinking of catching the killer to do that, then we failed." Belle paced Flour Sax.

Taylor didn't remember Belle volunteering to catch a killer but didn't correct her.

"Your focus just needs to shift, that's all." Roxy was organizing the little quilt patterns that had gotten mixed up the day before. "Readjustment isn't the same thing as failing."

"You've known Dayton forever. Where would she hide?" Taylor asked.

"My first thought would be their family cabin up in the mountains, but I don't think she's brave enough to hide there alone."

"How isolated and rustic is it?"

"One hundred percent isolated and rustic. It's an old shack off the grid. No electric, no water. They bring water in gallon jugs for drinking and boil creek water for everything else. They heat with an old cast iron wood burner they brought up there a few years back."

"If she was trying not to be found, that might be a good place to go..." Taylor mused.

"But not if she wanted to be able to summon help. No phones, patchy cell service."

"Which could explain why she rarely answers our messages." Taylor fussed with a chicken wire basket full of rolled-up fat quarters. They kept spilling out of the large hexagonal holes. Chicken wire, no matter how trendy, was not the best for a quilt shop.

"She would be fine while the sun is out, but once night hit, I just can't see it."

"What kind of family does she have in town?"

"She's a Reuben. What family doesn't she have in town? Aunts, uncles, cousins, grandparents. And her mom was a Love. There's a handful of them around still." Flour Sax Quilt Shop sat on the corner of Main and Love. The Loves founded the town, but there weren't many left.

"With a family that big, don't you think she's just hiding in someone's spare room?" Taylor gave up on her basket of discount fabric rolls. She removed a dusty baby quilt from the front of their cutting table. It was long since time to hang new work, but none of them had made any.

"Go to the cabin first," Roxy directed. "You won't be easy in your mind till you do. Then come back and go door to door. Visit every Reuben and Reuben-adjacent house in the town. Someone knows where she is."

Belle nodded, "It's not a bad idea," but she didn't stop pacing.

Roxy was right, nothing Taylor could say or do would give Belle any peace. "I wish I could go with you."

"Sorry," Roxy's apology was tinged with sadness. "Poor Jonah has been waiting over a year to take his driver's test. I can't reschedule it again."

"I get it." Taylor ran her hand across the clean surface of the cutting table, feeling anchored to the little metal grooves that guided the scissors. Her mother had been so proud when she'd found this old table at a going-out-of-business sale in Salem.

Clay announced his arrival with thudding footsteps as he ran down the stairs. "Good morning, pretty ladies." He was glowing.

Taylor's brows drew together as she looked at him. He looked happy, really, really, happy. Happy like the day he brought home his Santa Fe Blur for their failed attempt at mountain biking. She hadn't seen him that happy in ages.

Surely Joey hadn't really stayed the night.

Joey wouldn't, would she?

She wouldn't actually hook up with Taylor's ex—the ex that lived rent free? That would be weird. Everyone in town would think so.

Clay needed to find himself and leave town, not find Joey and stay.

"I can go alone." Belle straightened up as though trying to look older. She didn't need to. As far as Taylor was concerned, her baby sister looked too old already.

"I'm not doing much of anything." Clay's giddy smile could only be called a grin. "Where do you need to go?"

Roxy brightened. "That's a good idea. Clay, Belle needs to go up into the mountains and see if her friend is at this cabin. We would both feel so much better if she didn't have to go alone."

"Say no more. I'm ready for an adventure. Your car or mine, Belle?"

Belle cringed subtly and looked at Taylor.

Taylor cringed, less subtly. Then laughed. "You've always been good at inviting yourself along."

"You'd rather she drive off into the woods by herself? She could get lost."

A shadow crossed Belle's eyes. "I could. Ugh. I don't need a babysitter, but it's true, I think I'd rather not go alone."

"I'm at your service. Let me grab a coffee and get out of here." He made for the classroom.

"I've got to get gas anyway," Belle said. "You can get your coffee at Arco."

"Aye-aye, captain." Clay winked at Taylor and went outside.

It wasn't that Taylor didn't trust Clay with Belle, but this felt weird. In the almost-year he'd been living upstairs he hadn't spent any alone time with Belle. If he had, he might have been able to win Taylor over. All she had wanted, after all, was for him to show he cared about her family.

That said, her own face brightened. Joey was definitely not upstairs if Clay was willing and ready to up and leave with Belle like that.

Taylor went through the motions of opening her store. Roxy's comments about Flour Sax not really being Taylor's business because it wasn't her passion nagged at her. She felt judged as though loving business in a general sense wasn't a good enough reason to own *this* business, or that you could only own a quilt store if quilting itself was your life's great passion.

Her great passion…

After unlocking the front door, she leaned on the register counter resting her chin on her fist.

Tucked deep inside, she had a longing for one thing and one thing only. But it was absurd to dream about, because it was never going to happen. And, anyway, life with her own store offered her plenty of variety.

And she liked quilting. She really did.

But if truth be told, she adored advertising.

In her years working for the corporate craft store in Portland she hadn't gotten to do one single bit of real advertising. No copywriting. No ad art. No negotiating co-op deals with product lines.

She planned classes and made fliers for them, and that had helped scratch her itch. But things were better here. With her own store, and the business account fattened with YouTube royalties, she could advertise to her heart's content.

She didn't need to work for Widen and Kennedy shooting videos for Nike to make her dreams come true.

"Earth to Taylor. Earth to Taylor." Roxy waved a scrap of maroon cotton covered in custard colored daisies at her.

"Sorry. Lost in thought."

"I can't blame you. You must be devastated with worry for Dayton."

Taylor blushed. It would have been very nice to have been worried for the missing girl instead of pining for a job she only imagined was a dream come true. "I can't do anything about it from here," Taylor sighed.

"We could print a picture of her and keep it by the register. Then, when folks make their purchases, we could ask them if they've seen her."

Taylor shook her head. "Not without talking to her parents first. Can you imagine the outcry if we declared Dayton Reuben missing to the world like that? A lot of Reubens shop here. They would call Dale and Dayna in seconds."

"Have you called them? What if she hopped a plane to Montreal to be with her folks?"

"She would have if she was smart. Maybe I will call them. Or, better yet, I'll ask Sissy to do it. I highly doubt Dale would answer a call from me, and I never did get Dayna on my side."

Taylor knew Sissy was stuck at her salon just like Taylor was stuck at the shop, but she sent a quick text anyway. After a few minutes Sissy sent a thumbs up as a reply. It wasn't much, but it was something.

She hadn't stopped to ask Belle where this cabin in the woods was, so she didn't have any idea of when she ought to hear from her. She spent the rest of the day in a sort of daze, cutting fabric, ringing up purchases, and hoping everyone was okay.

Around closing time, the shop phone rang. "Flour Sax Quilt Shop, this is Taylor."

"Good. Glad I got you." The familiar voice of Reg was on the other line. "Some of the guys were telling me about the missing person you reported. I thought I'd call and offer to help."

A great big sigh of relief escaped. "Oh, Reg, that would be amazing. I don't deserve it, but I will absolutely take you up on it."

"Why don't I swing by your place tonight?"

"I'll make sure there's something to eat. You don't know how much this means to me."

Reg cleared his throat. "It's the right thing to do. See you around eight?"

"Perfect."

She hung up. There was no one in the shop to celebrate with —Roxy had taken her son for his driving test a few hours earlier —but she was light on her feet as she closed up anyway. After the disappointing meeting at the café, she had given up hope of help from Reg.

As she made her way home, her happiness at having Reg on her side wiped out all concern about not having heard from Clay or Belle yet.

CHAPTER FIFTEEN

*E*llery offered to take Grandpa Ernie out to dinner when Taylor told her Reg was coming over, but she took a pass. She didn't want Reg to get any ideas. This was one hundred percent a meeting of minds—a concerned citizen and an officer of the law discussing an endangered teen, or something like that.

She was annoyed to find all she had to serve for dinner were two frozen pizzas, not even the rising crust kind. And there were no soft drinks to be had in the house. The local grocery had closed an hour ago, and she'd never make it to a bigger town and back by eight. She thought about running back to her shop to get some of the generic soda out of the small fridge, but it was old. She hadn't refreshed the stock since their fall wall hanging class. The only thing worse than generic soda in a can was stale generic soda in a can. She tossed the pizzas in the oven and made a pot of coffee. It was better than nothing. She scavenged the cupboards one last time, and unless she wanted to stop and make some oatmeal cookies without raisins or chocolate chips, they were out of luck.

"You should make that Ellery go to the store for you. All she does is sit around and play cards." Grandpa Ernie poured slightly dry baby carrots into a cereal bowl.

"I presume she plays cards with you." Taylor set the table for three.

"She doesn't bring boys over, that's for sure."

"I'd hope not. Now, did you want coffee or just water?"

"It's eight at night, you want to go to sleep or what? Who drinks coffee at this hour? You're not giving Belle coffee tonight, are you?"

"No, this is for Reg."

"Reg? Who's that?"

"My friend."

"Why are you giving him coffee but not a plate?" Grandpa Ernie pulled out his chair at the table.

"He has a plate, Grandpa, calm down."

"And where is Belle supposed to eat then?"

"She's out tonight. With Clay."

"You kids make me dizzy. What's that little turd doing out with your sister? She's just a baby."

"It's not a date, Grandpa. They were um…" She tried to think of a non-stressful way to explain what her sister and her ex were doing in the woods at a cabin, but she couldn't, especially as now that she thought about it, they really should have been back or at least called. Fortunately, a knock at the front door saved her from having to make sense of it all for herself or her grandpa.

UNLIKE MOST PEOPLE who willingly live on the good will of more generous folks, Clay was not a stingy man, not with his money or his time. Especially when he was in a good mood, and Joey Burke had put him in a very good mood.

Belle's memory of where the Reuben cabin was hidden away wasn't so good, but they had found it after just two hours of hunting.

The shack had been built sometime in the dark ages, and the primordial trees that loomed over it still seemed to resent its presence.

It ought to have been deadly silent, but a healthy forest never is. In addition to the babbling of the creek that skirted the clearing, birds sung and squabbled and smaller tree rodents...maybe chipmunks...hollered at each other. Clay wasn't up on what lived in the coast range mountains.

"Some vacation place." He whistled and kicked a large pinecone. Fir cone? He knew there was a difference, but didn't know what it was.

"Some Reuben built this thing a million years ago, and now the whole family shares it." Belle poked her head into the cabin.

"I wonder how many places like this are hiding in the woods?" Clay sat on a stump and checked his phone. "No reception."

"No Dayton, either."

"Could she be off hiking?" Clay asked.

"There's no sign of life. No ashes in the woodstove. No blankets or bags or anything like that." Belle sat with Clay and shivered.

"You're worried." He smiled avuncularly at her. He liked that word. Fancy for uncle. Though he supposed he would have been her brother-in-law if Taylor hadn't gone crazy when their mom died. He still couldn't understand why she had thought she could uproot their entire life without even a conversation.

"She's such a pain." Belle looked at the palms of her hands. "She ran away three times in middle school. I thought she'd outgrown it."

"But right now you're worried that she didn't actually run away."

"Yup."

"Where did she go those other times?" Clay stood and walked to the edge of the clearing. The woods were dark and damp, even on this early summer day. Rainforest. He knew he'd learned that in school. There were rainforests in Oregon, and this had to be one. But cold rainforests. Not the tropical ones that had mangos and monkeys.

"Not out here, that's for sure. Can't ride a bike this far."

"Sure, but where did she ride her bike? I bet she went back to one of her previous hideaways this time."

"We had a fort in the woods by the creek. We made it out of fallen trees and branches, like a teepee. She went there twice, but the fort only lasted a couple of years. There's nothing there to go back to."

"What made you want to set forts up way out there? Shelter? Water?"

"Yeah, it was right on the creek, so that was good. And there were some big shrubs that made a kind of V where we could go to the bathroom. Or at least we said we could. I never did."

"So, shelter, privacy, and water. What would keep her from setting up a tent there?"

"The cold?"

"It's June. Have you checked the old fort?"

"I mean, no. I just figured…"

"Let's go there next. You said she ran there twice. Where did she run the third time?"

Belle scrunched her face up. "Her aunt, um…what was her name…Debora. Her aunt Debora, who used to build computer motherboards from home, had property. So, the last time she ran away, she went there, camped out in the woods."

"Was there water or anything?"

"No. When they found her, she was miserable. I don't think she'd go back there."

"But does Debora still live on the property?"

Belle shook her head. "I don't remember, but we can always check."

"Lead the way to the fort. We'll check there first."

Getting to Belle's old fort only took half an hour, but there were no signs of life.

They immediately headed to Debora Reuben's place, but there was a gate shut across the long driveway.

Clay parked on the shoulder. They both got out.

Belle hesitated. "We don't even know if Debora still lives here."

"Only one way to find out."

He climbed over the fence, but Belle was glued to her phone. After a moment, she looked up, shaking her head. "I asked Dayton's cousin, Aviva. She said Debora moved to Salem three years ago."

"And you're sure the woods weren't a good place to hide out?"

Belle scanned the property, her hand shading her eyes. "I don't even see the woods anymore. Do you?"

He had seen trees and figured they counted but taking a few steps back and really considering the situation, he had to admit there were no woods.

"I can't see her trying to hide in that windbreak."

They got back into the car. "We've got all day, Belle, where do we go next?"

"What's easier, hiding where no one goes and no one expects you, or hiding where there are so many people no one would notice you?"

"Think she might have gone to Portland?"

Belle stared into the distance, not responding for a while. "If she did, we'd never find her. We wouldn't even know where to start looking. It's not like we could trace her phone records."

"She just graduated high school, right?"

"Yes."

"What was she planning on doing in the fall?"

"She wanted to go to Comfort College of Art and Craft, but her parents wouldn't let her. It was too expensive, and she wouldn't get any federal aid, because their income was too high."

"Trapped in the middle," he said it softly and with sympathy.

"Yes."

He started the car and got back out on the road, heading for the highway.

"Where are you going?"

"There are other arts colleges in this state. Maybe she called one and set up a tour. Those smaller colleges do that kind of thing."

Belle pursed her lips but didn't respond.

He settled in for the drive, sure and confident he'd cracked the code to finding Dayton. And in four years of living with Taylor Quinn, queen of arts and crafts, he had learned where all the schools that might possibly rival her alma mater were located.

It was a long drive to Lake Oswego where Oregon College of Art and Craft was located.

Clay had been called glib more than once in his life, but having Belle alone in the car with him led his thoughts away from those easy things to talk about and on to the failure of his relationship. Even with the happy thought of Joey Burk in the back of his mind, he still had things he wanted to ask his captive audience. "It was like a divorce, really, since we'd lived together for so long." He spoke out of the blue of his breakup.

She lifted an eyebrow, which he caught as he took his eyes off the road for a second to check her mood. Her attention was still trained on her phone.

"And it hurt like hell. I'd had one other relationship as serious as this one. That one had broken my heart too."

Still no response. Clay wasn't fazed. "I still wonder if she was going to break up with me anyway, and this was just her excuse. Otherwise, why not have a conversation about it?"

Belle let out a short, sharp breath. "Have you thought of asking her this?"

He shook his head. "What's the point? She's made herself very clear."

Belle snorted—though it was a very feminine, teenage girl

sort of snort. "Has she? Because I remember coming home from school in May for a quick weekend and seeing you two saying goodbye on the back stoop. It didn't look even remotely decided."

He too remembered the kiss goodbye, a little bit fueled by the wine they'd had with dinner, but mostly fueled by the happiness over the success of their spring ad campaign. He'd hoped that the kiss would have been followed with an invitation inside, but it hadn't.

"You don't know your sister."

"She kisses everyone like that?"

A quick slide show of the men he knew were his rivals, plus some of the other men in town who kind of intimidated him, like Hector, who was running Café Olé, spooled out before him. "Yeah. She does."

"Then I guess I don't know her. But if I did know her, even a little bit, then the thing I would know is that she is unsettled in her mind about her life right now, and having you around all the time is the thing that has unsettled her."

"Not the more obvious stuff?"

"Like Mom? Sure. That doesn't help. But if you weren't here, she could move on. At least that's what I think."

He felt judged by this teen and changed the subject. "What about you? How're things with Levi?"

"Poor Levi." She said it softly.

He frowned. Poor Levi? Was he the next to have his heart broken by a Quinn girl?

They rolled up to Oregon College of Art and Craft. The parking lot stood empty, and the landscaping was unkempt. "What the heck?" Clay frowned at the abandoned school in front of him.

"I could have told you this place had closed."

"Why didn't you?"

"You didn't tell me where you were going."

"We need to eat." He started the car again and roared out of the parking lot. Annoyed with the person sharing the car with him in a way he hadn't felt for many years. Not, in fact, since he had lived at home with his own little sister.

He drove to the nearest Taco Bell and took them to through the drive-through. "You're not a vegetarian, are you?"

"Not usually." She didn't smirk, but she still wasn't paying attention.

They got back on the highway with their sodas and tacos.

When they were finally out of the sprawling suburbs, Belle looked up from her phone. "If you love her, you need to be serious with her about it. My sister is serious in general. This thing where she's dating everyone in town isn't the real her."

"Sure…"

"Did she date a million guys before you?"

"Nope." He squinted as he concentrated on balancing his taco, merging into traffic, and remembering Taylor's past. "Before me, it was just some guy she knew in grad school. Some real numbers geek."

"So, a guy like you."

"Uh…"

"Her two serious relationships were with numbers guys. You really think Hudson is her type?"

"Hudson is every woman's type."

"Then why does she still go out with that banker guy? Hudson's not her type. She likes geeks like you. She always has."

"Thanks?"

"No offense. I like geeks too."

He cringed. He did not want Taylor's eighteen-year-old sister making a pass at him.

She laughed and reached toward his knee.

He jerked away, turning the wheel.

She laughed again, holding up the chip she had been reaching for.

He exhaled. And clenched his soda. The lid popped off, and

in an attempt to catch it, he tipped the cup of icy Pepsi over himself.

"Damn it!" He tried to mop up his legs with a napkin, but only managed to drive the aging VW Rabbit into the Amazon Freight truck as it attempted to merge in front of him.

"WE'RE NOT DEAD," Belle's voice, though clear and unshaken, had a hint of apology.

"Excuse me?" Taylor stared at Grandpa Ernie, comfy in his recliner. She always told herself that her fears were nonsense and that her sister wasn't going to die in some kind of unexplainable accident. Just because fate had taken both of her parents didn't mean it would take Belle as well. And yet, whenever Belle didn't answer a call or a text, that is what she thought.

"There's been an accident, but Clay and I aren't dead. I didn't call sooner because there wasn't any point. I knew you were at work." Belle put a little sauce on that last sentence, her regular taunt that Taylor loved work more than family.

Taylor leaned against the wall. "What kind of accident?"

"Car. Your idiot ex drove us into a semi. We've been checked out by docs and are fine. But we had to wait forever to get insurance to pay for a rental. He's cheap, did you know that? Wouldn't just use a credit card. Also, he's in a little trouble. An accident caused by distracted driving is no joke apparently."

Taylor slid down the wall. Everything about the call was hitting every one of her most sore spots. "Are you, um, coming home?"

"Yeah, we'll be leaving shortly. If I was twenty-five, I would have rented my own car and abandoned him." She laughed, but it didn't sound natural.

"Are you really, really okay?"

"A little whiplash. My head is killing me. And I do wish I

could drive myself." She dropped her voice. "I'm a little scared to get back in the car with him. Isn't that dumb?"

"Where are you? I'm coming to get you."

"No, don't. It's not that bad. We're about an hour away."

Taylor pressed her hand to her eyes. Clay could kill them both in an hour. "If you don't want to get in the car, don't. I will come get you. I promise."

Belle murmured softly, maybe to herself, "No, we'll come home. I'm sorry."

"What? Don't be sorry. Please, whatever you do, don't apologize for getting in an accident. Put Clay on."

"I can't, he's already in the car and starting it up and stuff. I'll be home soon."

"Love you."

"You too."

Taylor rested her head on her knees. Everything was fine.

Everything was fine.

Everything was fine.

But where was Dayton Reuben? Had they found her before the accident?

Taylor sent Dayton another text, but knew, deep in her heart, she'd never get a reply.

Her phone buzzed a text. She nearly leapt for joy.

But it was just Reg. "Sorry. Can't make it. Talk soon."

CLAY'S ARM was in a sling, and it was cute.

Joey Burke could have made very good coffee for herself in her own kitchen at work but had been inexplicably drawn to Café Olé. And as she stood with the small cluster of early morning customers waiting for her *café con leche*, she watched the goofy grinned, somehow injured, newcomer to town as he ambled down Main Street in her direction. Breakfast service was to begin at Bible Creek Care Home this morning, but she had time for a quick coffee and chat beforehand. And, anyway, it would be good for her mental health. She needed a friend or two who wasn't likely to die of old age in the coming year.

And despite the injured arm, Clay looked young and healthy to her.

CHAPTER SIXTEEN

*A*ll day Friday, Taylor was torn between yelling at Clay for damaging her sister and spoiling her sister for still being alive.

Clay had met her in the store with coffee and *conchas* from Café Olé, looking and sounding sincere in his regrets and looking pathetic in his sling. She limited her yelling to just three short bursts and only when they were alone.

After the third, he stared at her, "You need to eat lunch."

"I *know,*" she hissed like it was his fault.

"Then go, because there is nothing I can do to unbreak your heart."

She exhaled sharply. "I'm going home to grab a bite with Grandpa Ernie as soon as Roxy gets here."

"Then I pray she gets here fast." He settled in at her desk next to the stairs and made a show of opening the shop laptop with one hand, then hunting and pecking as he typed.

Taylor ignored him till she could escape.

It was a long, uncomfortable day, and she was ready to collapse when she finally made it back home.

Before she could collapse, the door swung open.

"Taylor." Sissy stood in the doorway of the little house

looking tired from a long day's work. She wore her smock embroidered with her name and salon logo in the corner. Her naturally curly hair looked like it had been styled nicely at the beginning of the day, but exertion and humidity had taken a toll on it. "Taylor," Sissy began again, "today was salon day at Bible Creek Care Home, and Marva Love didn't come."

"Come in, come in." Taylor led Sissy into the kitchen. "Can I get you a cup of tea?"

"I don't think you heard me." Sissy did not sit down in the chair that Taylor pulled out for her. "Marva Love did not come to her weekly appointment at salon day. This is the first weekly appointment she has missed in six-and-a-half years. I have been setting her hair for her in exactly the same style since I took over salon day from Lorena."

"I see." Taylor put a kettle of water on the stove, the normalcy of the action, of the plastic kettle handle in her grip, of the sound of the water filling it, made more sense than Sissy showing up agitated about a hair client. "Are you worried something has happened to her?"

Sissy looked as though Taylor was the slowest student she had ever had the chance to work with. "Yes. There have been two murders at the care home, and my most faithful client did not come to her regular appointment. Of course, I'm worried."

"Did you call the police?"

"First, I called Marva, but no one answered, so I called Karina at the front desk. She said Marva had been receiving her meals all day and was at home. So, I talked to Joey in the kitchen, and Joey said that someone had delivered a meal to Marva at lunch and had seen her. What exactly do you think I should have told the police, given that information?"

"Don't get testy with me, Sissy. I can't know what you don't tell me. If you're not worried that she's been murdered, what are you worried about?"

"I *am* worried that she was murdered. That is exactly the thing I'm worried about. For all we know, she accepted her meal, and it was poisoned. She had an after-lunch appointment."

"Did she get her dinner?"

"Dinner service started after I left. They opened the dining room today, but residents who wanted to have meals delivered could. She was on the delivery list. This is also fishy because she's one of the most outgoing residents there, besides which she's not very old, just seventy-six on her birthday, so it's not like she was too tired or frail to come to dinner."

"I suppose I'm an idiot if I ask you if you went to see her?"

"I called again after I closed up shop, and she didn't answer. I did go to her apartment and knock, but she didn't answer. I could hear the TV through the door. And one of her neighbors, June Fischel, said Marva always falls asleep in front of the TV and that she'd never hear me."

"I think I understand now." The kettle began its piercing whistle. Taylor poured herself a cup of tea and then held the kettle out towards Sissy. Sissy shook her head no. "You can't go to the police because her behavior is seen as normal by everyone else, but you are concerned that something dreadful has happened to her."

"Exactly."

"I hate to be the one who constantly says stupid things, but what am I supposed to do about this?"

"I was afraid you'd say that." Sissy sat down and took a deep breath. "Have you started cooking yet?"

"I literally just stepped into my kitchen. I've been at the shop all day."

"Never mind. You and Ernie come to my place with me. I've got tetrazzini in the crockpot. We'll eat and make a plan."

That worked for Taylor. It got her out of one of her least-liked chores and gave her someone to talk about this murder situation with. She dismissed Ellery for the day and helped Grandpa Ernie into Sissy's van. With a name like Marva Love, the missing resident might just be one of the many relatives of Dayton

Reuben, as Dayton's mom was Dayna Love before she got married.

While Grandpa Ernie appreciated the good old comfort food, he did not relish babysitting Sissy's youngest daughter, Breadyn. That said, as Sissy and Taylor drove to Bible Creek Care Home on the edge of town, they both agreed he took it better than he would have if he'd realized that the soon-to-be thirteen-year-old was actually babysitting him.

"Did anyone explain the lockdown situation to you?" Taylor asked.

"I got an email saying the campus was open." She snorted in derision. "It didn't feel open to me, but they claimed the police have said the residents are safe."

"But if they'd had a major break in the case, it would have been in the news."

"What news? That pathetic shadow of what was once a great newspaper? Or the radio that can't be bothered to give more than a traffic update?"

Taylor had to acknowledge the pathetic nature of the major sources of news, not just in Comfort, but in all of Oregon. She had a lingering sense of guilt about it as she had never paid for subscription to any newspaper and rarely listened to the local radio. She got all of her news on those rare occasions she listened to NPR or from headlines that popped up on her phone.

The front desk at Bible Creek Care Home was closed, as it was evening. This was just as well as far as Taylor was concerned. She and Sissy signed the visitor book and made their way to Marva Love's apartment.

"What do we do if she won't let us in?" Taylor asked.

"That's when we finally get to call the sheriff. According to my email, they've stationed a deputy here with the security guards."

"So...it's not completely safe after all." Taylor didn't like it. Why were they pretending all was well but keeping a deputy on hand?

"Exactly."

Sissy marched down the long west wing like she was under orders.

Marva's TV was still audible in the hallway. Taylor recognized the screeching voice of a competitive cooking show host. A funny thing for an older lady to watch, but it was popular with Belle. Taylor's heart pattered with excitement. If Belle liked the show, surely Dayton did too.

Sissy knocked and got no response. She called with the same result. The neighbor next door, a real thin man with a bald head and suspiciously black mustache, came out. "Asleep at the TV again." He patted the top of his bald head. "You did good work today."

Sissy grinned.

The old man had a thin edge of hair just around his head that was trimmed to a clean line of white. "Marva keeps a key in her pot." With two pale, thin fingers he lifted a house key out of the plant that, Taylor realized with surprise, really was marijuana.

"When it's in bud, we make her put it in the bathroom and run the fan." He handed the key to Sissy.

She knocked again and then let herself in, calling out a greeting as she did.

A pungent rotten smell hit them like a wall. Taylor reeled. She covered her nose and mouth with her hand and grabbed the sleeve of Sissy's coat like a child. Something had died here, and it had happened a long time before lunch.

Taylor braced herself against the smell, feet slightly apart, one in front of the other. She bobbed like a boxer, putting both of her fists up. Though the heady odor of decay meant whoever had died had done it quite a while ago, everything in her sensed someone living was still in the apartment.

The recliner faced the TV, and over the top of it, Taylor could see the curly white hair of the elderly woman who had missed her appointment. How long had she been there? Should Taylor call 911 or check her for signs of life first?

Sissy leaned against the wall, eyes closed. This strong presence, this woman who seemed to carry the world on her shoulders, had collapsed.

Taylor took a deep breath, regretted it, and exhaled slowly. She reached for Sissy again and led her towards the body of Marva, towards the small sofa opposite the lady, and helped her sit.

The springs of the far-from-new leather-like sofa let out a grown as Sissy sat.

"Who dat?" The recliner popped up.

Taylor fell back.

Sissy screamed.

Marva leaned forward in her chair, eyes squinting. "Sissy? Is that you? Where are my glasses?"

Sissy was breathing hard.

Taylor pressed her hand to her forehead. She must keep Sissy from hyperventilating.

No, Sissy wasn't hyperventilating. She was laughing.

"Marva Love, you scared me senseless. What died in here? Where's your cat?"

Marva scrambled in a dish of pens and crochet hooks and remote controls that sat on the small table by her chair. Finding her glasses, she slipped them on. "What do you mean, 'what died?' What are you talking about?"

"Marva, the smell. Can't you smell that? Like something has rotted."

"Ahh." She nodded, lowered the footrest of her recliner. "I haven't been able to smell anything since I had that procedure for my bloody noses when I was in my forties."

"Do you have a mouse problem?" Sissy stood and looked behind the sofa.

"No, no. It's that...." She paused. "A friend of mine wanted to try something she saw on one of these goofy cooking shows. A weird fruit, what's it called? Darren?"

"Durian?" Taylor offered, remembering the fruit that's

supposed to smell like rotten flesh.

"Yes, that's the one. It's supposed to make great vegetarian barbeque, though what's the point in that?"

"I think that's supposed to be jackfruit, isn't it?" Taylor was finding it hard to think straight with the smell. "Is your friend making it right now?" She looked around the generously-sized apartment. Marva lived in one of the units with multiple bedrooms and even two baths. Taylor was surprised it didn't have an open kitchen.

"Yes, hold on." Marva turned the TV off. The clattering sounds of cooking came from behind a wall. She didn't offer to introduce them to her friend.

"Marva...." Sissy raised an eyebrow. "Are you allowed to have overnight guests here?"

"Why else would I have an apartment with a guest bedroom? What do you think I am, an invalid?"

"How big is this place?" Taylor asked.

"I've got eight hundred square feet here, and I pay a pretty penny for it."

"It's lovely."

"Why, thank you." Marva's smile was forced, and her eyes kept bouncing over to the kitchen behind the wall.

"You missed your hair appointment." Sissy seemed to remember the reason they had come. "I was worried about you."

"I forgot." Marva patted her hair. "Maybe I can come by the salon...later?"

"Please do. Just been busy with your company?" Taylor raised her voice, hoping to be heard by the person she suspected was Dayton.

The clattering stopped.

"Yes. She's been kind enough to entertain me during this dreary lock-in. I'm glad for all the room I have. Don't know what those folks with the studio apartments do at times like this."

"Can I have a tour?" Taylor stood up.

"Oh, um...."

Taylor popped her phone out of her pocket and called a number she'd been trying to reach for days.

She was annoyed that it didn't ring somewhere in the house, but then, whoever has their ringer turned on?

"I'm rather tired, ladies. I'm sorry. Do you mind if I let you go so I can get a little shuteye?" Marva batted her eyes at them sweetly.

Taylor knew failure when she saw it, so decided to shoot her last shot. She leaned in close, as though to give a quick hug and said, "Just keep her safe, okay? We're all worried about Dayton."

Marva froze.

Then she batted her eyelids again and yawned. "Must rest. Tomorrow is a big day." She wrenched the footrest back up and reclined her chair.

"Oh?" Sissy sat back down.

"We're taking a memorial trip to Spirit Mountain in honor of Pastor Leon's memory. There was a man who knew how to have a good time." She smiled sadly.

"And Cricket, too," Sissy spoke softly—for her.

"Ah, yes. Leon took a real a shine to her."

"I'd heard that Cricket and Leon were engaged." Taylor sat down next to Sissy and got comfortable.

"Oh, I'd heard that, too, but I never saw a ring on her finger. Though...I often thought he hadn't gotten over his wife. Sweet Annie."

"Divorce is so sad," Taylor murmured.

"Indeed, it is, but I sympathize with Annie. A man like Leon can't be easy to be married to."

"What caused the rift in their relationship?" Taylor found the complete silence in the kitchen as disquieting as the stench of the durian.

"Annie was a good, religious girl. You'd have to be to be married to a pastor, but he wasn't that kind of pastor, if you know what I mean."

"I'm sorry, I don't," Sissy said.

"He was a flirt, always teasing the ladies. And he did love his casinos. He had a mind for money, actually, investments and the like. I think it was all too much, too flashy, for her."

"She's a very talented artist," Taylor offered. She hadn't gotten the sense the woman was religious, but she supposed you'd have to be to want to marry a chaplain or a pastor or whatever.

"Yes, a real gift from God." Marva pointed at a wicker shelf by the window. "That vase is one of hers. It's my favorite." A ceramic vase with the same luminous glaze as the mug Taylor had used at Annie's house sat on the shelf. It was filled with dusty silk flowers, faded with time, but with a lovely, expensive look. The kind you had to look twice at to make sure they weren't real.

"Who do you think would want him dead? Him and Cricket?" Sissy said it with a deep sigh, not like an interrogation at all.

"Oh, I just can't imagine. We all loved him, and he did so much for us. Cricket was a nice lady. It was such a shock she had been killed. You'd think murder was something that happened to folks who drew much stronger reactions from people than Cricket did."

"Maybe someone was jealous of her relationship with Leon?" Taylor suggested.

"I wonder, but though Leon flirted with all the ladies, I don't know anyone but Cricket who took him seriously. And his wife, bless her soul, she wouldn't have wanted the father of her children to die."

"No? Not even if he had been having an affair or something like that?" Sissy asked.

"I don't think so. The killer would have to be someone vicious and cold to do it in front of all of us like that. Not a sad, hurt wife, or a jealous girl. Someone who could stab a man in the back while he was talking on a microphone to a crowd of people has nerves of steel and no conscience, don't you think? This was a real killer."

"Maybe Cricket knew who it was?" Taylor chewed her bottom lip. She didn't want to be scared, but Marva was right. This was no crime of passion. Not in front of a crowd. And Dayton had every reason to seek shelter where she couldn't be found.

"That's what I thought. I hadn't seen her all day, so I don't know what she was doing before the tea party. I can only guess she had a run-in with the killer, and that was that."

Sissy stood. "Give me a call when you want me to set your hair."

"I will love, and now I'll have a bit of a sleep."

"Light some candles to get rid of this smell, will you? You don't want the neighbors calling that awful Karina over to see if you're still alive."

Marva laughed. "Karina's all right, I suppose. She's entertaining, anyway. Watch out for her though, Taylor," Marva said. "She's been in love with Hudson for an awful long time. So have a lot of girls." Marva shook her head, then closed her eyes. "You're one lucky girl for winning his heart."

Taylor cleared her throat awkwardly. "Um, thanks." They left quickly and took deep breaths of the stale, but at least not rotten, air of the hallway.

"What do you think, was Annie nothing but a good religious girl or could she have been a cold-blooded killer?" Sissy led the way down the long hall as quick and firm as she had earlier.

"Neither. I think she's a perfectly normal woman who had been stuck in a bad marriage. But I wonder about Karina. Maybe her over-the-top declarations of love for Hudson are a cover for the crime. Maybe she really loved Leon. Loved him enough to kill."

"She strikes me as the kind of woman to kill in a screaming fit. Not the kind who would sneak up behind him and then saunter away like nothing happened."

"People can surprise."

Taylor pondered it for the rest of the evening. People could surprise. Like Dayton sneaking away to stay with a great aunt at the old folk's home.

Later that night, the rustle of the trees outside Taylor's window sent shivers of panic through her core. She pulled her dresser in front of her door and double checked the lock on the window. In bed, she wrapped her Dove-in-the-Window quilt around her tightly, despite the heat of a summer night in an un-air-conditioned, second-story bedroom. A cold-blooded killer was out there and had killed two.

Maybe there was always a cold-blooded killer running loose? The statistics of murder indicated it was so.

Maybe she'd panic like this every night for the rest of her life?

She took a deep breath and tried to think of something nice. Hudson came to mind, but then so did all the other women who seemed to love him. Clay was in the background, grinning at her and waiting, but then she remembered he wasn't really waiting anymore. Not with that cute little chef on the scene.

It was a happy, bright moment when she remembered her date with John Hancock. Good, uncomplicated John who liked to go to fancy restaurants and symphonies and things like that. He knew where he stood and didn't mind. And so did she. She sunk down into her pillows and let herself imagine the upcoming evening—she'd need something new to wear. Even though they lived in casual-country, John Hancock dressed for things. Tomorrow she'd go to Salem and find something new and fancy, but not try-hard. A dress and some shoes, maybe.

Even the imagined ritual of finding something and trying it on and ringing it up seemed to calm her nerves. God bless John Hancock, being just the friend she needed right now.

CHAPTER SEVENTEEN

aturday morning Taylor rose bright and early. She shoved her dresser out of the way and opened her window for some fresh air. Her sister had survived what was really just an accident. It was good that Clay was showing interest in some other women, and she needed to get something sexy, casual but fancy for the Alan Thicke Theme Song Symphony thingy tonight.

She skipped out without a "good morning" for her sister or Grandpa Ernie. She didn't owe them any explanation of where she was going or why. Salem was less than an hour away, and she could get some breakfast at the first Starbucks she found when she drove into town. She knew just where it was.

She didn't let the surprise of gray skies get her down as she parked a nice long way from her favorite discount store. Fresh air and exercise and new clothes. All of these things would work together to shake the gloom, the megrims, and woe-is-mes. She stared at the mall for a moment before she went in.

It had been remodeled years ago.

It wasn't the same place she and her mom had snuck off to when they needed to escape the suffocating sympathy of their friends and relations in those early days after her father's death, but it was at the same time. It was the same physical spot on the earth, and it had worked its magic many times before in her life.

In the store she was drawn to the small selection of little black dresses, but each time she slid one off the metal rack, it had some sort of glitter or sequins or plastic sparkle attached. Such a pity. One of them looked like it might be easy to de-sparkle, if it fit right. She was holding it up in front of the mirror trying to decide if it was for her or not when she spotted a newly familiar face behind her. "Annie!" Taylor lowered the dress and turned to Leon's sort of widow. "How are you doing?"

Annie held up her own little black dress. "I'm trying to find something suitable for the joint funeral of my legally separated spouse and his girlfriend." She shook her head, a look of mixed humor and despair in her eyes. "I never thought I'd be shopping for this particular outfit."

"I'm finding their selection is heavy on the sparkle."

"Indeed." Annie tapped the large clear plastic squares that framed the neck of the dress she was holding. "But what can we do?"

"We could go get brunch."

Annie's smile was warm and appreciative. "I'd love to, but my kids are around here somewhere finding something nice to wear to their father's funeral." She rolled her eyes then froze. "Oh! I'm sorry."

Taylor shrugged. "This will be really hard for them. But I can kind of get how you're feeling."

"You know, you're a really nice person. I've heard so much about you, not just since your mom died, but before, too, that I was ready to hate you."

"Yikes." Taylor stepped back and tried to get the "working at the store" smile to stick on her face.

"Sorry. That wasn't nice. I'm not in a nice mood, and I'm having a hard time reacting appropriately to basically everything."

"It's the grief." Taylor slipped the dress back on the rack. She had little black dresses at home. Some she hadn't even worn yet.

"Small town gossip. The good and the bad. And, boy, every time *you* do anything, it spreads through Comfort like wildfire. You'd have thought when you moved home you were going to be sainted."

Taylor lifted a shoulder. What could she say to this? The woman in front of her was probably in shock still. She was dressed in skinny jeans with artfully torn holes but covered in clay. Her flannel was baggy and clearly of the "wears this to do my pottery" collection, but her hair and makeup were perfect, as though at least part of this morning she had been aware of what she was doing.

Taylor sighed.

Annie was a mess.

"Do you have anyone to talk to? Like a counselor?" Taylor wondered if she had asked this already. She ought to have, but she too sometimes didn't react appropriately. Especially when talking about dead parents. It was like the grief would jump out and surprise attack her. She'd be going along taking care of her responsibilities, doing her best to live that good life her folks would have wanted for her, and wham. There it was. The misery and loneliness and fear, out of the blue, and she would say or do something that hurt someone or didn't help them or just didn't make sense.

It happened a lot.

Always had.

Shopping, no matter how much her mom had believed in it, hadn't fixed the problem.

"No. Not yet. Who has time?"

"Or money?" Taylor remembered the straits Leon had left his family in and wished she hadn't said anything. Annie hadn't inherited a profitable business, fat savings account, and popular YouTube channel when her soon-to-be-ex had died.

"Funny you should say that. I got a call just yesterday from a bank I didn't know about. He had quite the stash set aside."

"What?" Taylor gripped the sleeve of a knit dress that swung on the rack next to her. Marva Love's words about Leon being good with money came back to her. She had been distracted by the nasty durian smell, and it hadn't registered as being untrue at the time.

"I don't know if it was his escape fund, or what, but it's ours now, and by God, we need it. Not quite the full thirty thousand he lost gambling, but very close."

"Be careful with it. No rash decisions."

"Yes, that's what the banker cautioned as well. I promise I'm using my pottery money to buy our funeral clothes."

A school age boy, Odin, Orrin? Taylor couldn't remember, ran up to Annie. "Here." He shoved a pair of pants at his mom. "Can we go now?"

Annie kissed the top of his head. He had a young face, but was rangy, tall like a weed, and came to her shoulder. "Not quite yet. Your sister and I aren't done."

"I think I am. It was nice to see you. Call if you need anything." When Taylor got to her car, she realized she didn't have anyone to run to with the news of Leon's surprise bank account. Since she was going out with John Hancock, she felt just a little too guilty to call Hudson, Sissy was working, and telling Belle didn't even occur to her.

"JOHN, GOOD TO SEE YOU." Todd, a well-dressed man Taylor had met on occasion when out with John Hancock, shook hands with her date for the night. The man looked at Taylor with a smile that turned to a frown of confusion. "Good to see you as well."

Taylor shook the hand he offered.

"No Tatiana this evening?" Todd drew out the name as though it were a fine wine he was sampling.

John Hancock stepped closer and spoke quietly, "She's back in New York defending her thesis."

The well-dressed man nodded in approval. "Good luck getting a girl like that to come back here for a sod like you."

The lobby of the University of Oregon's Beall Hall was crowded and hot. Though Taylor's blouse was a light satin, she was damp with sweat. Someone had said the central air was broken, but they said it in a way that made her think it was a joke. Her shoes were too tight as well.

Who was Tatiana?

She had tried to hold John's hand as they walked to the auditorium, but he had taken a few steps forward, out of reach.

And yet, dinner had been pleasant. Laughing at the same old jokes. Glad to eat together.

He looked more casual than usual. Jeans this time, though he did have a sport coat on.

Her slim linen pencil skirt felt like too much. No one else was wearing a skirt.

But who was Tatiana?

She couldn't ask because the lights flickered, and they had to find their seats. His seats. His regular seats.

He had a season pass, but this was the first one he had taken her to since before Christmas.

Had he been taking this…doctoral candidate instead?

Not that it mattered.

They had been in too much of a hurry during dinner to talk about the murders. She'd tried to bring it up, but John had merely nodded and said it sounded like a bad deal. Then he'd told her about how his brother's pub was the go-to place for quiz nights.

He hadn't said anything about some girl named Tatiana.

Tah-ti-ahhhh-na as Todd had said.

Like she was some supermodel who only had one name.

"Earth to Taylor." John took her elbow. "Time to go in."

Taylor did not enjoy the TV theme song symphony.

On the drive home, she felt sullen and moody.

"So, this murder really is getting to you," John said after a long, silent drive through the country from Eugene back to Comfort.

"Who's Tatiana?" It was a bold decision to flat-out ask her date about the other woman, but she'd get no rest till she knew what she was up against.

His face brightened. "Ahh. Tatiana." He grinned. He beamed even. The light emanating from his happy face lit up the whole car, despite the dark outside. "Tatiana is the most beautiful, brilliant woman I have ever met in my life. I can't even begin to describe how much I love her. She's working on her thesis right now—it's a finance thing, but so far above my pay grade I can't even begin to understand it. I met her at quiz night. She dominated. Dominated." He drew that word out too.

"Sounds lovely." There was a distinctly poisoned tone to Taylor's voice, but she wasn't about to admit it.

"Hold on." They rolled to a stop light, and he looked at her. "Don't tell me that Taylor-Friends-Zone-Quinn is jealous?"

"I'm not." And yet, she sat in the car with her arms crossed. She couldn't change her physical position now because it would look like she realized it was a jealous way to sit.

"How's Hudson?" He smirked when he asked.

The light changed.

"Fine."

"When you play with fire…"

"Whatever. She sounds amazing. Have you ever in your whole life once met a woman who got excited about hearing how great some other lady is?"

He laughed. "That's not very feminist of you."

"Whatever."

They were almost to her house.

"We're still friends, right? Tatiana doesn't change that for me."

"How does Taaaah-ti-aaaaaah-na feel about it?"

He shrugged. "She's not here, is she? And it's no fun to go out alone when you can go out with a friend."

She pictured all of their friendly dates, the hand holding, the intimate laughing, the one or two stolen kisses.

They weren't really just friends.

She had been playing with fire.

And it was her feelings that got burnt.

"I don't dare say that you already had your chance, do I?" He had hoped to take their casual dating to the next step the year before, but like all the men she'd been dating casually, she'd kept him at arm's length.

"I'm not jealous." They were stopped at her house now. She got out of her car before he could open the door.

"Great. I'll call you when Tatiana gets back in town. We can all go out to eat. Me, Tatiana, you, Hudson, Clay, Reg, and maybe that kid that works at the Arco? I hear he's single." John's eyes were laughing. He was thoroughly enjoying the moment.

"Sounds great. I'll line them all up." She shut his door with a bit of a slam and went up her front steps stomping a little.

He didn't drive away till she was safely inside.

The front room was empty.

The whole house quiet.

Taylor was left alone with her thoughts.

Had she really, honestly, and truly expected to keep all of the men she was dating to herself? She was not willing to admit this might have been true. Not even close.

A loneliness settled over her as she got ready for bed. Her reason for not committing to Hudson had been the advice not to make major decisions after a crisis. But what if that was just an excuse? What if she knew the honest truth was that she didn't love him? Wouldn't ever love him? Even after that lovely night where he'd had no expectations of her and had just let her sleep? What if her four years with Clay had been the only years of love she'd been granted?

Her parents had been together for about fifteen years when

her dad had died. They'd met in high school. By the time they were twenty, they had married and had her already. Only eleven years after that, he was gone. And her mother never fell in love again.

It had seemed so short and tragic. Not seemed. It had been short and tragic.

What if the only love she'd ever have was even shorter? Just four years?

She snuggled into her bed, wrapping herself in the quilt her grandmother had made her for high school graduation. Both sets of her grandparents had decades of marriage. What if she never even got a wedding?

She supposed she should be happy for the four years she did have with love. Some people never got that. Her life wasn't a tragedy just because.... no.

It was only fair to say her life was a tragedy.

But Clay Seldon was just two blocks up the street, in her apartment above the shop. If he was her one true love—if those four years were the only four she'd ever get as a real couple—why didn't she go back to him? Couldn't she forgive him for abandoning her when her mother died?

Others had hinted to her that quitting her job, selling the condo, and moving home to Comfort without even discussing it with him had made her at least partially to blame for their breakup.

Sure, he ought to have been mature and able to cope with those changes. He ought to have been willing to give it all up and come with her. But the same impulse that had driven her to make all of those changes had made him dig his heels in. He ought to have come. She ought to have had a conversation with him about it first.

If she could acknowledge that, then maybe there was a future for the two of them. Maybe she and Clay and John Hancock and Tatiana could be couple-friends and go to the symphony together. Clay liked fancy things like that. They could all vacation somewhere sunny together during the rainy season. It would be lovely to be part of a couple again. A real couple that was committed.

She pulled up Clay's number on her phone, but her gut clenched with anger.

He had abandoned her when she needed him most.

Whether she had been wrong or not, that pain wasn't going away anytime soon.

She opened YouTube instead and found her mom's show. There was one in particular that she watched when she was sad or lonely or the weight of missing her got to be too much.

It was a silly one. Just a how-to for hand quilting. Her mom poked herself in the finger a few times, and her eyes started with tears.

Taylor fast forwarded to the important moment.

Laura Quinn, popular quilt YouTuber, quilt shop owner and mother, stared down at the tip of her finger as though it surprised her to feel pain. "I swear…" She was about to say something she shouldn't and bit her lip. Then she sucked the tip of her finger and looked at the camera. The tears were there. Ready to spill. "I don't know how many times I've told my babies to wear thimbles when they stitch." She smiled through the tears. "Because I would do anything in the world to save them pain. But do I protect myself? Nope. We moms, we always think we can tough it out. Take one for the team. I mean, not you all. You're smart enough to wear your thimbles. Mine's not in the sewing kit because I loaned it to my baby, Belle, and forgot to get it back, but I'm standing here, in the middle of my *quilt shop*," she emphasized with a laugh, "and I didn't just grab one. Like I'm invincible. Or like it doesn't matter if I hurt anymore. But you know what? It does matter. I'm not talking to myself. I'm talking to you guys. To all of you who give away your thimbles or your lunch or your last spare minute. It matters if you get hurt. You matter."

Taylor paused the video and stared at her mom. Did a kid,

even a grown-up kid, ever really recognize all the little ways their mothers sacrificed for them? The tears in her mom's eyes were paused, like the video. Ready to spill, but not spilling. Real, but not real anymore. Taylor gave in to her sadness, letting her own tears spill, letting herself hurt, because her mom said she mattered.

She pulled her quilt up over her head and let herself feel like that scared kid again.

Shuffling footsteps in the hall seemed to echo her heartache, slow, shaky, heavy.

Not like Belle's footsteps.

Not like Belle's footsteps.

Taylor held her breath.

Someone was in the hall, and it wasn't Belle.

The sound stopped right at her door.

"Taylor…" a low voice called out. "Taylor." Then a cough.

Taylor screamed.

Like a girl.

Like a scared child.

She didn't think about waking Belle or Grandpa. She didn't think about anything. She wrenched the quilt in her hands and screamed.

"Taylor?" The voice, again, then the door opening.

A stranger stood there in boxer shorts and a t-shirt, backlit from the hall light.

"Taylor, what the hell?" Belle's voice rang down the hall. "You could wake the dead. Levi, come back to bed."

Levi.

Levi with the flu.

Levi coughed. "I just wanted some aspirin."

Belle sighed dramatically. "It's in the bathroom."

"It's not," he had a whiny voice.

"It's the middle of the night." Taylor was still clutching her quilt.

'It's only eleven."

"Why are you still at our house?" Taylor asked.

Levi coughed.

"You have a twin bed." Taylor rubbed her eyes.

"He's sleeping on an air mattress. Come on, buddy, I'll get you some aspirin." She took his arm, and he followed her with his heavy, shuffling step.

Taylor pulled her quilt over her head again.

Levi needed to go home.

CHAPTER EIGHTEEN

*T*aylor was haunted all day by the idea that she was selfish, greedy even. Her mother's video about self-sacrifice and thimbles seemed to call her out. At least that's what her guilty conscience said. She felt like she owed Hudson an apology. He was the one she had toyed with the worst. She held her phone, ready to text him several times throughout the day, breathing in relief every time she was interrupted by a customer.

Around closing time, Clay sauntered down in his sock feet.

"You look comfy." Taylor frowned at his wooly toes pointedly.

"Staying in tonight." He yawned.

"We're not closed yet."

He glanced at the wall clock behind the register and laughed. "Sorry. He pulled a tall stool up to the worktable. "I'm ordering a pizza. Want to join me?" He patted his slinged arm, almost begging for sympathy.

"No." She could feel her eyebrows drawing together against her will. The shocked, maybe even horrified, look you give a child who has a stupid idea.

"I thought you'd like that I was staying put. Not driving and all that."

She pressed her hand to her forehead. "I've been trying to forget your little accident since it happened."

He gently touched his bruised nose.

"I'm surprised you don't have plans with Joey." Taylor wasn't sure she'd pulled off a casual sound. She didn't want to feel jealous, and she really didn't want to sound jealous.

"She took some old folks to the casino again. Won't be home for another hour or so and will probably be wiped out." His eyes were bright, but Taylor sensed disappointment.

"Too bad you couldn't meet her out there."

"Hadn't thought of it."

"There's a good restaurant. Maybe the gang is staying to eat."

He was already texting, probably Joey. He looked up with a grin. "This was not the official Leon Farkas Memorial Gambling event, just another one of many. They are staying to eat at the Cedar Plank Buffet."

"Could be worse."

"Come with?"

She grimaced again, like his idea was remarkably stupid. Then she paused. She could get the shop closed for the night pretty fast. Grandpa Ernie was far from alone with Belle there and Levi skulking around the house. And...there just might be someone at the casino who could shed light on Leon's death. Surely someone in this town knew something. They had to. They just didn't know they knew it. Especially if any of these folks were on the cusp of needing to move to the memory care wing.

"Yes. Actually, I could use a good old-fashioned buffet."

He lifted an eyebrow with a cheeky smile, patted his sling again and said, "You drive."

She closed up shop in record time, and the drive to Spirit Mountain Casino was quick and painless. The party from Bible Creek Care Home hadn't made it to the buffet yet, but Taylor and Clay found them cashing in their bingo wins.

Clay and Joey spotted each other, and the moment was electric.

Delicate little Mrs. Sylvester giggled.

Boggy Hudson gave Joey an avuncular look of pride as she smiled at Taylor's ex.

Taylor stiffened, but reminded herself she wasn't here for his company. She was here for the mystery.

She joined Mrs. Sylvester as they walked to the buffet. Boggy, Hudson's grandpa, had smiled at her and seemed to want to join them, but that guilt that had been riding her all day, the guilt that she hadn't been fair to Hudson, made her look away in embarrassment. Instead she asked Mrs. Sylvester how the day had gone. "Win anything?"

Mrs. Sylvester rolled her eyes, such a youthful, casual expression it took Taylor by surprise. She looked around the crowd as they made their slow way to their dinner. They were all casual, relaxed. Not the same formal company they had been at the tea party. Boggy laughed loudly at something a short woman in a red denim jacket said to him. She swatted at his arm.

What had Taylor expected? It was a day at the casino, not a trip to church. But she was still surprised. "I'm glad to see everyone having such a good time."

"The casino is always fun."

"I wasn't sure. I thought it might be quite sad this time, because of Leon."

Mrs. Sylvester clucked. "He wouldn't want us to be sad. Besides, the dividend checks came in, so we're celebrating him."

"Dividend checks?"

She put her finger to her pursed lips.

"What do you mean, though, did he help you invest?"

"We really weren't supposed to talk about it. I wasn't sure what would happen once he passed. We're all celebrating that today." She paused and lowered her voice to a whisper.

Taylor had to stoop to hear her.

"Someone has suspected that it might be a scheme." She said "scheme" as though it were a bad word. "And they suggested we would lose all our money after my poor boy died."

"You must be relieved." Taylor flagged the word "scheme" and filed this with the news of Leon's secret savings account. But she put an asterisk next to it. After all, Mrs. Sylvester and her friends had received their dividend.

"I wouldn't mind a dividend. I wonder if my banker could invest in the same funds..."

Mrs. Sylvester shrugged. "I wouldn't know. Leon handled all of it for us."

Taylor counted heads. Twelve retirees, all who looked to be between Boggy Hudson's seventy-something years old and Mrs. Sylvester's ninety-four.

"Is this the group of investors?"

"Almost," Mrs. Sylvester said. "Marva couldn't come. She still has company."

So, at least for now, Dayton was still safe.

They arrived at the buffet, and Mrs. Sylvester sat down, breathing a little heavily. It was hard to remember how close she was to one hundred years old. After helping her settle into the wooden chair, Taylor brought up the investment again. "How long did you have money with Leon?"

"Two years. And the checks came every quarter like clock-work. I suppose we can talk about it now that he's gone, but he did say we ought to use discretion as it was a limited opportunity."

"I do wonder if it's something I could afford." Taylor gave a soft little sigh. "Was it terribly expensive to get involved with?"

"No, no. I gave him a rather large check right away, but then monthly checks of only fifty dollars."

"That's hardly anything." Taylor worked hard to keep her face happy. In her opinion, at their age they shouldn't have been actively investing anything. And she worried their "quarterly dividends" wouldn't be equal to their fifty-dollar monthly payments. She rallied to ask. "And it earned money every quar-ter? Not every investment has done that. The market has been quite up and down."

"Not this investment. It's done very well." Mrs. Sylvester narrowed her eyes.

Taylor backed off. She didn't need to know all of the details. If it was a scheme—a Ponzi scheme—then those big first investment checks were paying the current quarterlies.

Boggy caught Taylor's eye again and smiled. "Will you excuse me a moment?" Taylor asked Mrs. Sylvester.

Mrs. Sylvester waved her away.

The woman in the red jean jacket took Taylor's seat.

"Boggy, can I be impertinent?"

"Most girls can," he laughed.

"Is there any chance this little investment with Leon was fraudulent?" She kept her voice low, though the odds of any of the guests today having hearing strong enough to hear from their places in the buffet line were slim.

He lifted an eyebrow at Taylor. "I never gave that old schemer any of my money."

"Then how did you get invited here?"

"I let my friends think I did."

"But why? Didn't that just…."

"Didn't it just support what he was doing? When you have as many old friends as I do—and I mean literally old—you do what you can to take care of them. They were giving that schemer their money whether I did or not. By pretending I did, I got to hear about it. I was keeping good notes."

"But what did you find?"

"Come by tomorrow morning before your shop opens, and I'll tell you all about it."

"Were you surprised they got their dividend checks?"

"Not at all. I'm sure it's automatic. And someone would have to know the account existed to shut it down."

"Then the next checks won't get cut," Taylor said. "Annie found an account just the other day. Said it almost made up for what he'd lost gambling."

Boggy took a sharp, deep breath. "I had hoped it wouldn't

come to this. Meet me tomorrow morning. We'll talk then. But now, let me buy you dinner. It's a very good buffet."

🍀

TAYLOR WAS BACK at Bible Creek Care Home the next morning at nine. Whatever Boggy had been hiding, he was going to reveal, she was determined, and also armed with a box of what Hudson swore were his Grandpa's favorite chocolates.

Boggy's apartment was on the larger side, like the one Dayton was hopefully still hidden at. He welcomed Taylor to his vintage pine dining room table, round and thick and dinged with living. His apartment had the aura of a man-cave with more wool plaid than Pendleton Mills, and a big fish hanging over a bigger TV.

"I've talked to the police already." He set a thick ceramic mug of black coffee in front of Taylor. "But Leon had kids, so I didn't want to say anything that might lead to gossip. Kids have it hard enough when a parent dies."

She nodded but didn't get a chance to reply.

"Like when your dad died. Just like that. From here on out, Leon was a man of God in this community and nothing else. It's the least we can do for the kids."

She jerked to attention. "Excuse me?"

"Let a man die a hero, if he has kids. That's all I'm saying."

Taylor's shoulders were stiff, and gooseflesh chased up and down her arms. Leon was far from a man of God, but her dad... he *had* been a hero. He literally died fighting a fire. Whatever Boggy was implying...

"But before he died," Boggy continued, "Leon Farkas was a con artist. I tried to warn that Cricket away from him, but she wouldn't listen. Wanted to get married, I think. But he wasn't even divorced yet." He grumbled something under his breath.

"What was that?" Taylor leaned forward.

"Homewrecker. Cricket, she was as sweet as anything, but

190

she only really liked a man when he was married to someone else." His face was angry as he remembered the pain his daughter had experienced because of Cricket and Doug.

"Tell me about the con Leon was running." Taylor's mind was stuck on whatever secret or gossip or dirt Boggy thought he had on her dad, but she needed to shove it aside. She was closing in on something big, and nothing else mattered. For now.

"Classic Ponzi scheme. No more, no less. Take money from the old folks and promise them impossible interest earnings."

"They couldn't see it was impossible?" Taylor wrapped her hands around the mug. It reminded her of Annie Farkas' work.

"The trick with a good con is to make it seem possible. Crazy, but not that crazy. You weren't born yet, but there was a time when 15% interest was common for a mortgage. So, us old folks…we see 15% as high, but not impossibly high."

"That doesn't seem all that high for a stock, though."

"He wasn't offering that. It was higher, but what I mean is, it wasn't so high that it seemed obvious. Not to folks who've been around the block a few times."

"Annie said she found an account with about thirty-thousand dollars in it." She traced the rim of the mug. It was similar, but not as special as what Annie had at home. Probably someone else's work.

"Sure. I could see that."

"It's a lot, but not enough to bankrupt anyone, right? Like maybe no one is going to be devastated by this."

"I couldn't say. It depends on how much he was paying out each month and how much he was gambling or hiding in other accounts."

Taylor exhaled slowly through tight lips. "Are you sure, I mean absolutely sure, no one else had figured out it was a con?"

He sighed, deeply and sadly. "None of the residents here who invested believed they were being conned."

"But what about their family?"

"That's a good question. Sure were lots of guests at the tea party."

"We all had to sign in, right? No way to sneak around that?" Taylor stared at Boggy. She had a list of suspects at her fingertips and had never even tried to look at it.

"Karina is a good bouncer. I'm sure everyone had to sign in. The line was pretty long."

"True. We had to kick our heels at the front door for a few minutes. But you're sure there aren't any back doors?" She thought of Dayton sneaking around, hiding in plain sight. Maybe the killer had done the same thing.

"All locked. We have pass cards that open them for us."

"Maybe we should go see who signed in for the tea party?"

"And hope they used their real names."

KARINA HAD a bulldoggish look on her face when Boggy and Taylor appeared. She wanted to turn them away. Taylor Quinn just made her feel like that. But, on the other hand, she couldn't afford to make Hudson's grandpa angry. At least not at her. "How can I help you?" The words themselves were kind, but even she could tell they didn't sound friendly coming out from between her gritted teeth.

"Hello, young lady." Boggy leaned on the counter and smiled at her, his big brown eyes sappy. She knew about his reputation with the older ladies. Unlike his grandson who was known as a good catch in large part because he didn't play around, Boggy liked to make sure all the ladies got some of his attention.

She softened under his flirty gaze. Who wouldn't, after all? "What do you need?"

"I was just wanting to look at the guest register, if you don't mind. This gal and I were arguing about who was at the tea party. I say, you know, what with the death and all, she just can't remember. But she swears she's right. You wouldn't help us out with that, would you?"

"I really can't." She crossed her arms. This had the stink of Taylor all over it. She was clearly doing some kind of detective something and had Boggy wrapped up in it. With Taylor's luck, Boggy would be the next one killed. Or Karina would.

"I know it's a lot to ask." He slowly pulled out a worn leather wallet. "I wouldn't assume something like this is...free."

She smirked.

"I probably have something you want...." He lifted an eyebrow.

She laughed. Even with a higher percentage of women than men, there were plenty of eighty-year-olds at Bible Creek Care Home who have offered to be her fella.

"You know...." He slipped a picture out of his wallet and set it on the counter.

She pulled it down. Hudson. Sure, it was his high school graduation picture in a cap and gown from almost ten years ago. But it was still Hudson. This time she lifted her eyebrow.

"You two used to be so in love."

Behind Boggy, Taylor's face went white.

This time Karina's smile was warm and satisfied.

"What went wrong, my dear? And do you think it can't be made right?"

Taylor coughed into her fist.

Karina attempted a demure look, glancing down and fluttering her eyelids. "Nothing is impossible to fix..."

"What you two need is a quiet dinner alone, don't you think?"

She stroked the picture with her thumb. Yes, yes, she did think. "Are you saying that I might..."

"I'm saying..." Boggy dropped his voice. "I'm saying that I would be grateful to prove this little girl wrong, so grateful that I would happily arrange a quiet dinner for you and him."

She slipped the picture into the pocket of her skinny jeans, got up, and went back to the workroom. Helping Taylor do detective work was abhorrent. But using Taylor's detective work to get alone with Hudson was delicious. She selected the pages from the sign-in book and ran them through the photocopier.

When she went back to her desk, Taylor was gone, but Boggy was happily looking at a smart phone. "Here you go." She held out the pages for him, but didn't let go when his hand was on them.

"Ah." He let go of the pages and held up the phone. "Talking to Hudson. How will Friday night do?"

"Just fine." She barely got the words out and could have kicked herself for that moment of weakness. The idea of this dinner being so soon had literally taken her breath away.

Boggy took the papers, and she let him.

Dinner with Hudson on Friday.

This was her chance and she wasn't going to waste it.

BACK AT HIS APARTMENT, Boggy scanned the pages on an almost vintage scanner and emailed them to Taylor. "Sorry we can't go over this together." He slipped his copy of the pages into a yellow Pee-Chee folder. "But I've got a hot date with Mrs. Sylvester."

"How is she doing?" Taylor lingered by the door.

"She didn't invest, if that's what you mean." He walked forward, pulled the door shut behind himself and Taylor.

"That's good, but I was thinking more about her grief at losing a nephew."

"She's sad. We're all sad." He looked down from his tall, slender height and shook his head. "You've lost a lot of folks in your young life, my friend. Gives you a lot of sympathy for folks who are suffering." He patted her shoulder. "It's a good thing, kiddo. I'll make sure young Mrs. Sylvester isn't alone. You go find out if someone on that list might have had a grudge against our man of God."

Taylor took a shortcut out of the care home and went back to her shop. Clay was good at data. A funny memory popped up as she thought of him hunched over a computer...the "Nigerian Princess" scandal from some years ago. She smiled despite it all. He'd been the amateur detective that time, and she'd almost forgotten about it.

Yes, Clay was good at internet sleuthing.

Between the two of them, they could get through this list and find something.

She texted Belle to make sure she was staying home with Grandpa.

"Who's the hot date with tonight?"

Taylor scrunched her face at her phone. *"No date. Just Data, with Clay."*

"And I'm just nursing Levi."

Taylor grumbled loudly to herself. She'd better be just nursing him.

"Can I order food?"

Where she thought she'd order from was anyone's guess, but Taylor figured it wouldn't hurt to try. *"Anything you want. Pizza, drinks, whatever. Use the cc I have in my desk drawer in my room."*

"Don't worry about rushing. We'll be here all night."

"I'm not staying the night with Clay."

"Whatever."

CHAPTER NINETEEN

*I*t was well after midnight when Taylor shut her laptop. She rubbed the dust and sleep from her eyes and yawned, laying down on the floor.

"You did good." Clay stretched across the couch. "Can I please go to bed now?"

"Yes, of course." She yawned again, more deeply.

"You didn't walk here, did you?" Clay sat up again, a look of disappointment washing over his face.

"You don't have to walk me home. It's less than half a mile." She sat up on her elbows. She had walked. She'd been walking all day. It was good for her nervous energy. But she wasn't looking forward to walking to her house alone in the dark.

"Want me to call Grandpa Ernie so he can come pick you up?" Clay had changed into his flannel jammies hours earlier, and his mussed hair and crumple look were more laughable than his joke.

Taylor flopped back down on the floor.

"Pass me that quilt." Clay pointed to the nine-patch she had made in junior high. Its soft worn cotton was draped over her bare feet. "I'll stay here. You take the bed."

"I'd call you a saint…."

"But it's your apartment. I get it."

"But, Clay, what did we actually learn from all of that?" Taylor stood and stretched, her T lifting enough for the chilly night air to hit her bellybutton and make her shiver.

"Three visitors had records, Tay. That's not nothing. Two of them were visiting folks you saw with the group at the casino. All you have to do now is find out which one was absent from the table while Leon was killed."

"Easy then." Taylor rubbed her arms. It was cold in the apartment. Too cold. But she'd ask Clay why he wasn't using the furnace some other time. She closed her eyes and pictured the tea party. It had been a huge crowd, but it would be easy enough to find out who wasn't sitting at the table. All you had to do was ask.

WHEN TAYLOR WOKE the next morning, she was freezing. She pulled the quilt up under her chin. Why was her room so cold? She squeezed her eyes tightly.

She took a deep breath, but something wasn't right. It smelled wrong. Familiar. But wrong.

She sat up and looked around.

The apartment.

A moment of panic washed over her as she looked for Clay, but no. She hadn't made a dreadful mistake in the night. Besides, she was fully dressed. She had come in, laid her head on the pillow, and that was that.

She pulled the quilt from the top of the bed—an afghan, warm and snuggly and a rare thing in a world of quilts. Her steps were slow, not wanting to see him. In all these months—well more than a year—she hadn't seen Clay in the morning, and there was a feeling, a sick feeling in her stomach, that if she saw him this morning, sleep in his eyes, hair messy, his goofy grin, then all those old emotions would come rolling back in, and she'd be home again.

But he wasn't in the living room. She popped open the door to the second bedroom that she and Clay both used for storage. He wasn't there. She knocked on the bathroom door, and he wasn't there, either.

Relief washed over her in waves. Maybe he hadn't wanted to see her in the morning either. Hard to say. But since he was gone, she took a quick shower, did her hair, and ambled down to the shop. It was only seven, still plenty of time since she hadn't planned to film today.

The shop was quiet and dusky feeling. Cozy and secretive. She made herself a whole pot of coffee and took one of the granola bars from the little chicken wire basket of snacks that stood on the coffee bar. The window-pane style mirror she had made room for on the wall was a challenge to check her whole outfit in, but her hair was looking nice, and she had time to run home to change into clothes she hadn't slept in.

But first she nestled into Grandpa Ernie's old recliner and opened YouTube on her phone. If she didn't have Grandpa Ernie to take care of, she could live above her shop, save all that money she spent maintaining the house, and have every morning feel this casual and comfy.

She didn't stop to think about where Clay would live. He was a grown man. He could figure it out.

Her mom's radiant face glowed from the screen. "My eldest daughter has been with her boyfriend forever." The voice she missed the most in the world sounded wistful. "And every year I think 'this is the year they will get married.' Not that I want to rush them, but I'm a mother, aren't I? So today, since Valentine's Day is just around the corner and this Valentine's Day might be 'the one,' I'm going to show you a way to make a wedding-ring like quilt block. Beautiful and traditional, but much easier."

Taylor paused the video. She'd seen this one before. Her mother's last Valentine's Day, spent wishing Taylor and Clay would get married. It seemed sincere, at least. But maybe it had been just for the show.

She knew why she had selected it this morning. To punish herself.

For what, she wasn't sure exactly. Probably for being so happy to have a morning all to herself without anyone else to care for. Certainly no one deserved that kind of peace, right? She hit play again, ready to feel lots and lots of guilt for never giving her mom a wedding.

Before she could really begin to wallow, the back door opened with a creak. She was well awake at this point and realized it was just Clay coming back from wherever he had been, so she didn't move from her spot. She turned off the video of her mom dreaming about her wedding and opened her email.

Before she could open a message and pretend to be absorbed in it, a girlish laugh flickered through the room.

She sat up.

Clay and Joey walked around the corner to the classroom space Taylor was hiding in. "Morning." Clay held out a *concha* from Café Olé.

"Morning." She accepted it, one eyebrow lifted.

"Hey, Taylor." Joey looked down at her feet, then up, making eye contact, but looking shy.

"Tay, my dear old friend, you will never believe who I ran into at the coffee shop."

"I'm going to guess...Joey Burke?"

"Sure, that's what some people call her, but I call her exactly the woman we need right now."

Taylor waved to the coffeepot. "Pardon my manners, help yourself."

"No, no. I had some at the café, but, um, listen, Clay and I were talking over coffee, and he got me thinking about those people on the list that you have."

"The visitors who also had criminal records?"

"Yeah. So, I'm pretty familiar with the residents and their

families. Lots of people come eat with their grandparents. And he was saying that, um…Rob Packard and Jerrod Brickell were both there, right?"

"Yeah, those were the two guys we found criminal records for from the guest list who were also visiting people at the casino. The people who were in on Leon's investment thing."

"Okay. So Rob, he's always seemed okay, but I know his record was for some kind of fraud. He tried to get a volunteer gig at the care home, but the boss wouldn't take him on. Didn't trust him."

"Whoa. That's good to know." Taylor smiled at Joey, trying to make the nervous woman feel more comfortable. As far as she was concerned, Clay was right. Joey was the right person at the right time.

"But, on the other hand, he's like six feet tall, and Clay was saying your potential killer was sort of smaller, right?"

"Yeah." Taylor didn't let that get her down. There was no reason to think Dayton's description was super-accurate, especially since Dayton, herself, was around six feet tall.

"So, Jerrod, his crime was possession—pot. No big deal, and I think he gets to have it expunged now that pot's legal. But he's smaller, shorter anyway. But he's a really mellow, soft-spoken guy, so I don't know."

"You never know with the soft-spoken ones…" Taylor nodded as she spoke, hoping to get Joey to say more.

"Maybe so. Especially because, now that I think about it, I think I saw him in the dining room around the time I was heading out to do the cake and all that. I'm not sure, but I think maybe."

"Is there something about him that stands out? Something that makes it hard to mistake him for someone else?"

"Not really, no, but he's cute. So, I do notice him sometimes." Clay winked.

Taylor didn't know why, and she didn't wink back. "Thanks, Joey, I really appreciate it." She pocketed her phone and stood.

201

"Leon was my friend." Joey looked at her feet again. "He wasn't a perfect guy, but in this world, you take the friends you're given, you know?"

"Yeah…" Taylor paused. She'd been living in this town for over a year now and hadn't once reached out to Joey, even though they were around the same age, both single, and both needing friends. Instead she'd spent all her time replacing Clay while pretending it wasn't about him.

But that was silly. Joey hadn't been forced to be friends with a sleezy hypocrite just because Taylor was dealing with stuff. Anyway, Joey hadn't reached out to her, either. Taylor smiled, but wouldn't let herself feel guilty.

"What I mean…" Joey cleared her throat. "Jerrod is a cute guy. And I did notice him, I'm sure of it. Because he was with Cricket when I saw him. And that was the last time I saw Cricket alive."

AFTER GOING HOME TO CHANGE, Taylor went straight to Bible Creek Care Home.

Karina stared at her from the other side of her desk. "Don't you have, like, a fabric store to run?" Her lip curled not at all subtly.

"Just wanted to pop in and have a chat with, um…" Taylor consulted the note on her phone. "Jenny-Sue Meyer."

"Old friend of the family, huh?"

"You know small towns." Taylor gave an apologetic shrug.

"You could always call, you know."

"Oh, folks like a visit."

"At eight-thirty in the morning? You know they have set dining room hours, don't you?"

"I mean, I just want to sign in and go say hi. It's not illegal or anything." Taylor's friendly façade was cracking.

"I bet ten dollars if I call *Mrs.* Meyer, she has no idea who you are."

"For heaven's sake, what's your problem?"

"Oh, me? Just trying to keep my residents safe in light of two recent tragic murders."

"But that's all I want." Taylor bit her words off before she started yelling. "Karina, you got a date with Hudson for giving us that list, what do you want so I can visit? His kid?"

"How about a whole night—a *whole* night with him," Karina whispered, her lips curled up in a cat-like smile.

Taylor just shook her head. Then she laughed. "Because I'm what, his, like, his pimp? Please. You know how hot he is. I could make real money, not these little favors." She laughed again, but it was forced.

Karina shrugged. "Let me call her and see if she wants a morning visitor. She's one of our older residents. Karina dialed a number. Taylor didn't know if it was actually Jenny-Sue Meyer's number or not.

Karina hung up. "So sorry. She's probably off at breakfast. You'll have to come back another time." She dared to flutter her eyelashes sweetly as she said it.

"No problem. I can swing by after work. We close up nice and early." Taylor kept her cool leaving. There was more than one way to skin a horse. After all, she had his name and a computer. She could look him up and call him herself. She didn't need to talk to the elderly lady he had been visiting.

"That isn't a great idea." Hudson was referring to calling the potential killer to see if he remembered anything in particular about the tea party. He passed a hamburger to Taylor. He'd been up in Keizer earlier in the day and brought them back burgers from the northernmost In-N-Out burger. They were cold.

"I don't think it's smart to call while I'm working, so I do have time to talk myself out of it."

"Good."

"You could always call." Taylor thought about batting her eyelashes at him a la Karina, but refrained.

"I could."

"Really?"

"I really could. I'm not saying I will." He finished off his burger before she'd even unwrapped hers. "The Joneses called."

"Bethany and Clark?" She nibbled a French fry.

"I hadn't heard those voices in years. I used to call them Nana and Pop."

"That's adorable."

"They were adorable." He grinned. "It's funny, I never forgot them, but I do have two sets of my own grandparents, so I didn't really think of them."

"They are lovely people."

"So, you won't mind having dinner with them, oh, say, tonight?"

"It would keep me from calling a killer..." She paused and looked at his face. Handsome, sure; rugged, yes. But a little vulnerable, the way both eyebrows were lifted and his cheeks slightly pink as though he were embarrassed to ask. "I would love to, honestly."

"But?"

"Grandpa Ernie. I made Belle stay the night with him last night while I did some research on this guy. I ended up sleeping in the apartment." This time she felt her own face turn red.

Hudson cleared his throat.

"Clay had the couch. I was beat, and I swear, after all that, I didn't want to walk home alone in the dark."

"He'd have made you walk home, huh?"

She inhaled sharply. "I don't expect much of him."

Hudson crumpled his bag. "Some other time, then." He

tossed it into a garbage can across the room with a thump and stood.

"Hey, what's wrong?" She took a quick drink from her Coke and followed him out the back door.

"I thought things were getting more serious than you thought they were, I guess."

"I did not sleep with Clay last night."

"No, but did you want to?" He stared at her, his eyes still vulnerable.

"Absolutely not."

"Okay." He shrugged and left.

She wanted to follow him, but she couldn't. It wasn't that kind of day at the shop. Just her and Roxy, and they'd been busy. She wondered if Boggy had already told him about the date he was going to have with Karina. She wondered what exactly had upset him. She hadn't been remotely interested in sleeping with Clay. He needed to know that, to really know that. She glanced back in the shop. Roxy was doing fine. Roxy could handle things for a minute anyway.

She bolted down the steps and around the corner. Hudson's truck was gone. She held her hand over her eyes and squinted, but it was too far down the road. He hadn't said where he was going next, but she doubted it was back to Kaiser. She ran back to her car. She'd try his house real quick. It wasn't that far outside of town.

HUDSON's modern hand-built A-frame was bathed in afternoon sun. It's wall of windows glowed, and the redwood- stained siding seemed to radiate warmth. The house felt like a warm embrace waiting for you on the hill.

Hudson was out front, in a slightly damp t-shirt, working his frustration out by washing his muddy truck.

Taylor came up behind him and put her hand on his back. "Hey."

He wiped the windshield, his long, strong arm reaching halfway across.

"I wasn't there to sleep with him."

"I know."

"Do you?" She turned and leaned on the front of the truck so she could face him.

"Yeah, I do." He dropped his rag and gave her a rueful smile. "I don't like feeling jealous, and I don't like acting stupid when I feel jealous. We haven't slept together, and it's been a long time. I don't know that you want to sleep with anyone. But you do want to solve problems and help people."

She nodded, tears smarting in her eyes. It felt magical to be understood.

"You wanted help or company doing it, and you didn't turn to me. You turned to him, even though it was basically my stepmom who got killed."

"But, Hud, it was only because he's good at..."

"At giving you what you need." He looked past her, quiet for a while. "You're different around him."

"Probably so."

"Comfortable."

"Before we lived together, we were friends, good friends, for like a year. Of course I'm different around him."

He raked his hand through his hair. "Sorry. I was disappointed. I shouldn't have stormed out."

"You are amazing. Kind of unbelievable, really." Her voice was gentle and the words, though they could have been so negative, were loving and kind. "What kind of man talks the way you talk? Opens up about his feelings the way you do?"

He chuckled softly. "I'm the product of modern public-school education, aren't I? We're real good with our feelings, but we can't write in cursive."

She laughed. "Clay is good with data. Finding stuff online. Come inside and I'll show you everything we've got, and you can help me figure out what we're supposed to do."

He looked at his watch. "I have to go bid on a job. I have an appointment. How about I come over after dinner? I can tell you all about the family reunion."

"You know…The Joneses are fond of Grandpa Ernie…."

He shook his head. "I'm fond of him, too, but…"

"He can be a lot at the dinner hour. Don't worry, I get it."

She leaned up and kissed his cheek.

He pulled her in and kissed her with passion, the kind of passion you can only share outside when you know you are all alone on a private piece of land far from prying eyes.

When he let her go, he had a twinkle in his eye. "And later tonight you can tell me what on earth Grandpa Boggy was thinking when he sold me out for that info you needed so bad."

CHAPTER TWENTY

I'm no third wheel." Grandpa Ernie glowered at Hudson from under his bushy eyebrows. Some days he loved the young grandson of his best friend. Some days he seemed to resent the flannel shirts and Carhart jackets. Grandpa Ernie, when the night fell, was a young fit tailor creating bespoke suits for the elite of the state. And whoever Taylor was to him at that hour, she deserved a man in a nice suit. He shuffled into his bedroom with the aid of a rolling walker and shut the door behind him. Soon the sounds of evening news at a volume that would damage the hearing of healthy ears vibrated against the solid wood door.

"How are your Nana and Pops?" Taylor held out a bottle of beer.

He waved it away. "Amazing. Man, we laughed and laughed together. They were a big part of my childhood, but I've always figured that since it was only maybe five years of their life, that they didn't have the same attachment. Especially since I never did hear from them again."

"I'm sorry." She put the beer back and shut the fridge. "Water? Coffee?"

"No, nothing. I'm good." He sat on the edge of the couch.

"They didn't throw my dad under the bus. Didn't even hint at him keeping them away, but once or twice Nana started to say something and Pop quietly touched her elbow, causing her to stop. I suspect they had tried to stay in touch, but Dad wasn't for it."

"Divorce is crap."

Hudson seemed on edge, his muscles flexed, ready for some kind of action. He leaned forward; his elbows pressed into his knees.

She took Grandpa Ernie's recliner to give him the space he seemed to need.

"I remember Cricket as being fun and young. When my parents were married, they made a lot of money, so they hired Cricket to watch me. I was so young I don't remember her not being there. When my folks broke up, it made sense to my kid mind—I was about five—that Cricket was still there. And then it made sense for her parents to be there. I hated going between houses and splitting my time, but Cricket didn't seem like the problem."

Taylor had a mug of tea and sipped it, letting him talk uninterrupted.

"But around the time desserts came, Nana and Pop's mood changed. I know with their daughter murdered it is going to be a long time before they have any untainted happiness. But they were apologetic, not grieving, you know? They kept saying how sorry they were for me." He seemed to caress Taylor's face with his eyes. "Dad's drinking is the official reason my parents broke up, but I guess he didn't drink before Cricket came along. And apparently he really did leave Mom for her."

"Oh...." Taylor made some other sounds of sympathy, but his look was heated, intense. And her heart was beating too loud for her to speak.

"I stayed with Karina far longer than was healthy for me, because breakups are brutal, and I didn't want to do that to anyone."

She nodded.

He shook his head and broke his gaze. "But then they apologized for something really specific, and I'm still trying to figure out exactly what it means—for you."

"For me?" Being released from his intense gaze was both a relief and a disappointment. She didn't care about anything at this moment except those eyes and that face and how badly she wanted him to stop talking so she could kiss him. She inhaled deeply, but it didn't help.

"Nana started to say how sorry she was about the house—Dad moved right after he and Cricket broke up. I was about ten. Pop touched Nana's elbow, but Nana shook her head and kept going. She said, 'It was a terrible loss for you all, and she never did accept responsibility.'"

"Cricket did something that made your dad lose his house?"

"That's what it sounded like. I didn't press for details. Dad stayed in the house in town for a few years, then bought the property he's on. It's got a doublewide on it. He's happy. I guess the house in town was a rental. He never explained any of it to me, and I didn't ask."

"We need to call your Dad."

He exhaled through tight lips. "You're right. If Leon was killed for being a crook, maybe she wasn't just killed because she was dating him. Maybe she was part of the problem." He took out his phone and called—but when his father answered, he took the call outside.

Taylor didn't want to think this implicated Doug, Hudson's dad, but losing a house could be motive for murder, even if it had happened fifteen years ago.

The wait for Hudson to return was intense. When he came back in, he gripped his phone in his fist. "Dad's pissed."

"About your questions?"

"Yeah, and me seeing the Joneses." She noted he didn't say Pop and Nana this time.

"Tell me everything."

"Mom had always done the bills, so Cricket did once she replaced Mom. But instead of paying the bills, she stole the money for drugs, and that's how he lost the house."

"Drugs! I'm so sorry."

"I would have never guessed. She didn't seem the type."

"And he holds her whole family responsible?"

"He says they're rich. She certainly had a giant diamond on her finger tonight. He asked them for a loan to help save the house. Not a gift, a loan. But since he had kicked Cricket out, they wouldn't do it."

Taylor bit her lip. She had liked the Jones family. For a long time, she had liked them. But right now, she hated them.

Hudson turned to her, and his expression changed, softening. "Dad was an alcoholic, Taylor. I wouldn't have loaned him money, either."

She pressed her hand to her forehead.

He stepped closer and took her hand in his.

"Cricket didn't have any kids…" Something occurred to Taylor, something that could be so useful.

"No, just me."

"That means no one in this town will feel compelled to keep her secrets."

His eyebrows drew together.

She kissed him first, then explained.

SPENDING the day at the quilt shop cutting fabric, chewing the fat, and dreaming up projects with customers was not the worst way to pass the time—if there wasn't a murder. But Roxy had to take her son in to Portland for something school related that went over Taylor's head. It had to do with film work and potential scholarships, though. It was an overnight trip. She was looking at two full days of sitting on the news about Cricket and the names of the visitors with criminal pasts. She didn't like it.

Then, shortly after noon, the little bells jingled on the door to Flour Sax and Grandma Quinny strode in, dressed for a day on the hobby farm in sturdy blue jeans that had never seen dirt, a crisp plain shirt probably from Eddie Bauer, and a jacket that looked exactly like the one Princess Kate wore in the family photos out on their country estate. "Darling," she addressed Taylor and gave her a kiss on the cheek.

Taylor's Aunt Susan had come in on Grandma Quinny's wake.

Taylor's mood improved immediately. Grandma Quinny knew everyone and everything, and Susan was a gossip. It wasn't nice to say, but it was sure nice to know right now.

Two ladies with a baby stroller had just completed their purchases. As soon as the door swung shut behind them, Taylor came out from behind the register.

"Let me make you a cup of coffee." She led her family to the little coffee bar and offered them the variety of generic Keurig cups.

"We don't have all afternoon to chat." This comment from Grandma Quinny was pointed at Susan.

"What can I do for you?" Taylor held her peace. She'd never get an answer from them before their own questions were dealt with.

"I hear you tried to see your great aunt but that martinet at the desk wouldn't let you."

"I'm sorry, what?"

"Jenny-Sue Meyer. Your great aunt. When word got to me, I almost spit nails."

"But how did anyone know? Karina and I were alone."

Aunt Susan laughed. "You told Clay. Clay told Joey. Joey yelled at Karina. Jenny-Sue heard."

"Um..." Taylor refilled her own cup. The chain of news spreading made sense when put that way. "But how is she my great aunt? And why didn't I know that?"

213

"I don't know why you didn't know that. She was always at family parties before she had to move to the home."

Many people were always at Grandma Quinny's "family parties." Taylor hadn't realized they were all literally family.

"Abe Meyer was Jenny-Sue's second husband. And he was a very good man. Her first husband was Arch Brickell."

"But Arch is married to your sister, Patty."

"Yes, Arch and Jenny-Sue divorced."

"So, she's not really my aunt."

"Don't be fussy, Taylor. Jenny-Sue is family and has been for longer than you've been alive, and that woman," her lips pinched as she said the word, "had no right to keep you from having a nice little visit. Jenny-Sue could use it. She's been lonely since Abe passed."

"If I were you, I'd lock that Hudson down. So long as he's not married, you're going to have no end of trouble." Aunt Susan's soft gentle voice had a harsh tone.

"I don't expect marrying him will make her nicer to me."

"No, it won't." Grandma Quinny gave Susan a disappointed glance. "But I don't know what has happened to this town. In Comfort, once you're family, you're always family. That Karina Wyandotte needs to settle down. We never used to hold vindictive grudges around here."

Taylor doubted that. Comfort was a nice town, but no town was that nice. "I bet it was a real trial for the town when Cricket made Doug lose his house."

Grandma Quinny's eyes narrowed. "Cricket wasn't from here."

"Neither was Pastor Leon."

"No, and it showed, didn't it? I know pastors are supposed to be forgiving and see the best in people and all of that, but how he could be dating a woman with a known history of drug abuse is beyond me."

The door jangled again, and Annie Farkas walked in. She was as casually elegant as ever, this time in slim jeans and a loose linen jacket that hung off her thin shoulders, but with clay-splattered boots on her feet letting out the secret she was a working artist.

Taylor held her breath, but Grandma Quinny had seen her.

Susan greeted Annie with a hug. "How are you hanging in there?"

Annie spotted Taylor, nodded, and went off to the side of the shop with Susan. They were quiet, so if they were sharing heartfelt secrets, Taylor couldn't hear.

"I didn't know they knew each other."

"Even if you count the students at the college, there are only 3,000 souls in this town, Taylor. Everyone knows everybody."

"And everything about everybody, right?"

Grandma Quinny smiled warmly and a little sadly. "Try not to listen. That's all I have to say. If you don't know, then you can't hold it against anyone. It's the very best way to keep peace in a small community."

"Did everyone keep quiet about Cricket's drug use? I mean, she had a job with the elderly, and she likely had a relationship with Leon's kids."

"Her drug problems were a long time ago, and she'd never been arrested. A lot can be swept under a rug if there's no criminal record."

The dozens, if not hundreds, of people at the tea party who didn't have criminal records crossed Taylor's mind. Sure, narrowing the field of suspects down to two men who had a criminal past might help, but then, any one of them might be harboring secrets worse than Cricket's.

Then again, Joey said she'd seen that "cute" Jerrod guy *with* Cricket. That was one coincidence too many. Taylor would find out about him by hook or crook. After all, if Jenny-Sue was her great-aunt, then she and this Jerrod were practically family.

"You tell me next time you want to see Jenny-Sue, okay, love?" Grandma Quinny said. "And I'll go with you. That Karina wouldn't dare keep me away from my sister-in-law." She patted Taylor's arm gently. "Susan, let's go." Her voice rang out, far louder than necessary in the little shop. Susan and Annie came out from their quiet corner.

"Can I help you with anything?" Taylor asked Leon's widow as the other two left.

"I wanted to make a photo quilt for the kids," Annie said. "Pictures of them and their father. But I don't know how."

"Sure, no problem." She led the woman to a shelf where she sold a few novelties like printable fabric. Technically it didn't match her oldy-timey aesthetic, but none of shops in the quilt guild had complained, and they all carried it.

Annie took a few packets, probably more than she would need, and held them to her chest.

"Is there something else? Fabric for the back maybe?"

It was obvious Annie had something on her mind, and it wasn't likely the fabric.

"I've heard a rumor that worries me a little." Annie swallowed and her eyes glistened.

"Come this way," Taylor led her back to the coffee bar and wondered if maybe she should add some sofas. "Let me make up a cup of coffee, or maybe tea?"

Annie shook her head. "You remember I found all the money hidden, right?"

This time Taylor swallowed a little note of emotion.

"I've heard he stole this from the folks at the home. The residents." She shivered, though the day and the room were warm.

Taylor nodded. "I've heard that rumor as well."

Annie passed her hand under her eyes to catch the rogue tears that might fall against her will. "I need to give it back to them, but how will I make it if I do?"

"Sit down, please?"

Annie took one of the metal folding chairs at the class tables.

"I am not going to pretend that I know the answers you need."

Annie looked away, but she couldn't have been surprised.

"And you probably already make more than you would if I gave you a job."

Annie swallowed what was probably a desperate sob.

"But you can have a job here if it would help."

Annie's brows crumpled inward. "You don't have to. As you said, I'd probably do just as well sticking to what I do. The trouble is, I am going to need to do a lot better. And I don't know how."

"Do you have a lawyer?"

"Yes, my divorce lawyer."

"You've got to talk to her, or him, and see what they can do for you."

Annie held the printable fabric on her knee, looking at it. "I don't know why I said I wanted to do this. I can't afford it." She set the packets on the table behind her and stood. "I can't afford much of anything."

"Have you talked to the school about things like free lunch? I know they can help with some things."

"No...I haven't. Thank you." Annie was far away in her mind, but didn't move, frozen in her spot.

"There must be something else that brought you here." As Taylor spoke, she could almost hear her mother's voice. The warmth, the comfort, but it was coming from herself.

Annie pressed her lips together, then pulled a paper out of her pocket. "I found this. And I really hoped you could help me, since you are... involved."

Taylor took the folded paper, but didn't try to read it. "Is it something you don't want the police to see?"

"Yes, in case it's nothing. It might be nothing. There's always a chance. But could you call the number? Could you find out first? Please? If I try, they'll know me."

Taylor unfolded the paper. Right there, in black and white feminine handwriting it said, "Leon--Call Jerrod. Make it right." And it had a phone number.

"Yes, I will. I promise. Do you want me to take it to the police if I need to, or do you want to do that yourself?"

"Please, just do it. I want all of this as far from my kids as possible."

"Whatever you want, Annie. I'm here for you."

If the paper had said any other name at all, Taylor wouldn't have been sure this was about the money and possibly the murder. But this? Call Jerrod and make it right? This might well be what both Leon and Cricket died for.

CHAPTER TWENTY-ONE

*T*aylor sent a text to both Clay and Hudson. *"Have a number for Jerrod. Will call tonight."* Though she had more than strong feelings for Hudson and appreciated his perspective, she didn't feel obliged to leave Clay out of an investigation he'd been such help for already.

Clay responded first. *"Cool."*

Hudson's text came while she and Grandpa Ernie were ordering their dinner at Reuben's diner. *"Do you want me to come if he wants to meet? Do you want me to be there when you call?"*

"yes and yes." She smiled at the phone.

"No phones at dinner." Grandpa Ernie scowled at her.

She didn't like how little patience she had for him at night. She knew he couldn't help being cranky. She knew he wasn't trying to make her life hard on purpose, but as she stared across the table at the man who used to be so different, she wasn't sure she could be as kind as she needed to be. "Sorry." She slipped the phone into her purse and did her best to pretend everything was just fine. "Do you know Jenny-Sue Meyer?"

"Jenny-Sue Middlebrecht," he corrected her. "She was real smart in school."

"Do you know any of her family?" She paused and then they

successfully ordered their soup and sandwiches from Aviva Reuben, waitress, karate expert, and cousin to their murder witness.

"Her husband was no good, so she got a better one." Grandpa Ernie said it like a threat, like if Taylor had a no-good husband, he'd make sure she got a new one too.

Taylor lifted an eyebrow. That spunk, it was exhausting, but kind of charming in its own way.

She tried to remember how Grandma Quinny had delineated the relationship. This no-good husband was…married to one of Grandma Quinny's sisters? Patty. He was married to Taylor's Great Aunt Patty. "Did Jenny-Sue and her no-good husband have any kids?"

He wrapped his spoon on his table. "You don't know your own cousins?"

"I guess not."

"That no good husband of hers got himself hitched to a Quinn, so his boys are your problem now. Jerry and Johnny."

"Jerry, short for Jerrod?"

"That's right."

"I think I remember Johnny, but there are always so many people at a Quinn party."

"When was the last time you went to one of those?" Grandpa Ernie grumped.

Aviva interrupted again with bowls of chicken noodle and their specialty—Reuben sandwiches—split in half.

Grandpa Ernie sipped at his chicken soup, and his face relaxed.

It had been a long time since Taylor had been to a family party. The last one might even have been her college graduation. The Quinn strawberry farm had been crawling with everyone from Comfort—family relationships extending to cousins of cousins and their kith and kin.

"I don't care how handsome he is, young lady," Grandpa said, "he's your cousin, so you can't marry him."

Taylor laughed. It came from deep inside her, somewhere past the pain of losing her grandpa slowly, somewhere beyond the loneliness of having both of her parents gone. This was her Grandpa Ernie, who had always made sly jokes, silly comments that you have to catch just right or you'd miss it. Trying to catch you off guard, just to tease.

She had to share her Grandma and Grandpa Quinny with the whole town, but with Belle away all the time, she had her Grandpa Ernie all to herself.

"I dunno, Grandpa," she said, "I might just give him a call anyway."

He grumbled and picked up his sandwich. "Don't make sauerkraut the way they used to."

"Nothing ever is, is it?"

Aviva brought Taylor the check in the little black vinyl folder. Grandpa Ernie made a pretense of taking it, but Taylor stood firm.

She flipped open the folder ready to stick her debit card in but stopped short. A copy of the receipt was covered in black Sharpie: DON'T CALL JERRY!

"I JUST WANT you to do what you need to do." Hudson sat on the couch, leaning forward so Grandpa Ernie could keep up with the conversation from his recliner.

"This thing you're doing, where you completely and totally support me without trying to tell me what to do is very cool on paper." Taylor fluttered the two pieces of paper. "I like it much better than, say, telling me what I absolutely cannot do. But...I don't know what to do. Do I call my so-called cousin Jerry and see how he's doing and do a little digging to see what he knows about Leon or not?"

"You want your girl calling some other man?" Grandpa Ernie interjected.

"It's okay. It's her cousin." Hudson was casual, comfortable even.

Taylor couldn't figure out why.

"Not her real cousin." He glared at his granddaughter. "And it wouldn't be the first time in this family."

"Oh, Grandpa!" Taylor swatted at him.

He grinned, clearly teasing, and glad to be included. His mood could tip at the push of a button, though, and she longed to send him to his room. But it was only eight. She didn't dare.

"Call the diner," Hudson suggested. "Find out what on earth Aviva meant."

"But she's working, probably another hour at least."

He smiled, his eyes crinkling. "You asked."

"Okay, I will!" She had to Google the number for the diner, but Aviva's Aunt Jess answered immediately and passed the phone over.

"Aviva, I trust you."

"Thanks." She sounded distracted.

"But I need to know what you meant about not calling Jerry."

"Aunt Jess told me to write it. She said you'd know what it meant."

Taylor swallowed her impatience. "Can you put Jess back on the phone?"

The phone switched hands again.

"Why should I not call Jerry?"

"I don't know what you want from him." Jess spoke in a voice just barely loud enough to hear. "But I dated him back in the day, and he's no good."

"I'm not planning on dating my cousin."

"He's your cousin?"

"Never mind." Taylor very much did not want to get off track.

"Anyway, he's too old for you, and, frankly, he's prone to violence. Stay far away from those Brickell men, they're not good. And really, they are much too old for you."

"I promise, I'm not remotely interested. But thanks for the warning."

She ended the call. "He's violent."

Hudson nodded, but didn't offer any more advice.

Taylor paced the small living room, circling it and considering her options. "Jerrod Brickell is a smaller man, soft spoken, so he wouldn't likely draw attention to himself at the event, was the last person potentially to see Cricket alive, and was prone to violence. And his mom had invested with Leon, right?"

"That sounds right to me."

"I think I need to call Bethany Jones. Do you mind?"

"Do what you need to do."

She stopped pacing and sat on the couch next to him. "But, really, is it okay? I don't want to hurt you."

Grandpa Ernie grunted. Taylor looked up expecting a derisive comment about manly men or something, but it had actually just been him falling asleep in his chair.

"Like I said, I wouldn't have loaned my dad money to save his house, either. I don't know that having a relationship with the Jonses is in the cards for me, but there's no reason for you to not call them about this murder."

"Okay then." She called immediately in case he was going to change his mind.

Bethany answered right away.

"I'm so sorry to bother you," Taylor said.

"It's never a bother when you call. And thank you so much for connecting us with Hudson again. He was such a charming boy, but now he's such a lovely man." She sighed softly. "What can I do for you?"

"You know, we're all still just reeling from the deaths, and we've been chatting with friends and all of that. A name came up, and I was wondering if you knew him...Jerry, Jerrod Brickell? He's actually my cousin, but I haven't seen him in years."

"Oh." Her voice dropped. "Yes. I knew him. Cricket dated

him for a while. I'm sorry he's your cousin, because I have nothing good to say about him."

"That's all right. I don't really know him. Not well. I just, his name came up, and I wondered. That's all." She paused, thought for a moment, then threw caution to the wind. "Actually, someone said they saw Cricket talking to him shortly before she was killed."

This was greeted by a long silence. Then, "I always knew he'd destroy her." Her voice broke. "She got clean, you know? She was clean for so long. Then she met him."

"Oh, Bethany, I'm sorry."

"If she was seen with him, then he's the one who killed her. I'm calling the police. You'd better tell whoever saw them to call too. I can't talk now. I have to do this." Her words sped up and went high, fear, anger, adrenaline all present.

"Do that, please. Call them. I'll talk to the witness and make sure she does as well."

She hung up and stared at Hudson.

He tilted his head slightly.

"I think we have the killer."

CHAPTER TWENTY-TWO

*C*lay had offered to work for Taylor so she could go hunting for her cousin, the killer, but Willa wasn't free to work with him, and the sunny June day was a busy one at the quilt shop. She couldn't get away till evening, which was fine with Grandma Quinny.

Early summer sun was just setting when they arrived at Jenny-Sue's little apartment. Taylor's shoe-string relation welcomed her guests from her tiny kitchen where she was baking something in a compact convection microwave.

Grandma Quinny took her place on the floral slip-covered love seat with a flourish. She must have visited before because the soft colors of her crisp striped button-down complemented the furniture. "Jenny-Sue, how have you been feeling?"

"Good, good." Jenny-Sue was a small woman with a rounded back. She wore an old-fashioned housecoat of polyester velveteen that made Taylor's fingers curl. She'd had a jacket made of that fabric as a child, and the memory of it was visceral.

Jenny-Sue carried a plate of scones to the coffee table. "Can I make you tea? I don't have coffee, I'm sorry."

"Tea would be lovely, dear, then sit. Relax. We just wanted to visit for a while. It's been too long."

"Not since dear Laura's funeral." Jenny-Sue clucked sadly.

The funeral for Taylor's mother was a blur in her head. People everywhere. Flowers. Disposable aluminum dishes filled with casseroles. Broken words from sad people.

"How are you holding up without her? I do hope that Ernie isn't giving you trouble." Jenny-Sue's eyes twinkled.

"He's no trouble." Taylor didn't elaborate. He was a ton of trouble, but that wasn't Jenny-Sue's business.

"He always was a darling. A real delight." Jenny-Sue looked away, a soft smile on her face.

As much as she loved her grandpa, Taylor was eager to get to the subject on the forefront of her mind.

"Ernie Baker is a gentleman." There was something in Grandma Quinny's voice that sounded like a warning.

"Grandpa's fine. He's doing well, but how are you holding up? That's what I'd like to know. There's just been so much sadness here and so much danger." The tag at the back of Taylor's polo shirt was irritating her neck. She reached back and scratched at it.

"Oh! Hasn't it just been awful? And we were stuck in our rooms for so long. It's really lovely now that we can get out again."

"Have you had a lot of visitors to help pass the time?" Taylor sat on her hands to keep from fussing with her shirt.

"No, not since the tea party. That's why it's just been so lonely. I tell you, now that we can eat in the dining room again, I'm feeling much better. Nothing like a little company to make things look right again."

"Did you have company at the tea party, or did you have to face that awful trauma alone?" Taylor asked.

"Darling, maybe she doesn't want to think about such a sad experience." Grandma Quinny took a scone and gave her grand-daughter a disapproving look.

"I haven't had anyone to talk about this with in ages, and let me tell you, I do have things to say!" Jenny-Sue matched

Grandma Quinny's look of disapproval. She nibbled her own scone and sat back in her oak glider rocker.

"Don't get yourself all worked up, Jenny-Sue. You know your heart."

"Pish, my heart is fine and so is my hearing. And during that tea party, after Leon fell, you know, you should have heard the things they were saying at the table next to me."

As much as Taylor appreciated the value of gossip when digging for the truth, she really only wanted to know if Jerry had been at the party and if he had been where he was supposed to be when Leon was killed. She tapped the heel of her foot impatiently.

"To start with, that Darlene Smith, you know the one, she's got her eye on Boggy Hudson. I could just smack her on the back of the head sometimes. She's much too young for him. There's older ladies here who deserve a shot at tall, handsome men who don't live in the memory care wing."

Grandma Quinny groaned softly.

Taylor bit the inside of her cheek to keep herself from interrupting.

"Darlene was terribly envious of old Mrs. Sylvester who was sitting with you all. And she knows how much Mrs. Sylvester loved her nephew, so she said right off how Leon had it coming."

"Surely that wasn't just because she liked Boggy," Grandma Quinny chided.

Jenny-Sue's lips curled up. "I think that was the primary motivation, but there was also the envy. She wanted in on the investment, but it had closed up before she could get her bid in." Jenny-Sue gave a little toss of her head like she would have done if she'd had a full head of hair to throw over her shoulder.

"Tell me you didn't partake in that nonsense," Grandma Quinny scolded.

"Why wouldn't I? I've always been ahead of the curve. Silly Leon thought he took me for a ride. I gave him a good bit of money, but..." Jenny-Sue leaned forward and lowered her voice. "I'm rich. I could afford to lose what I gave him if the rumors were true."

"But what were the rumors?" Taylor hoped this might give her the chance to turn the conversation back to Jerrod.

"Everyone who didn't get invited to invest said he was taking our money to gamble. I don't think he was." Jenny-Sue held her head high with her little round chin jutted out. "I think he was investing like he said, but I think he was investing in something awful like cocaine or heroin."

Grandma Quinny stared with wide eyes.

Taylor had never seen her Grandma lost for words. She wondered how she could ever have missed a woman like this Jenny-Sue at a family party. Surely...surely! But, no, she hadn't gone to many recently, and when she was younger, she spent her time off in the strawberry fields goofing around with her cousins. "You wouldn't have wanted to earn money from something like that, would you?" Taylor asked.

"Why not?" Jenny-Sue countered. "Drug money spends as good as anything."

"Jenny-Sue," Grandma Quinny's voice rose, "after the troubles your boys had, you can't possibly mean that."

"You know how much of my money I've spent on rehab? It's about time I make some money from all of this." She crossed her arms defensively.

"I can't imagine if your, um, boys had gotten clean, they would have liked to think you were um...making money selling drugs." Taylor had trouble piecing the words together. Jenny-Sue was not like any of the other older folks in her life.

"I don't know what Johnny thinks. He hasn't spoken to me in years."

"What about your other son?"

"Jerry? Oh, he's just a wonder, that Jerry. But I didn't tell him a word about it. None of his business. He's had enough of my money already. How else would he have gotten that little Minnie

Winnie of his? But at least he uses it to visit me. No guest room in this place. But now he can park out by where the woods start. There's a and no one ever tickets him there. He never leaves until I tell him I'm sick of him. Pretty lucky, I'd say."

"I'm sure his work doesn't like that." Grandma Quinny had managed to find a few more disapproving words.

"Oh, he doesn't work. Early retirement because of an injury."

"But he's younger than my David!"

David was one of Taylor's many uncles. The youngest Quinn son.

"So? He's doing fine and isn't bothering anyone."

Jenny-Sue glowered at Grandma Quinny.

Grandma Quinny stared from under lowered eyebrows.

Taylor wondered why on earth these two women considered each other friends, much less family. She cleared her throat quietly and asked the question she'd been dying to ask, "Was he at the tea party with you?"

"He came to the party, but he'd excused himself before Leon was killed. I'm glad he did. I didn't want to hear one more person saying Leon deserved it. No one deserves murder." Jenny-Sue's black eyes were practically sparkling, but her frame seemed to lose a little of its strength.

"Let me get you that cup of tea, Jenny-Sue." Grandma Quinny went to the kitchen. She was back in form, the weakened state of her friend having rallied her own spirits. "And, Taylor, please, if you could just drop this subject, I'm sure we'd both appreciate it very much."

"Yes, sorry, Grandma." Taylor dusted scone crumbs from the legs of her jeans. She had gotten what she had come for. Jerry was not at the table, where he was supposed to be, when someone knifed Leon Farkas.

"Now, tell me how that new great-grandbaby of yours is doing." Grandma Quinny set a small china cup on the table next to Jenny-Sue, but before Jenny-Sue could answer, the air was filled by the squall of a fire alarm.

Jenny-Sue sighed and stood slowly. "Not everyone in this place deserves to have their own oven."

As if by some kind of pointed bad luck, a light drizzle had started to fall, and the residents of Bible Creek Care Home were huddled together under the weak shelter of an old oak tree in the far parking lot.

It was the dusk of an Oregon summer day. Everyone stood in grey shadows, the sun long gone, but not dark enough for the lights in the parking lot to have come on. Taylor counted heads —not hard as they weren't a rambunctious crowd—but she didn't know how many there ought to be. Marva Love stood on the far side with a tall, slender person wearing an over-sized coat with the hood up. Likely Dayton. Though Taylor had known the girl was safe, she was hugely relieved to see her with her own eyes. She also spotted the tall Boggy Hudson, but Mrs. Sylvester wasn't around. Wait staff, kitchen crew, and cleaning crew stood between the residents and the building as though they were the safety line.

"Well, this just beats all." Jenny-Sue squinted into the crowd. "Chef Joey is over there with Karina from the front desk, what's her last name? Don't remember. Her people never were worth much. Last I heard, those two hated each other. What are they up to?" She leaned heavily on a black lacquered cane decorated with a green snake curling around it.

"I would think the staff would be great friends," Grandma Quinny murmured, but her eyes were on her sturdy Volvo station wagon, so close but so far away at the same time. The car was blocked by the fire truck.

"Does this happen a lot?" Taylor asked Jenny-Sue. Her mind at the moment was on her Grandpa Ernie and his mobility issues. Having to rush outside in case of a fire didn't seem ideal for the elderly man with the shuffling gate and the walker.

"No, no, less than twice a year." Jenny-Sue's attention had been taken by two firefighters who had come out of the building.

They looked relaxed, as they should. The building hadn't burst into flames, and no great choking clouds of smoke had billowed forth. They stared at the front door for a moment. The taller of the two scratched his jaw, then they parted and walked in opposite directions still looking at the front of the building. The timed lights around the planting beds popped on, like the footlights of a stage.

The sheriff's Chevy Blazer pulled into the parking lot, but it didn't have its sirens or lights on.

Taylor checked her watch, antsy to get on with things. If the fire situation was taken care of, she was keen to see if she could grab the sheriff's deputy before he left again. She squinted at the sheriff's car. It would be great if it was a deputy she knew.

Before she could figure out who it was, a great echoing boom reverberated through her chest. She grabbed for the trunk of the skinny little tree next to her, then exhaled sharply. She was shaking and her ears felt clogged. She caught Grandma Quinny's eye.

Grandma Quinny frowned, the worry line between her eyes was cut deep.

The two firemen froze.

And great billowing clouds of smoke poured out of the kitchen wing of the old folk's home.

Taylor spun and checked the crowd again. Dayton was still safely with her great aunt. She spotted Boggy. And the sheriff was out of his truck talking on a cell phone.

She wanted to push her way through to get to him, but to be frank, she knew better.

Grandma Quinny placed a hand on her back. "It looks like we may all be here a while. Why don't you go over to the staff and see if you can help. These folks are going to need seats."

"Yes, Grandma." Taylor joined Karina and Joey who were in mid conversation.

"Because that's what Molotov cocktails do." Karina's tone left no doubt about her opinion of Joey's intellect.

"But who would do that? Who would throw a firebomb into an old folks' home?"

"Should we get chairs?" Taylor interrupted.

Karina rolled her eyes.

"I don't think we can go back in there," Joey said.

Taylor chewed her bottom lip. "But these folks, they are going to need to sit. They can't just stand out here forever."

"We know that. But no one's letting us in an exploding building."

"Benches!" Joey looked excited. "We've got benches all along the exterior of the building. They'll let us bring those over, come on."

She and Taylor left Karina and found one of the firefighters, who had stopped to have a drink from a water bottle. They got permission to drag benches over, and Joey enlisted the help of her kitchen crew.

Taylor let them work and rejoined Karina. "Why do you say it was a Molotov cocktail?"

"Plural." Karina shifted the low neckline of her stretchy shirt. It was getting chilly. "Someone tossed them in. One caught fire right away and set off the alarm. Another one must have hit the gas in the kitchen to make the explosion. There were probably others."

"But why? Who?"

"Why would I know? We've had murders, now arson and explosions. Probably connected, right? I know someone's been asking a lot of questions." She sneered at Taylor. "Maybe the killer got antsy and wanted to get rid of evidence. Or witnesses."

What if the killer knew Dayton was here and had tried to kill her this horrible way?

But how would he know?

If it was Jerry...and Jerry made long visits when he came by...

She wanted to go ask Jenny-Sue more pointed questions, but it might be too late.

Instead, she sent a lengthy text to Reg, the only deputy whose number she had saved in her phone. She begged him to pass the info on immediately, and said she was going to look for a "Minni-Winnie" off where there was a wide shoulder by the woods.

She didn't plan on accosting Jerry, she just wanted to see if he was still there.

"I've got to walk around a little," she whispered to Grandma Quinny. "I'm getting anxious. Do you mind?"

Grandma Quinny gave her a little side hug. "If you don't mind, could you go to my car? I've got several quilts in the trunk and at least one spare coat."

"Give me a minute, okay?" She scanned the crowd of residents again. They could use the extra warmth, but she desperately wanted to prevent that little Winnebago from driving away.

She hoofed it as far around the building as she could before shouting arrested her.

She couldn't really make out the words, but assumed it was, "Hey, you, stop!" So, she did.

She turned sheepishly. One of the firefighters pointed to the crowd under the tree. She walked toward him slowly, not wanting to give up so easily. "No one leaves till the Sheriff says so."

She didn't say anything but went back where she was told, skirting the edge of the crowd. Once there, she texted Hudson and begged him to see if the little RV was parked by the edge of the woods. He sent a thumbs up and then called.

"Did you hear about the fire?" he asked.

"I'm here right now. I think the guy in the Minnie Winnie did it, and I think he killed Cricket and Leon too."

"Taylor, this isn't safe."

"I know. Don't get out of the truck. Just go see if it's there, and if it is, text me. I already sent the info to Reg, and I'm dying to talk to the sheriff."

"Got it. I'll send pics if I can."

She hung up and looked for a way to escape again, but from across the crowd her grandmother spotted her and nodded toward the Volvo. Taylor did as she was told and collected the quilts and the coats.

In a matter of minutes, Hudson sent his text. The Minnie Winnie was there. As she headed back into the parking lot to see if she could show it to the sheriff, two more SUV's with the Yamhill County Sheriff's Department logo emblazoned on them rolled up.

She took a deep breath and trudged forward anyway.

The door of one Chevy flew open and the tall, heroic Reg in his khaki uniform hustled to her. "I've got a man headed to the location you gave us. This is serious. Are you sure you're not insane?" Though his words could have been some kind of flirty joke, his face made it clear he was dead serious.

"I'm not crazy. I swear." She held her phone in her grip, not sure if she should show the pic or not. "I've tried to keep you guys informed of anything I found. And I was only doing this to protect my sister's friend."

"Come with me." He didn't drag her off, but he was oozing anger and strength, and she followed him as though she were under arrest.

Reg exchanged a word or two with his boss, who looked Taylor up and down, nodding.

He didn't say a word to her.

Her heart seethed.

Surely, he'd at least ask her how she had learned about the guy.

She'd done all of this work.

She'd gotten them the clues. Surely, they weren't going to go off and arrest Jerrod Brickell without even talking to her first?

She stepped forward. "Excuse me."

"What?" the head man, the sheriff himself, snapped. He was short and stocky like a competitive weightlifter. A vein on his forehead looked like it was ready to burst.

"I..."

"Got it, sir." One of the young firefighters came running up with a shard of green glass in his gloved hand. "Amateur job. Desperate guy."

The sheriff pointed to another man, and the young firefighter nodded and took his prize over there.

The sheriff turned to Taylor again. Though he had to look up ever so slightly to make eye contact, it was still clear he was the one in charge. "You did this."

"No! I know who did it. That's what I was trying to say."

"If you hadn't interfered, the Reuben girl would have been safe with her aunt where we put her, and we would have been able to arrest the murderer without anyone else getting hurt."

"But! But...." She swallowed and her eyes burned with smoke and tears, fear and confusion.

"But *nothing*, young lady. I have a lifetime of respect for your father, may he rest in peace, but if you ever try this bullshit again, I'll lock you up, do you understand?"

"But I helped! No one else got hurt. If..."

He pointed at the crowd of elderly people, some sitting on their walkers, some in wheelchairs, some on the benches, all shivering. "This building will have to be condemned. You might not think we're fast enough at our job, but by God, we do it right." He sniffed, and for a moment, Taylor wondered if he was about to start crying.

But he didn't. He turned and left.

She shivered.

She was sure she had helped. And Dayton had begged her to. And this couldn't actually be her fault, could it?

CHAPTER TWENTY-THREE

*"T*he only man I respect more than the sheriff in this world is my father." Reg stood in the middle of Flour Sax Quilt Shop, his black ball cap with the logo of the county sheriff's department literally in hand.

She had let him in at five-thirty in the morning, though neither of them had any reason to be there that early. It had been a long night, and she hadn't slept. Dread, confusion, regret, and that unwelcome fear she had thought she was getting past took turns torturing her through the hours. Had her attempt to help Dayton really made all of those grandparents homeless? Surely not.

With a greater strength of will than she thought possible, she had not shoved her dresser in front of her door in the night, but dread soaked her like a winter storm. Long before dawn, Taylor had been up, pacing up and down the stairs, touching her grandfather's door, then Belle's, convinced her best intentions had brought danger to those she had tried hardest to keep safe.

When she could bear it no more, she went to the shop. She knew Clay was upstairs or ought to have been. There was some comfort in that. But, in reality, she longed to drive to town where she could walk into a twenty-four-hour Walmart and fill a cart

with things. Just so many things. Instead, she sorted and orga-
nized the things she had to sell and told herself it was almost the
same.

When Reg knocked on the front door, she hadn't had any
panic left, but opened it automatically, letting him into the sanctuary, partly thinking he might need it as well.

"If you breathe a word of this to anyone, I will deny it." Reg
continued his halting explanations. "But the sheriff was working
his case up against the widow—Annie. In most cases, a murder
is done by a close relative, and he didn't like Annie's alibi." He
stared at Taylor, but she didn't respond. "Annie had a great
motive. The sheriff had a stack of notes from your phone calls,
but they weren't considered legit tips."

"Do you think it was my fault?" Taylor shoved her hands in
the pockets of her khakis so he couldn't see her hands shake.

"That the killer was caught? I wouldn't call it a fault."

Taylor stared at the smiling face of her friend. His eyes were
sad and tired and the smile was weak, meant to comfort her, but
it didn't register as anything, really. "The bomb." The two words
fell from her like bricks.

"No one was hurt. Don't feel guilty about that." Reg stood so
still, not even his jaw twitched. He was a good man. Someone
would be really lucky to marry him.

"But all those residents."

"They'll be okay. They all have beds for tonight anyway.
They'll get their stuff out, and the owner will make sure they
have somewhere to go."

"But why is the whole place condemned? It was just the
kitchen, wasn't it?"

"Someone had turned the gas on. The kitchen exploded when
he tossed the firebomb in there. But he hit a couple of apartments
first."

"So, he was out in the dusky evening, tossing bombs while
we were all just…there? And while the firemen were there?"

"It looks like it, but we'll get the whole story eventually." Reg cleared his throat and moved one foot slightly.

Taylor registered it and knew that it meant he wanted to go now, but she couldn't let him. Not yet. "But he wouldn't have done that if it hadn't been for me."

Reg shook his head. "He was after the witness. He'd been coming to see his mom every day after the murder so that he wouldn't look suspicious, and one day he spotted the girl."

"But Dayton never left Marva's place. Even I couldn't find her for the longest time."

"He claims he saw her through the window."

"I can't believe he's confessed already. That doesn't seem..." Taylor stared at the slipper chair in the corner of the room. Somehow she thought she ought to sit in it, but the shock was too fresh still.

"I think he's after a mental illness plea, but we'll do our best to keep him from getting it."

"Why did he do it? Was it because of his mom's money?"

Reg's head turned a slight angle, as though he were looking for the way out. "He rambled all night long. Me and another guy were there with him, and I'm spent. I don't know what part of his ten-hour confession was true and what was invented. But he said he did it to keep kids off drugs, but Farkas wasn't involved in selling drugs, so that couldn't have been it. He also said he did it because Farkas was corrupting his mother. That seems more likely. And, yeah, I expect it was because of the money. It's almost always because of the money."

"How did you know I'd be here?" Taylor yawned. She pressed the ball of her hand to her head.

He shook his head. "I was headed towards Café Olé. I'm beat, but I don't get to go home for a while. Saw your light on and wanted to make sure you were okay."

"Thank you."

"You got a murderer off the street. Here's hoping that with

some time and space the boss will see it that way. You deserve our gratitude. But in the meantime…"

"Stay out of police investigations?" She rested her hand on the register counter. Sitting or even lying down again suddenly seemed like the only good idea.

"Yes, please. For your own good."

She nodded slowly. "Let me just say this: if I ever see a murder again, I'm running far and fast from it, okay?"

He shoved his hat back on his head. "Thanks."

She considered going home; going to bed. Not opening for the day. The whole town would be upended with the explosion and the fire. She was sure no would be out shopping for fabric.

But she underestimated the need for local gossip. Her shop was full all day.

Newly homeless residents of Bible Creek Care Home made their way up one side of Main Street, visiting quilt shops, the cheese factory outlet, and the rest of the stores, and down the other side for antiques and a hearty meal at the diner. Both Clay and Roxy were on hand all day to keep up with the work.

Sissy stopped by to say that Dayton had moved permanently in with the family. She said Dayton had been offered a scholarship at the College of Art and Craft she'd been dreaming of attending as well, and Sissy would make sure she took it, no matter what Dayton's parents said. Cooper had one more year of high school—having his two best friends both graduate early had been hard on him, but she thought having Dayton around all summer would help.

Taylor doubted having a live-in teenage girl would be the help that Sissy thought she'd be, but she held her tongue.

She called Grandma Quinny just to check in, but Grandpa Quinny said she was resting.

Eventually the end of the day came, but it offered no respite from her overwhelming doubts and no comfort from the fear that getting involved had made everything worse.

As she turned the lock of the front door, she let out a sigh that shifted slightly to a sob.

"Buck up, my friend," Clay said, his voice soft and lazy. "Let me take you out."

"I don't know."

"I do, and I've planned it all. You and me. That banker fellow you love so much and his date. Dinner at an English pub. I suggested it, but the banker says it's good."

"You planned this already?" Her heart softened toward the man who had worked so hard all day in her little shop.

"I did, but before you thank me, it's dinner and a show."

"What's playing?"

"Hudson and Karina."

Taylor stared blankly.

"Joey told me that Karina told her that she had a date with Hudson, tonight, at said pub. I thought you'd enjoy watching the fruits of your efforts."

"You've got to be kidding me."

"I am most certainly not. I know you. You would hate to miss this."

"But what about Joey? Aren't you seeing her?"

"Oh, she'll be there."

"But..."

"I suspect you won't be odd man out for long. Dinner with crazy Karina Wyandotte can't last long. But hustle, Hudson's picking her up at eight, and we want to get there so we can be inconspicuous in a back booth before they arrive."

Taylor looked down at the rumpled khakis and pathetic pastel polo. "I'll do my best."

JOEY BURKE WAS every bit the dimpled, dark haired beauty she'd seemed. And funny and kind too. Taylor liked her and not begrudgingly. She would happily let this girl take Clay off her hands.

John Hancock's *Tatiaaaaana* on the other hand…She'd come back from New York, having successfully defended her thesis, so she was smart. And she did have a sexy Eastern European accent. But otherwise she had the indifferent mousy hair and unfussy clothes of any math genius. Taylor didn't hate her, but her feelings were a bit ruffled. Even when John had wanted a romance with her, he hadn't looked at her the way he looked at *Tatiaaaaana*.

Tatiana.

If this romance was going to last, Taylor was going to have to practice saying her name non-sarcastically, even when just saying it in her head.

Taylor might have been the spare singleton in the crowd, but at least she had the best seat to watch Karina and Hudson on the date he'd been roped into. She hoped for some excitement from this. With Karina's short fuse and malicious nature, things might get explosive.

Hudson winked at her from across the room. He had on a fresh plaid shirt—not even flannel. His thick, dark hair looked like he had tousled it purposefully, and his face hadn't been shaved in a day or two. A couple other women in the bar also noticed him, and Taylor felt little pin pricks of pride. He may be waiting for another woman, but technically…

"He's really been great. I am grateful, honest. If I can fit a cheese reference in here, I could use grate one more time." Joey blushed.

Clay laughed.

Taylor turned her attention back to the couple sitting across from her.

"But Klamath Falls is so far away." Clay gave the pretty chef a big puppy eye look.

Joey's eyes were just as big and sad. "I know, but what else can I do? My kitchen exploded. He owns a few of these places, and the one in Klamath Falls has an opening. As soon as I find something better...."

"You won't be working in Comfort." Clay managed to make it sound like a pun, like Klamath Falls would be a particularly uncomfortable place to live.

"Probably not, but there are plenty of great restaurants around here...." She glanced at John Hancock who had been whispering to his date.

He pulled his eyes away from his beloved reluctantly. "I'd love to get my brother to take you on. I can ask anyway."

Joey shook her head. "That's a nice thought, but my plans are all made. Anyway, Klamath Falls is beautiful. I love it down there. You'll all have to come see me sometime."

Clay grabbed her hand. "Absolutely."

But Taylor knew the truth. Clay wouldn't take a four-hour drive to see a girl he'd just started dating. It wasn't his style. In fact, he seemed to be looking just over Joey's shoulder already, to the bar where three ladies in their twenties seemed to be having a girls' night out.

Taylor watched them too. They laughed, tossed their long thick hair, and kept glancing at Hudson, sitting alone at his table.

The food arrived for Taylor and her friends before Karina arrived.

And then more drinks.

Then an offer of dessert.

Still, Hudson sat alone. Maybe standing him up, trying to humiliate him, had been Karina's plan all along.

"Go ahead." John Hancock nudged her gently. "You haven't heard a word any of us has said for the last half an hour."

"Sorry." Taylor's face heated up.

"If you don't go get him," Clay said, "one of those kids will."

The ladies from the bar had moved to the table next to Hudson. They sat so close to him in their tight, sleeveless tops, laughing much louder now that they'd had plenty to drink, their glances his way much more direct.

Taylor'd been watching him, laughing, and texting him all evening.

But her friends were right. It was time to go to him. He may have been waiting for his ex, Karina Wyandotte, but he was there for her sake.

The restaurant was crowded, chairs and tables close together. She had to push and twist and fight her way to him.

As though he couldn't wait, he stood and reached for her, grabbing her as soon as she was close enough.

He pulled her into his arms and kissed her, warmly, and with love. The pub and the crowd, the friends and the girls all fell away.

Then he let her go and looked down at her. "This couldn't have been better."

"We saved you a seat." Taylor laced her fingers through his and took him to the group.

As she sat, her phone pinged a text. She glanced at it, wondering if it was an update from Dayton or maybe Reg.

A number she didn't recognize had sent a text. *"You owe me. You owe me big."* She shivered and showed it to Hudson.

He laughed. "That's Karina's number. I wonder how she'll make you pay for this?"

Another text came through while she pondered her fate. This one from her sister. *"Levi's mom came and got him. She's the worst."*

Taylor sent her sister a heart and sent up a prayer of thanks for Levi's mom. Funny, it was the first time she'd prayed as she investigated the murder of a pastor.

Her mind wandered as she sat next to Hudson on the long bench seat in their inglenook of a booth. Leon Farkas had no integrity. He was rotten, just like Cricket and Jerry and probably half of the people in this bar. But his lack of integrity had cost him his life.

Her mom had said something about that in one of her videos. How the whole project was only as good as the materials it was made out of.

Clay sat across from her, laughing at something Tatiana had said, one arm around Joey, but also glancing at the bar, where a new set of ladies were ordering drinks and laughing.

Clay Seldon. The love of her youth. He had already moved on mentally from the girl next to him. He wasn't a quilt that would survive in a washing machine, so to speak. His character was too weak.

But Hudson East. He was pretty much the real deal. He was himself, through and through, and that was one reason to respect him. And maybe, if she'd give him half the chance he deserved, she'd find she could fall truly in love with him too.

ALSO BY TESS ROTHERY

Dutch Hex

A Taylor Quinn Quilt Shop Mystery

Two years after the tragic death of her mother, Taylor is living her best life. She's got a steady boyfriend, stable business, and the coup of hosting a hugely popular quilt expo in her small town.

If that weren't enough good news, outtakes of her mom's old YouTube show have exploded online, bringing fame and money to everyone involved.

Things are literally perfect until the quilt expo's keynote speaker fails to show up for her morning class. It appears the young woman died of a tragic allergic reaction—but looks can be deceiving.

Since murder has a way of killing business, Taylor is willing to do anything to make her town safe. But a tangle of troubled teens, amateur detectives, and haunting clips of her dead mom have her tied up in knots. This might be the murder that makes her pack it all in for good.

Buy Dutch Hex to wrap yourself up in a cozy mystery today!

Visit TessRothery.com to learn more about the Taylor Quinn Quilt Shop Mysteries.

FLOUR SAX ROW

2019 Taste the Experience

COMFORT CAFE

Inspired by Cup and Saucer and French Cafe

Rows 1 and 3

two 3 inch half square triangles, dark
two 3 inch half square triangles, light
two 2 inch half square triangles, dark
four 2 inch quarter square
    triangles, dark

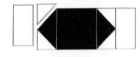

Row 2

two 2 and a half inch rectangles, light
two 2 inch half square triangles, light
four 2 inch quarter square
    triangles, light
one 3 inch square, dark

ABOUT THE AUTHOR

Tess Rothery is an avid quilter, knitter, writer and publishing teacher. She lives with her cozy little family in Washington State where the rainy days are best spent with a dog by her side, a mug of hot coffee, and something mysterious to read.

Sign up for her newsletter at TessRothery.com so you won't miss the next book in the Taylor Quinn Quilt Shop Mystery Series.

Tess Rothery is the general market pen name for Traci Tyne Hilton.

Made in the USA
Monee, IL
15 August 2021